Kori & Linnea,

Thank you for buying the executive
version of the book, with 33%

SuperGuy

more adverbs.

The Generic Alternative:

Less Superhero Hype,

Same Superhero Quality

[signature]

KURT CLOPTON

Published in the United States by
Not a Pipe Publishing, Independence, Oregon.
www.NotAPipePublishing.com

First Edition

ISBN-10: 0-9896352-9-5
ISBN-13: 978-0-9896352-9-5

Author's Note: While most of this book takes place in the city of Milwaukee, WI, I made up 95% of the locations, so any similarities to real places are purely accidental. And don't worry, there is no Cereal Factory of Evil[1].

---

[1] As far as I know

For Sarah, Julian, Evan and Greta

1

CONSCIOUSNESS came to him somewhat slowly, as if on a leisurely stroll in the park. Awareness followed at a bit quicker pace; call it a brisk walk, like those women with the hand weights who passed him while on his leisurely stroll in said park. This awareness was accompanied by a fluttery feeling in the pit of his stomach as if something was wrong, he just didn't know what. And then came panic. No leisurely stroll or speed walking there. This was the shock of every nerve in his body ramping up to eleven in an instant. So in the speed comparison of states of mind, panic hauled ass. SuperGuy twisted his body and kicked his legs frantically, his eyes alternating between the heavy chains binding his wrists above his head and the boiling vat of dark liquid placed, rather inconveniently he thought, twenty yards below him. The wild kicking and flailing caused SuperGuy to begin swaying back and forth while also starting to slowly rotate in a circle, but otherwise the larger state of panic wasn't doing much of anything very useful. Besides, due to the benefits of being a chemically enhanced superhero, the panic SuperGuy felt quickly subsided, and he began to more calmly assess his situation. Unfortunately after a quick reappraisal, SuperGuy realized the panic hadn't exactly hindered him in his first assessment. Now he just had a bit more detail. There were definitely chains around his wrists which suspended him above a large vat containing some kind of unknown liquid. That liquid, a dark greenish-brown in color with an accompanying odor somewhere between rancid and rancid's morning breath, was either bubbling or boiling. It was hard to tell exactly which, but it was probably bad either way. So, to sum up, he was chained above a vat filled with liquid that one probably shouldn't touch, let alone soak in like a hot tub. Not really any more complicated than that. For a split second SuperGuy allowed himself to be impressed by his ability to accurately assess a situation even while panicked, but he knew that assessment was only the very basic picture, and there was more to his predicament. He could usually break chains easily, but these particular ones resisted his efforts. They were either superhero quality metal (simply called that because the names of the various super strong metals were almost always harder to pronounce than aluminum) or SuperGuy's super strength had somehow been sapped. He realized quickly that both were true. A close examination of the chains made him certain they were indeed superhero quality and therefore nearly unbreakable even for the strongest of heroes, but he also felt an unusual weakness in his body, probably an after effect of the all the punishment he had endured as he was captured. Any other time SuperGuy could have used his strength to flip himself up to the rafters above and out of danger, but right then all he could manage was some more weak kicking and flailing.

"Oh my god, would you hurry up?!" came a frustrated scream from behind SuperGuy. "Obviously your super powers don't extend into your brain at all."

Twisting his head around, SuperGuy tried to see who was talking, but with his arms held above him his mask was knocked slightly out of place and restricted his field of vision too much for him to get a good look. He made a mental note of that uniform flaw, in case this ever happened again.

"Couldn't be bothered with super-deduction, could you? Or supra-deduction. Or even just a little above average deduction," continued the voice in obvious despair. "Just the good old run around and smash things superpowers, right? Don't think about it, just punch it. Typical."

No longer turning in a circle from his initial panic, SuperGuy kicked at the air again and twisted his body until he started to spin. It was the most he could accomplish in his weakened state. His tormentor slowly came into view.

"Gray Matter!" said SuperGuy, a bit louder than he meant, but it seemed obligatory on his part even though he wasn't surprised. SuperGuy's slow turn came to a stop and began to reverse its direction, taking the evil villain out of his field of vision once again. The criminal mastermind, dressed in his customary three piece suit of all gray and set off by his slicked back, bright white hair, was standing on a metal platform attached to a wall about ten yards away from where SuperGuy hung suspended above the vat. There was a door in the wall behind Gray Matter and metal stairs leading down from the platform to the factory floor below. And a factory it was, SuperGuy realized as he scanned the expanse around him. Machines of various sizes and shapes filled the floor of the cavernous room but, since it was the middle of the night, they all sat dormant, waiting for work to start again in the morning. Thick metal rafters, from one of which SuperGuy hung, ran the length of the ceiling with some criss-crossing catwalks hanging here and there just below them, although none close enough for the chained hero to reach. He did notice there was only the one bubbling vat of questionable liquid in the room, probably ruling out that it was just bad luck on his part he happened to be above it.

"Excuse me?" said Gray Matter, after clearing his throat to get the superhero's attention.

SuperGuy kicked a few times so he twisted back around. "What?" he asked, once the villain came into view.

"Not to rush you or anything, but you really should be asking me questions to stall right now. You know, maybe try to figure me out, get to the bottom of my plan, even throw in a 'You'll never get away with it' sort of thing. Generally just try to buy time."

More kicking. Gray matter came back into view. "Why?" asked SuperGuy.

"Wh-? Why? Well, to buy time like I said. Kind of standard procedure at this point really." Gray Matter nodded, urging SuperGuy to understand. "You know, so you have time to formulate a plan of escape or be rescued by a fellow hero, or a sidekick. Both of which are impossible, of course. Or at the very least, improbable, but I like to encourage the effort."

Yet more kicking. "No, I don't mean why-why, I mean what's the point?" asked SuperGuy.

"What's the point?" repeated the villain, with a mixture of anger and confusion.

"Yes," kicking, kicking, kicking, "What's the point? I can't break the chains, and eventually you're going to drop me into the soup down there, which I'm betting isn't good, so why bother talking to you in my last few moments? I'd rather spend my time thinking about distinctly un-superheroish topics. Like women. Specifically bikini-clad models. And maybe donuts." He looked down at the vat below. "Maybe I'll pretend there's

a bunch down there—bikini models, not donuts—
They're waiting for me in the pool, or hot tub as the case
may be. Oh, that does raise a question. Is that bubbling or
boiling? Just a technical detail, but it makes a difference
as to whether I go with the models or switch to donuts."

"Wha? What are you talking—? Stop it! No! I put
that vat in specifically for this purpose. A custom-made
superhero quality metal vat with superhero quality acid
and a few spoiled super serums tossed in just for kicks.
This is a *cereal* factory, no need for vats of acid in here at
all, not to mention it's an extremely safe, modern
workplace, with nothing at all you can fall into or get
crushed by. Bit of a pain in the ass to tell you the truth.
Why couldn't I buy a knife factory or a foundry?
Anything with sharp bits or molten metal or something
that crushes stuff, but no, I went with cereal. The only
dangerous thing in here before was the high sugar
content, so I had to go to some trouble to get this
equipment in place. And it's sure as hell not a hot tub!"
yelled Gray Matter. He looked down at the metal grating
under his feet and composed himself before looking back
up, only to find he was staring at the back of SuperGuy's
head again. "Oh, screw it!" He waved dismissively at
SuperGuy and walked over to a device he had sitting on
top of a pedestal on the platform. Stepping onto a little
stool next to the pedestal, Gray Matter set his hand on
the device.

"Okay, this is a laser that will slowly cut through the
chains suspending you above the vat, after which you will

plunge into the liquid below," Gray Matter continued in a monotone voice, showing he was clearly no longer enjoying himself. "Considering the mix of acid and super serum overdose, it will do things to you I can only imagine but wouldn't want to witness personally. It may turn you into something totally twisted and demonic, something I could proudly call a friend, but at the very least it will provide you with a death that will no doubt be incredibly painful and not terribly fast." Without any more ceremony, the villain sighed discontentedly and flipped a switch. The laser began emitting a bright green beam that shot across the gap, hitting the first of the three individual chains connecting SuperGuy to the rafter above. A thin trail of smoke immediately started snaking its way upward from the spot. Gray Matter watched for a second, and then without much enthusiasm said, "Not that it matters, but I chose to use three chains to add a little suspense. Oh, and the liquid is neither bubbling nor boiling. The bubbles aren't real, at least not produced by any kind of chemical reaction. I had some air pumped in for effect, not that you'd appreciate it. I just want you to know I did make quite a bit of effort for you. Obviously you could not be counted on to return the favor. Just some simple professionalism would be nice," he concluded bitterly. Then Gray Matter walked over to the door, opened it and paused to look back before exiting. "I hope they fill your position with someone of much better quality," he said, slamming the door shut behind him with a dull clang.

SuperGuy kicked his way back around to make certain the supervillain had really left. He saw the laser and looked up to verify it was doing its job, which it seemed to be with ruthless efficiency, steadily slicing through the thick link in the first chain. Slowly twisting back around, SuperGuy groaned in annoyance at his predicament. He wondered how he had let himself get stuck in this particularly odd mess. A cereal factory of all places. A cereal factory of evil, sure, but still a cereal factory. How did he end up here?

"Oh no, no, I didn't just think that. I gotta find a way out of this! I don't have time to think about that!" SuperGuy yelled and shook his whole body, but it was too late. The memories of those first days were beginning to play inside his head and there was nothing he could do to stop them.

"Well, crap," he said.

It all began...

2

THERE were a couple of things Oliver Olson hated about his internship. First was the Look. It wasn't just the ordinary everyday look someone gave you when you first met, one that was warm and welcoming and initially open to the prospect that you could become good friends, it was one certain Look which never failed to appear in that brief moment Oliver was introduced as an intern. There was a distinct pattern which Oliver had seen repeated over and over. That little introduction triggered such a complicated yet concise cascade of emotions that was really incredible to behold once you knew what to look for. The pattern usually shifted from surprise to suspicion to pity in a split second. Some of the more imaginative people could slip in a couple other emotions—the record was seven distinctly different ones—but three was the standard.

The surprise aspect of the Look came because Oliver was a bit older than the average intern in the office. In his defense, he was only twenty-nine, but when you're doing a job that usually falls to someone who may or may not be able to legally drink, it generates that instant of surprise. For some reason that gap between low twenties and high twenties is huge; a vast chasm between those who are hip and those who don't know any better than to use the term hip. Oliver assumed people noticed the age thing not because he had 'I'm 29' tattooed on his forehead, but because his rapidly receding hairline would allow for such a tattoo to be quite largish. It was a genetic thing. He considered himself somewhat lucky since his brother had started going bald as a sophomore in college, but fate had countered that bit of good luck with his very blond hair, which was so fickle that in some light, particularly the type of fluorescent lighting commonly used in offices, it looked almost white. This color issue plus the receding hairline didn't exactly combine to make Oliver look young. And, as if to drive the point home, the city government offices where Oliver worked had uncommonly bad fluorescent lighting.

It might have helped if Oliver was better looking. It seemed like you could get away with a lot more if you were. There had been a twenty-one year old stud of a college guy in the office as an intern the year before who needed written directions to get out of his cubicle, but he could have dropped his pants and peed in the corner of the cubicle and folks would have only noticed his tight butt. Now, Oliver wasn't bad looking in any way, just ordinary, being of average height and weight and attractiveness. He wasn't a hideous monster, but he didn't rate a second look either. He was in good shape, surprisingly better than most would guess, but they just didn't notice. He seemed to be, in his own estimation, a half step below noticeable. But that's a helluva step. Oliver had a theory that many people had one period during their life when they looked good, whether it was only one short year they peaked or an entire lifetime like some actors seemed to have. Maybe it happened when they were very young, just a baby, the cutest baby ever, but they redefined 'awkward-looking' from the moment they got up on two legs. Maybe they were the chisel-chinned football star in high school but a pot-bellied townie thereafter. Or maybe they eventually grew into their looks as they aged and hit their stride in their thirties or forties, like the girl from high school you're now friends with on Facebook that you wish you would have noticed back then. Oliver was pretty sure he'd hit his peak for about a week when he was twenty-six, but unfortunately he had been sick in bed with mono.

The second part of the Look, suspicion, followed quickly on the heels of surprise because people immediately wondered why someone of Oliver's age is only doing an internship, and the answer to that question couldn't possibly be good. Perhaps if he'd been older, maybe fifty and probably a woman, a non-traditional student as they like to say, then it would have been okay. But to be pushing thirty and still not have a paying gig, that was just plain wrong. The real story was much more boring than their suspicions, simply being that Oliver had taken two extra years to complete college due to several changes of major, all of which were variations on the theme of 'not useful for getting a real job.' Not to mention he also took a year off before college to earn money to go in the first place and then took the better part of a year off afterward to travel, spending money he didn't have. That was followed by two years of crappy jobs in a misguided attempt to pay for the travel, during which time the repayment of his school loans began. Those loans had somehow achieved an obscenely high total Oliver could not comprehend, especially while working at Joe's Jiffy Copy and Internet Coffee Bar. Eventually, realizing the best way to deal with the school loans was to defer, Oliver was led full circle back to school, but this time with the goal of a useful major and the determination to do it with alacrity and no new loans. He chose computer science because the market was huge, at least right up until he was pretty much done with school and then the economy tanked. So Oliver ended up grabbing a low paying internship, which had little to do with real computer work, and hoped to ride out the bad economy. Maybe, just maybe, there was a decent job on the other side of the long, dark tunnel.

The last part of the Look, pity, came when the observer decided they didn't actually want to know why Oliver was only an intern at his age and just assumed he'd served the sentence for his crime (which was almost certainly a spree of some kind) and was at least attempting to start a new life. They could get behind that. They could forgive. It's what we do in our culture, especially if the person in question plays professional sports. Secretly they didn't give him much of a shot at success, but they would be supportive, right up until the inevitable relapse. In their minds they were picturing the office hostage situation that is the almost unavoidable conclusion to the story. Whatever the outcome they definitely wouldn't be the ones on the news saying he seemed like such a normal guy.

Probably the most annoying thing about the Look for Oliver was, even though he was over halfway through his internship, he still met new people all the time. It didn't seem fair. This happened because he worked in a very large office complex, though not in the cool, campus-like idea of some ultra successful Silicon Valley startup, but more in a haphazard network of several mostly outdated buildings that were all parts of the city government offices of Milwaukee, Wisconsin. Some of the buildings were next to each other while others were blocks away, but there wasn't any logic to it. This is the result when the city simply buys the nearest vacant space when it needs more room. Soon everything has spread out. The particular department or office you may need could be two floors away, two buildings away, or, if you're really lucky, two blocks away. And let's face it, it'll be the one that's two blocks. It'll also be winter with a subzero forecasted high and a windchill of -40. But you're resourceful and know you don't have to go outside at all if you use the skyway, then the tunnel, cut through a law office, then use the underground parking garage, then through another law office to another skyway to get there. Of course with all the stairwells, elevators and backtracking, you've made a two block trip into something closer to two miles, but you never went outside. Needless to say, the city government offices sprawl. And Oliver's internship was just vague enough he found himself walking through every little inch of that sprawl, although his cubicle resided specifically in a section housing mainly law enforcement related employees.

That brings up the second thing Oliver hated about his internship. It wasn't being stuck in a tiny beige-ish cubicle in particular, or having that cubicle nestled among the seemingly countless others in the law enforcement section of the office, or even working alongside most of the employees inhabiting those other cubicles. Most. Sergeant Joseph Przybylinski, assigned to desk duty due to some dubious back injury, was another story.

Sergeant Przybylinski (pronounced 'Shi-ba-linski' for some reason), whose official capacity was difficult for an observer to ascertain except that it had something to do with keeping a very accurate accounting of his days left until retirement, took it upon himself to mentor Oliver. That mentoring took the form of Sergeant Przybylinski passing on any of his own real work to Oliver and supplementing that with obviously pointless, but time intensive tasks. In turn, most of those tasks would require multiple revisions and later, in a fit of clear-sightedness, would be abandoned as useless. Oliver was working on one such vitally useless revision on a Monday morning when Sergeant Przybylinski appeared in the doorway of his cubicle.

"Olson." Sergeant Przybylinski seemed to believe impersonating a drill instructor was the best way to interact with people, and most everything he said was delivered in a manner that made you think he was either in the middle of a bowel movement or fighting off an aneurysm. Or both. Or maybe fighting off a bowel movement. Whatever the reason, there was a strain. This strain also seemed to be reflected in the Sergeant's consistently reddish complexion, overly large bulbous nose, and a collar on his uniform shirt that was undoubtedly too small, making it look like his neck was lava spilling out of the mouth of a volcano. It was surprising he didn't have steam escaping from his ears.

"Sergeant." Oliver didn't bother to look up. He had incredibly little to fight back with in this torturously long and losing battle, but he thought giving the sergeant any extra attention even in the form of eye contact would only give the man more satisfaction.

"Olson, that disk you gave me Friday with that safety presentation? I seem to have misplaced it. I'll need you to redo it."

Oliver didn't react at all, only barely paused from his work to reach up and grab a cd from the shelf above his computer. He checked the label. "Here's a copy, made an extra just in case." He handed it to the Sergeant without looking, keeping his ever so slight look of triumph hidden. "Oh, and actually..." Oliver closed what he was working on and saved a copy to a thumb drive. He pulled it out and handed it to the Sergeant also. "Just finished the revisions on those stats tables. Took a long time but they're ready for tomorrow morning." Oliver thought he could feel the glare as Sergeant Przybylinski took the thumb drive and he decided he'd like to see the annoyance first hand since these small victories weren't common. But when he looked up at the Sergeant, instead of annoyance, he found Sergeant Przybylinski was smiling. The usual smug, deflating smile.

"Ah, well, thanks for this," said the Sergeant, shaking the cd in his hand. "But on this stats thing, I know I told you to make all the revisions according to the 2012 data. Well, it seems that's not what they want, it's the 2013 data, so I'll need you to adjust it." He handed the thumb drive back to Oliver with a wink. "Sorry about that. Still need it by tomorrow, nine a.m." He turned and walked off. Oliver wasn't positive but he thought he could hear the Sergeant whistling. Or maybe it was the ventilation system taunting him.

Oliver was resting his head on his desk, and had been for nearly ten minutes, when Roger entered his cubicle.

"Looks like someone is having a good day," said Roger, dropping into the extra chair inside the cubicle. Roger Allen was about the same height and build as Oliver, with a shaved head and John Lennon granny glasses. He was a big Beatles fan. Roger was also the main computer support person for the office and had become a friend of Oliver's early on in the internship. He tried to send useful, more interesting computer related tasks Oliver's way when he could, but there was little he could do to really help him, other than listen to his complaints. "Um, whatever this is," Roger motioned vaguely with one hand at Oliver's lowered head, "It's not going to screw up basketball, is it?" Basketball was the reason the two had met after Oliver started the internship, both playing in regular pick-up games after work at a nearby gym. Oliver was a more consistent shooter but Roger handled the ball better and claimed to have the overall edge in basketball talent because he was black. He said it was the stereotype and he was going to take advantage of it. The truth of the matter was that, while they were both decently athletic, they were decently more nerd, better at compiling and running their own code than running a pick and roll, but they loved it nonetheless.

"This will absolutely not interfere with basketball, in keeping with the rules," said Oliver. There were only a couple acceptable excuses that could keep you from playing ball and those were being injured (preferably badly) and being out of town, though the latter was frowned upon because a man has control of his own schedule. Everything else, like work, visitors, or relationships, could be planned around basketball. You just had to have priorities. "It won't interfere with that, just everything else tonight, and by tonight I mean all evening plus that little thing I like to call sleep. I was supposed to see a movie with Kate, but that's not going to happen now."

"Bummer," said Roger. "How's it going with Kate anyway?"

Oliver shrugged without taking his head off the desk. He didn't want to drain his energy reserves any more by actually getting upright to perform the gesture. He wondered how much of the rest of the day he could get through like this. "Good. Things with Kate are actually good. I think there's a lot of potential with her."

"Well, other than Kate—a definite anomaly—you don't have any life to speak of, so it seems working all night shouldn't really affect you much at all. I was just worried about how this head on desk thing would affect me."

"Very thoughtful of you."

"Least I can do. So why don't you give me the rest of the story?"

"Just the usual," Oliver said, finally lifting his head off the desk. "Good old Sergeant Przybylinski. Had me spend hours doing something with the wrong data and now he wants the right stuff by tomorrow morning. The same old thing. I really should just get some cards printed so I don't have to repeat this every time, or maybe make a little audio clip for my phone. Like, 'I've been Pryzbylinski-ed again'." Oliver rubbed his forehead. "I can't wait for this job to be over. Not so much a job as some kind of prison sentence. What did I do? Did I kick God's dog or something?"

"Oh, come on, you know that's not the way to think about it." Roger stood up and looked out over the cubicle wall at the rest of the office. "You need to change your perspective, put a little spin on things. It's all about the spin." He snapped his fingers. "Think about it this way. What you have here is a very prestigious—it is city government after all—a very prestigious, slightly salaried consultancy position."

"The only part of that description that's accurate is the slightly salaried bit. The only consulting I do is with you in determining just how much more of this I can take."

Roger rubbed his shaved head as he gave the problem a bit more thought. "Okay, obviously we haven't spun it enough yet. The pay scale puts you on par for a real job in say, 1967. That's a good year. So it's kind of a retro thing. Retro is cool right now. You are a retro consultant. Start listening to Sgt. Pepper and dropping acid, and it will all seem sensible."

"Hmm, hard to say for certain, but I don't think you're helping."

"Hey, this'll help," said Roger, nodding his head slightly in the direction of one of the outer offices that surrounded the main floor of cubicles. "It's Joan."

Oliver was up from his chair is a flash, then immediately tried to look subtle as he eased up next to Roger. Joan was practically a celebrity around the office, at least with the male population. Long black hair, long perfect legs. She was the object of every man's lust, and unfortunately she knew it. She didn't acknowledge your existence if you weren't someone important, which meant she was practically alone in the office because barely anyone was important enough to her. Oliver was a definite nonentity, although she had once asked him to get something for her off a high shelf, which he considered the highlight of his internship so far. If you were a city councilman, you might get a hello, but she gave most everyone else the same amount of attention she gave the fake plastic plants which dotted the building. You really hated her for it, but you would also lick her shoes clean if she asked.

Coincidentally Oliver was picturing just that image when a small sharp pain shot through his knee. "Ouch," he said, reaching down to rub it. He took one more look at Joan, who was now disappearing down a hall, and settled back into his chair.

"Knee still bothering you?" asked Roger.

"Occasionally," Oliver said with a shrug. "Which is to say just when I stand, sit, or move. You know, generally make use of it. I wonder if I should have it looked at?"

"You keep saying that."

"That's about as far as it will go too, as long as it doesn't get any worse. Can't afford the co-pay on the doctor visit, which is another place where your 'retro consultancy' theory doesn't pan out. Today the co-pay on the exam alone would probably be enough to have had my knee scoped back in 1967. If they even scoped knees back then."

"Okay, retro may not really work if you insist on looking at it that closely, but I still like the sound of it, so I'm going with it. And if the retro consultant is available, I do have a small project that came up this morning."

"Did you not hear the story I was telling you earlier? Sergeant Przybylinski, stats, no more sleeping? Any of that ring a bell?"

Roger feigned thinking for a second, then shook his head. "No, doesn't sound familiar. I really have a hard time following your stories if there's no car chase in them."

"Smart-ass."

"Look, don't worry, it's a small project that's not due anytime soon so you can put it aside and deal with this Przybylinski thing first." Roger moved to the doorway of the cubicle. "Anyway, I forgot to bring it with me so I'll have someone drop the file off later."

"Sure, sure, pile it on. Just tell them to look for the retro consultant. Maybe I'll put that as my job title on Facebook."

"You should. Take pride in it. Seize the day," said Roger. Seeing he wasn't going to get much more out of Oliver, he decided to move on. "Okay, I'll send the file over. See you at ball," he said, walking off in the direction of the elevators.

Oliver sat staring at the cubicle wall a moment longer until he put a hand on his forehead. It seemed a little warm and he felt a little funky. "Great," he said to himself. "Now I'm getting sick. Obviously has to be some kind of cool retro virus. Like the plague."

3

THE Mayor needed something big. Something really, really big. Well, maybe not really, really big, because that sounded like money and the Mayor knew his campaign coffers were getting a little low, so maybe something more in the realm of big enough. The most recent polls weren't as good as they were two months ago, and the Mayor could feel his re-election bid stalling, so first thing Monday morning he called in his key people for a little brainstorming session to help get things back on track. Those key people were in his office now. The more important ones, like his personal assistant Lily, the Deputy Mayor and the Police Chief, were sitting on the chairs closer to his desk while several other people, more staff members and such, lined the walls behind them. He didn't know them all, but a couple looked familiar. His campaign manager, Phil, sat on the window ledge behind his desk at the moment, but would routinely stand up to pace back and forth. The Mayor sat in his chair waiting until everyone was settled. Then he began.

"Lily says we're down another two points over the weekend," he said, going right to the heart of the matter. The Mayor liked to do that, to seem like the kind of guy who didn't flit around the edge of the party but was right there front and center, first in line for the keg. De Niro would be like that, he thought. He wondered if De Niro had ever played a mayor. He would have Lily look into it and see if there was anything. Or he could just watch Casino again; he owned the Blu-ray. Regardless, he could use a little inspiration—a performance on which he could model his own—and maybe a mole. Something more distinctive about his face would be helpful. He knew it was probably a bit too plain. He was a handsome man, with dark hair going a little gray at the temples, but somehow that gray didn't make him seem distinguished, just old. His chin was good, but not really special, with the cheek bones to match, and his teeth were perfect but everybody had perfect teeth nowadays. He was basically the department store catalog model of mayors, attractive sure, but no one was taking that summer swimwear issue into the bathroom and locking the door. So maybe a mole. Would anybody notice if he suddenly got a mole?

Or a scar. Yeah, a scar. Now that would be cool. Nothing too big or he might seem scary, but perhaps just a little one that hinted at some violent, though heroic past. Suddenly the Mayor realized he was getting a little sidetracked. De Niro never gets sidetracked. He looked at the Deputy Mayor. "How do we lose two over the weekend? I didn't do anything over the weekend. I didn't even shower. It was the weekend."

The Deputy Mayor, a tall, thin man with a hawk nose and trendy glasses, waved a hand slightly as if fending off a gnat and shook his head. Internally, he was conflicted by how much he disliked the Mayor but also by how much his political future was tied to the man winning a second term. "Sir, you can't worry about small fluctuations in the polls. Two points is well within the margin of error. It's practically a non-story."

"But it is a story," replied the Mayor, "Especially when it follows several other polls in which we've lost a point or two each week. Those tend to add up and someone in the press will eventually work out the math. Or ask a friend to help them." He stood and walked around to the side of his desk. He rapped his knuckles on the dark wood for emphasis. "Look, I don't want to play the ignore it game. I want to attack this thing head on. I want to do something to pick the numbers back up. It's way too close now, and their guy isn't going to do anything stupid and give it to us. We need to take it. Plus he's killing us on these latest crime figures. That might just be the edge he needs in these last few weeks." He turned his attention to the Police Chief. "Speaking of the crime stats, Chief, what the hell happened there?"

"Yeah, what the hell?" threw in Phil, who for a campaign manager seemed to be a step behind things an awful lot. It wasn't his fault since the Mayor would never let anyone else have control of his campaign, but he didn't help himself by being a bit thrown by all the complexities of politics. The simple truth was that he was the Mayor's cousin and his mother was a big contributor who somehow saw potential in her boy. The Mayor didn't, but he did see the potential in his aunt's money.

The Police Chief grimaced. He was a career officer who sincerely cared about the real work of policing and didn't like the political side of the department, but just enough luck and scandal above him had conspired to put him at the top. Now he was trying to walk the line between keeping the Mayor happy and doing his duty. Unfortunately, his sense of duty was coming out on the losing side too often lately. It didn't help that he knew whatever he said about the crime rates wouldn't matter anyway. The numbers could have been glowing and he would still get yelled at. He squeezed the brim of his hat in frustration. "Well, Mr. Mayor, those rates are pretty much the same as when you came into office. The numbers may sound bad when you look at them alone, but in comparison with other cities our size, we're average. It's just bad timing on the report."

"Bad timing is an understatement. Why right now anyway?" asked the Mayor. "Don't we have some control over that?"

"Well, it was part of your initiative, sir," the Deputy Mayor chimed in. He couldn't resist himself. "You ran an anti-crime campaign the first time around and regular reporting of crime statistics was one part of that. Unfortunately your challenger is using it against you rather effectively."

The Mayor glared for a second at the Deputy Mayor, then looked back at the Police Chief. "What have you been doing for four years if it's still the same?"

"Four years..." said Phil, shaking his head.

"Actually it's not quite the same," said the Deputy Mayor, once again not resisting. "The crime rate has risen in the last six months, hasn't it, Chief?"

The Police Chief gave a reluctant nod while shifting in his chair. "Sure, a bit of a rise, but that will average out in the long run." He brushed his hand against the side of his head, smoothing his white hair above his ear. If anyone in the room had been a regular of his Tuesday poker night they would have recognized this obvious tell. Despite his words, the Chief was secretly very concerned about the recent rise in crime because it wasn't a typical increase, and he had quietly formed a small task force to look into it. Truth be told, he wondered if he wouldn't mind the Mayor losing the election so he would then be replaced with the incoming administration and not have to deal with this apparent new problem. He had been in law enforcement for a long time and it smelled like something big to him, maybe organized crime, and that meant he had a fight on his hands. Not that he minded a fight, but without backing it wasn't something he could win.

The Mayor gave him a dismissive wave. "Oh, I don't want to hear it. Okay, so what do we do? I ran on anti-crime, as the Deputy Mayor so helpfully pointed out, and crime is what's killing us now. That doesn't look very good. We need something to turn that around quickly. Some big step against crime." He snapped his fingers. "Maybe some new policies?"

"We did that first thing in office," said the Deputy Mayor. "Nothing changed."

"Well that's because most of the policies spent money on useless things," said the Police Chief, his distaste clear in his voice. "Consultancies and feasibility studies if I recall correctly. New paint jobs on the cars. Didn't put any new officers on the street where the problems are, where it would make a real difference. Got some nicely bound reports, though. Really top notch work."

"Okay, okay, enough." The Mayor sat down in his chair. "Do we have any money to work with and can we move any of that money around to get somebody on the streets? Getting more officers out there might do it."

"I doubt that," replied the Deputy Mayor. "I believe most of this year's budget has been paid out and going over will just look bad. I had the fiscal office send Lily the latest numbers." He nodded toward Lily but didn't look at her. That was another area of contention for him. He had the biggest crush on this young woman, with her short brown hair and dark eyes, but even though they were both single, he never did anything about it because he sensed her total dedication to the Mayor. If they spent any time together at all, she would undoubtedly realize he didn't like the Mayor and the relationship would surely be doomed. So now he just passively-aggressively hated her since he believed she loved the Mayor he hated. It made perfectly good sense.

Everyone looked at Lily, who was sitting on a chair at the side of the room with a mammoth sized stack of files on her tiny lap. She was already paging through one of them. Shortly she nodded her head without looking up. "Yes, it looks like the Deputy Mayor is right. Most everything has been allocated and spent."

"Great," said the Mayor, obviously without enthusiasm. He rubbed his chin, trying to think of a De Niro movie that could help. Ronin was good. He liked Ronin. That girl in it sure was pretty.

"Oh," said Lily with a touch of surprise. "There is something that hasn't been used yet."

"What's that?" asked the Mayor.

"The Hero position," said Lily. "It's never been filled."

"Oh, crap, not a hero," said the Police Chief, rubbing his temples. He felt a headache coming on. This was the last thing he needed. The hero topic was almost always discussed whenever two or more police officials got together. The pervading theory was that it was never good for a police department. Whenever there was the inkling of some big crime, let alone a supervillain, the city always demanded a hero. A regular cop couldn't even get a free donut after that. The Police Chief recalled O'Hara crying in his scotch about it at the last conference, complaining about the commissioner always running to the red phone the instant some bad guy pulled into town. He didn't get a chance to do anything. No detectives on the case, no special patrols, not a single task force. Nothing. O'Hara went on and on, talking about other 'complications' concerning his wife and their private time. He was a real mess. The Chief shuddered at the memory.

"Hero position? What Hero position?" asked the Mayor.

"I have the file for it right here," said Lily, pulling one out of the middle of the stack. This file was different than the other variously colored ones on her lap. It had a metallic sheen, like brushed aluminum, and had the letters D.S.F etched across the front. They stood for the Department of Superhero Funding, the federal entity that approved and created Hero positions.

"Oh, the Hero position," said the Deputy Mayor, nodding his head in recognition.

"The Hero...yeah," said Phil.

"And...?" prompted the Mayor.

Phil looked up at the Mayor, realizing he wanted him to say something for real. That didn't happen often. "Oh, it was part of the anti-crime campaign, and also part of the budget, although we've never filled the position. I think we only allocated the minimum amount to create it in the first place, thus keeping our promise to create the position, but then also keeping it vacant to use the money as a slush fund."

"Yeah, that's right, I remember now," said the Mayor. "Voters love their heroes. That was always good for an applause break during a speech. And even more brilliant not to fill it and use the money to cover other stuff. Who thought of that?"

"Williams," replied the Deputy Mayor.

The Mayor looked around the room. "And where's…"

The Deputy Mayor shook his head. "No longer with us," he said. "Under indictment."

"Oh." The Mayor hated these awkward moments. He pushed on. "So this Hero position then. Conveniently not yet filled, so we appoint someone. Get a hero out on the streets and we look good, tackling the crime issue."

"I must object," said the Police Chief. "If it's a slush fund, why not move the money so we can get more cops on the street?"

The Mayor shook his head. "No, I like this better. It's bigger. A few cops can't compare to a hero."

"Can't compare…" said Phil, shaking his head.

"A hero just makes my department look bad," argued the Police Chief. "Makes us look incompetent."

"Well, that's you and your department. However, if I appear incompetent then we lose the election and how your department looks doesn't matter. If you have a better idea, then let me hear it, but I doubt you'll match this. As I said, the voters love their heroes, and they haven't had one of their own since, what, ten years ago when what's his name…?"

"Mystic Man," piped up one of the lower tier staffers, who then immediately hunkered back down in his chair as if he were a little boy who had spoken out of turn.

"Yes, that's it. Mystic Man. It's been ten years since he dropped us to go full time in Tampa. It's like losing a pro sports franchise. The people will want it back even though they didn't support it when they had it. I like this better the more I think about it. This will kill the crime rate thing and push us back up in the polls. If no one else has another similarly brilliant idea, then I say we get our hero." The Mayor got up from his chair and looked around the room, waiting for any dissension. There was none, at least not vocalized. "Okay then, it's settled." He walked over to Lily, who was smiling at him shyly, and took the hero file from her. He thought it would be heavy, considering its metal appearance, but it was amazingly light, almost as if it weighed nothing at all. He walked over to the Deputy Mayor. "This is extremely important, so I want you to handle the appointment personally. Find someone for the position and then set up the requisite announcements, appearances and photo ops. And do it fast, like today. I'm counting on you."

"I'll take care of it," said the Deputy Mayor, already thinking of which aides he could drop the task on.

Everybody had their priorities, and while this was the Mayor's, the Deputy Mayor had a few of his own that took precedence. Obviously one was hating the Mayor. Next in line were a couple of new plans he had that might ensure his personal political future was secure no matter what happened with this election. This hero might save the Mayor, but the Deputy Mayor wasn't taking any chances. His priority was himself right now. He would get someone else to deal with this hero thing.

"Good. Excellent meeting. Now everybody clear out," said the Mayor, walking back around his desk and dropping into his chair as the people shuffled out of the room. Damn good meeting, he thought. Not exactly the Untouchables De Niro, but he could never get away with the bat thing. Maybe he should get a bat for his office though, just for a little secret motivation.

4

BOB never enjoyed the first couple of hours after the Deputy Mayor had been to see the Mayor because his boss would sulk at his desk for a while before leaping up with his head full of new plans, schemes and angles. Unfortunately the most direct result of this was usually a bunch of new tasks for Bob, several of which he didn't understand the reasons behind because he wasn't privy to the Deputy Mayor's thought process. Bob chalked it up to not understanding all the intricacies of city government, or policies, or administration, or spinning, lying, backstabbing, jealousy, cheating, stealing, and misrepresenting. Just politics really. Bob wiped his clammy palms on the sides of his pants while staring nervously at the two folders on his desk. They had been given to him by the Deputy Mayor. He scratched the side of his rather large, thin nose and ran a hand through his short brown hair three quick times, a nervous habit, while trying to think of what to do next. The first file folder, the rather garish metal one in his opinion, the Deputy Mayor had handed to Bob right away once he returned from his meeting with the Mayor. The second file folder, just a normal blue one, the Deputy Mayor had brought out of his office after a rather shorter than usual session of sulking. He simply said they were a couple of consultancies that he wanted filled today. Emphasis on today.

"By who?" Bob had asked. While he was an assistant to the Deputy Mayor, he was only a part time assistant. The full time assistant, Cheryl, was on vacation this week in Tucson. Surely this was the kind of thing Cheryl, or someone else of at least full time status, would be assigned.

"I'm giving them to you, aren't I?" the Deputy Mayor had said. "Then I'm guessing it's you. Oh, and by the way, the blue one is my priority, so get that done immediately. But get that silver thing done immediately too."

That was all very clear then, although Bob had never done anything quite as important as hiring consultants before, and it made his stomach a bit queasy. At least it seemed important. Or maybe it wasn't. It was hard to know how vital things were when they were the result of a post-Mayoral meeting sulk. At least the metal one wasn't as important. Regardless, he had to take care of them fast, and Bob didn't have any clue how to start. He had looked through both files but the language was very bureaucratic, essentially gibberish. Only lawyers and Klingons could possibly decipher it. Not being able to even ascertain what the positions were he was supposed to fill didn't exactly help Bob's nervousness either. He sat at his desk with the two folders in front of him, trying to come up with a solution. Then it finally hit him. Irene. He would go ask Irene. She was an older red-headed woman with a motherly air about her who worked in the city budget office. She knew things. She would know what to do about this.

The very Irene in question had been staring at things on her desk too. Things to do, assignments, paperwork, tasks to complete. Irene was not a fan of said things, which made her choice of profession a bit odd, but she had worked hard for many years in these offices to make sure she had fewer responsibilities, not more. Delegation was the key, in fact it was her motto really, and now was the time to delegate. Irene just needed someone to delegate to and a smile slid fleetingly across her face as she noticed Bob walking toward her desk. She didn't know what he wanted, but it was plain from the befuddled look on his face and his white knuckled grip on a couple of folders that he wanted—no, needed—something, and Irene was already calculating what tasks he could take off her hands before he said a word.

"Irene?"

"Bob!" said Irene, giving him a good show of bubbly excitement. The various piles of paper and files on her desk made it obvious that she was very busy, but despite that she still gave Bob her full attention. This was part of her technique. She knew it helped to make most of her victims, Bob included, feel a little special before dropping work on them. Most people didn't realize the majority of the stacks on Irene's desk were just old items waiting to be tossed into the recycling bin. Irene worked on the theory that a clean desk just attracted more work, and even if that method is working well and you don't have much to do, you should still delegate as much of the remaining work as possible in case some emergency comes your way. She didn't look at it so much as ducking work, more like being prepared for the big project lurking just around the corner that no one else would be able to handle because they were already overloaded. She was thinking of the rest of the office. Really. She gave Bob one of her biggest smiles, in proportion to the list of tasks she had drawn up in her head. "How are you?"

"Good, Irene. I...I just have a question or two on something the Deputy Mayor gave me a few minutes ago," he said, holding up the two files.

"Sure, fire away," said Irene, with extra cheerfulness.

"Two position appointments or consultancies, I think. Well, as far as I can tell. The Deputy Mayor didn't really say what they were and I can't get much out of the language. Perhaps you might know what they are? I've never done anything like this before." Bob's hands were sweating again and it was getting on the files.

"No problem," said Irene, taking the folders and flipping each one open in turn. She skimmed the top couple pages of each and closed them back up. "Nothing too complicated. This one is for the maintenance department," she said, placing her hand on the blue file. "And this metal one is for someone in the Justice Department, or law enforcement."

"Okay. S—So how am I supposed to find people for them? This seems really important. Cheryl's not here. I've never done this type of thing before. Shouldn't someone else be doing it?"

"Oh, no, no, no," said Irene. Having Bob feeling overwhelmed wasn't going to get her tasks done. She needed to fix this. "Don't sweat it, Bob. These aren't as important as you think. You see, it's almost election time, which means all these things suddenly come up that have to be dealt with yesterday, but it's all political. The administration is just making sure they've done what they promised by running all these things out right before the deadline. Happens every election year, especially here in the budget office. Shift money to this, shift it to that, move it back again. Forget we ever did that, burn this memo after reading. It's all just smoke and mirrors, basically meaningless a week after the election. It doesn't matter if the appointments are done well, as long as they're done. Chances are they'll dump the position later to save the money. It's all part of the dance we do at the end of every budget year, and right before an election. So don't worry about who gets appointed, just get someone. Undoubtedly that's why the Deputy Mayor chose you, because you wouldn't waste time, you'd just get it done." She held the folders out to him.

"Um…yeah. Uh, so maintenance," he said, taking back the folders and pointing first at the blue one, then the metal one. "And Justice Department." Irene nodded. Bob nodded, but less certainly. "That's what they're for?" Irene nodded again. So did Bob, still uncertainly. Irene could see he was going to need more guidance if he was to be of any use to her.

"Look," said Irene. "It's simple. Get some CPA for the maintenance one, it's just a review of their budget. Go over to Accounting and find a consultant—they give them all cubicles along the south side farthest from the elevators—find one who's already working on something for us and appoint them to this one too. Almost all of them do more than one project at a time and this one is small. Then for the Justice one, find a consultant over in law enforcement…" she said, thinking for a moment, then holding up a finger. "I know, I think they are having meetings with law enforcement consultants all day today over in Building C. Let me check." She clicked her mouse a couple of times to bring up the calendar for the meeting rooms on her computer screen. "Yep, there it is. Meeting rooms A and B in Building C are reserved for Justice Department consultancy reviews all day. The reviews mean their current consultancies are ending so I bet most of them would be happy to take on a new project. So go over there, find one of them, and you've got your appointee. Just fill out the appointee page—that's the first one in the file with their name, social, and employee number—have them sign it, give them the rest of the file and drop the appointee page off at Human Resources. Simple. The hardest thing you'll have to do is the walk over to Building C. You'll have both appointments done by lunch."

Bob's face brightened with obvious relief. "That's great, Irene. I've just never done anything like this before."

"So you said."

"I really owe you," he said, turning in the direction of the elevators.

"Oh, not a problem, Bob," said Irene, letting him get a couple steps away before continuing, "But you know, I could use a little help with something. It's a lunch we're having today." She tore a piece of paper from a pad and held it out toward Bob. "We're having a meeting over lunch and this is the order I need filled from the deli. That's over in Building C, right where you're going. Maybe you could get it filled and bring it back here by noon. Bill it to our account, the number's right there at the bottom. Thanks, Bob, it's a big help." Irene plunged her head back into her stacks, making herself look as instantly busy as possible. She could sense Bob hesitate, looking at the lunch order, and then finally turn and go. She had wanted to give him more tasks but right at the moment he seemed a little too fragile with those appointments. Besides, he'd have to stop back by at noon with the lunches and once the appointments were done she would be free to pile more things on him. He'd be so thankful he wouldn't care.

Oliver could feel himself getting worse. He had just sat down with his lunch in one of the nearby conference rooms, but he didn't feel much like eating. The conference rooms were a good place for lunch because they were usually unoccupied during the noon hour since the people important enough to merit a conference room for a meeting could go out for food instead of brown bagging it. At least Oliver liked to believe those folks were enjoying extravagant three martini lunches so he could resent them. Oliver couldn't even afford a brown bag on his salary, so he repurposed plastic grocery bags. Unfortunately today he had only managed to dump his lunch items out of the bag before his motivation to eat anything deserted him. He had a tickle in his throat, a dull ache just behind his eyes and very little energy. All he could think about was a nap. That didn't bode well for either basketball after work or the project he had to finish for Sergeant Przybylinski. Obviously he felt worse about the basketball part. He was ignoring his turkey sandwich and eating a potato chip here and there while paging through one of the binders left on the table. It had a Justice Department seal on it and looked to be an outline and reference materials for the meetings they were having that day. Oliver didn't have any interest in it but he had forgotten to bring something along to read and it was within arm's reach. Sometimes other people ate in the conference rooms but no one was around today so conversation wasn't an option. Not that Oliver even felt like talking much. He was reading through a short paragraph about the merits of certain police unit sirens as compared to others (Some are really loud, and others are really, really loud.) when someone stopped outside the conference room door, looked intently at the board showing the day's activity, and then stuck his head inside.

"Ah, hey," said the guy, glancing around the large room. His eyes settled on Oliver, sitting alone at the table. "Um, meetings, huh?"

"Yeah, nothing but meetings. Gotta love 'em," said Oliver, patting the binder he had been reading. The guy seemed nervous, or at least well out of place. He kept wiping his free hand on his pants or scratching the side of his nose. He didn't say anything, so Oliver did. "My name's Oliver Olson," said Oliver, "Can I help you with something?"

"Oh. Yeah…" said the guy. He looked at the sign next to the door again and then inched into the room.

"Um, you are the…a consultant…here?" he said, vaguely pointing down, apparently indicating the room or the building. It wasn't too clear.

Oliver was about to say no when he remembered Roger's new position title from earlier that morning. Retro consultant. This must be the guy dropping off the new project. "Oh…Consultant. Yes, the consultant. Absolutely. That's me. Surprised you found me in here."

"Uh, yes," said the guy, looking confused for a second, but then he smiled. "Well, where else would a consultant be, but in a meeting room for consultants?"

"True, can't argue with that logic."

"No, no. No, you can't," the guy trailed off. He looked around the table. "So…are you a busy consultant?"

Oliver laughed. "Of course not. Barely have enough work to make it worth getting up for in the morning. Heck, by tomorrow morning my latest project will be done."

"So, you'd be happy to have another one?"

"Of course. It's what I live for."

"Great!" said the guy, smiling happily. "You're perfect for this then." He set a folder on the table and opened it up, pulling out a piece of paper. "Oliver Olson," said the guy out loud as he wrote the name on the sheet of paper. "What's your social security number? Oh, and employee number?" Oliver recited both, a bit surprised since he didn't usually have to give them for a project, but he didn't really care. Just one more bureaucratic formality to complicate things. "Okay, excellent," said the guy, "If you could just sign right here." He set the paper in front of Oliver and pointed to a line with one hand while offering his pen with the other. Oliver took the pen, signed with what he thought was the appropriate flourish despite feeling a bit under the weather, and pushed the pen and paper back toward the guy. The guy picked them up, checked the paper and then slid the folder toward Oliver. "That's for you, then. Um, well, that was easy enough. Thanks." The guy stuck his pen in his breast pocket and folded the sheet of paper in half. He started toward the doorway but turned back before he exited. "Oh, what's the easiest way to the deli?" he asked.

"Down the hall to the stairs at the end and up two floors. Deli's right there as you come out," answered Oliver.

"Great, thanks," said the guy.

"No problem," replied Oliver, watching him go. Then he turned his attention to the folder the guy had left behind. Oliver hadn't noticed it at first, but it was fancier then the ubiquitous paper folders that filled the office. This appeared to be metal, a sort of matte silver finish, about two inches thick. It was the expandable kind, with a flap that went over the top and could be tied in place so nothing would fall out. The letters DSF were etched in huge type across the back and also again, only smaller, on the other side in the center of the flap. Oliver lifted the flap, noticing that it seemed to magnetically seal to the side of the folder. He played with it a couple of times, letting it slap back against the side before flipping it all the way over. He knew Roger said it wasn't urgent, but the folder was way too cool not to look inside, and besides, it had to be a better read than anything about police sirens. Maybe if Oliver was really lucky the project would be as interesting as the folder it came in. He'd owe Roger big time if that proved to be true.

Reaching inside the folder, Oliver pulled out a bundle of papers, setting them on the table in front of him. As he did so, an object dropped from the folder, bounced on the table once and flipped inside his potato chip bag. Oliver set the folder down and retrieved the object from his potato chips. It was cylindrical and made of a shiny silver metal, measuring three or four inches long and about an inch and a half in circumference. And now it had salt all over it. Oliver brushed off the salt and examined the item more closely. One end was rounded off smoothly and the other contained a hole, showing that it was hollow. On the side it had 'Insert index finger here' etched in blue on its surface, with an arrow pointing to the end with the hole. Oliver stared at it for a second, then did what it said. For a split second he thought he felt pain as he slid his finger inside, but the sensation changed immediately to cold, then warm, then somehow both at the same time, then nothing. Oliver sat staring at the silver cylinder on his finger, as if waiting for something to happen. He wiggled it a couple of times and tapped it lightly on the table. He wondered what it did. Maybe some kind of pointer device that synced with a computer.

Had to be bluetooth capable. Could be a cool little toy. Eventually he glanced around the room, realizing how odd he must look sitting there staring at his finger.

"Good point," he said to himself and put his hand down. He slid the metal cylinder off and set it aside, turning his attention to the bundle of papers. "If all else fails, look for the owner's manual," he said, starting to sift through the small stack. But just then his watch beeped, warning him that his lunch time was over, which was a little annoying since it seemed his appetite was suddenly coming back. Oliver didn't see anything in his quick glimpse of the paperwork that gave him the gist of the project, just lots of jargon, policy speak and words no one ever used in real life. He didn't have enough time to make any sense of it. Rather than aggravate the headache he had felt coming on earlier, he decided to take Roger's advice and set the project aside for now. He slid the papers back inside the folder and tossed the metal cylinder in on top after giving it one more quick examination, mostly for any remaining salt. He'd figure out what the hell it was later.

5

OLIVER pulled his dark blue Dodge Omni to a stop in front of his garage door. Technically it wasn't his garage door, it was Mrs. Lundquist's, the elderly woman who owned the house and from whom Oliver rented a tiny second floor efficiency apartment. Living there did have one perk as Oliver liked to think of it, and that was the garage, a very useful thing to have if you went through winters in Wisconsin and had to drive to work every morning. You had to clear the driveway of snow occasionally, but at least you didn't have to scrape the frost off the car windows every morning. Of course the garage, like the apartment, was tiny and came with no extras. It was detached from the house, had no power so you couldn't see anything inside at night, and the door was obviously a manual one you had to raise...well, manually. Since he had to stop and get out to open the garage door anyway, Oliver always emptied his car of whatever he needed to take into his apartment before driving it inside. The garage was so small that the gap between the car and the wall made it hard to get out if you were unlucky enough to be wearing a winter coat, let alone the ridiculous idea that you might try carrying something too.

This particular evening, Oliver unloaded his gym bag, his backpack with the work he had to do that night and the plastic bag of various medications he'd purchased at the drugstore on the way home in preparation for whatever cold or virus he had contracted. Setting them aside, he approached the garage door and mentally prepared himself for turning the handle, which was always a battle. He had closely examined the old metal handle a hundred times and coated every inch of it and all connected machinery with various types of oils and lubricants, but the thing was still both a test of will and a feat of strength to get turned. Lifting the old, heavy door was a breeze compared to turning the ancient handle. Oliver centered himself in front of it, planted his feet firmly on the ground, and bent his knees slightly. Exhaling slowly, he counted to three in his head and then twisted the handle with both hands, letting out an unconscious grunt as he did. The handle, apparently forgetting its usual role in this mythic tale, turned with a simple click, almost as if it were made to do that. Oliver opened his eyes, which had been closed in anticipation of the strain, and looked at the handle. It was the same old handle—no one had replaced it with a new working version. He looked around at the garage and then over at Mrs. Lundquist's light yellow house, wondering if this were some look-alike at which he had mistakenly arrived. There were a lot of similar old houses with detached garages in the neighborhood, so it was feasible Oliver had stopped at the wrong one, possibly because of the delirium accompanying the early stages of his illness. But after a couple of turns back and forth between the garage handle and the house, it seemed he had indeed arrived at the right one. Looking up at the sky, Oliver wondered if this particular night held some perfect blend of temperature, humidity and barometric pressure (whatever that was) which had made this possible. No doubt a complex combination of factors that would never be repeated again in this millennium. After a couple of seconds, he shrugged and lifted the door. Perhaps it was simply a little good karma for all the bad he'd had lately. He pulled the car inside, shuffled sideways out of the garage, and shut the door behind him. The garage handle clicked quickly and competently into place, which also never happened, and Oliver carried his stuff up the exterior wooden staircase toward the door of his apartment.

About halfway up the stairs Oliver noted that his right knee didn't hurt. Usually he did a bit of a funny, stiff-legged walk up the stairs because it took some of the weight off his knee, which routinely ached a little extra following a couple of hours of basketball. Tonight it wasn't hurting at all. Oliver guessed it was just a fluke but secretly hoped his knee had finally given up hurting and gotten better. That was possible, wasn't it? Or maybe this night of perfect weather conditions responsible for the easily functioning garage handle had done the same for his knee. He wasn't sure if it was a good thing or not that what fixed a rusty, ancient metal apparatus also fixed his knee, which was presumably made of different stuff, but one can't be too picky.

"Maybe it's a little more of that good karma," Oliver said to himself as he climbed the last few stairs to the landing. "A few million more similar things and it might make up for the rest of my life." Unlocking his door, Oliver thought about it some more. He did have a particularly good night at basketball, so maybe there was something to this idea of good karma, especially since he hadn't even expected to play after the way he had started feeling earlier in the day. But maybe it was the sickness that was responsible for it. Sometimes you play well in spite of an injury or illness because you're not focused on your play, just surviving. Oliver had not missed much at all shooting the ball and even surprised himself with a couple of the passes he made, the kind where he wasn't even sure he had seen the opening before the pass was out of his hand. That wasn't a common part of his game. And there had been some defense too, even a blocked shot. Oliver never blocked shots. Maybe he was actually having a run of good luck. It's certainly not something he would have recognized, it being the most endangered species in his world. However, in the very next instant Oliver was cursing himself for believing it possible as he scraped his knuckles against the side of the doorjamb. He had done this same thing so many times in the past it was ridiculous, but it wasn't really his fault. It was a hazard. The handle was placed so close to the edge of the door that if he wasn't extremely careful as he turned and pushed, his hand would scrape along the doorjamb and he'd leave a sizable chunk of skin behind. Of course he didn't know what was worse, the fact that he kept forgetting and doing it repeatedly, or that he never just replaced the knob with one in the proper location. Oliver froze, waiting for the pain to start and not wanting to look to see how much of the back of his hand was scraped off, but as the seconds wore on, no pain arrived. Looking down at his hand, Oliver found it to be in surprisingly good shape with no bleeding at all. There were a couple of light red marks but no long scrapes or broken skin at all. Maybe his streak of good luck or karma, whatever it was, was still intact. He examined the doorjamb and noticed the thick metal plate that usually did the bulk of the damage was bent. That must be what kept it from drawing blood this time around but Oliver didn't know how it had gotten bent, or for how long it had been that way. It looked like the door would still close and latch properly, so he decided he would leave it, seeing as it might save him from future injury.

Inside the apartment, Oliver dropped his backpack on the coffee table where he'd be slaving away on work the rest of the night, tossed his gym bag onto the bed he assumed he wouldn't be using because of the work, and set his bag of meds on one of the tiny slivers of counter in the kitchen. The truly amazing thing about how Oliver had deposited each of his bags in their place, which gives a person a true sense of the smallness of his apartment, was that he was still standing just inside the front door. If he wanted, he could probably go to the bathroom from there too. Real one stop shopping. But at least the apartment was cheap. It could possibly be classified as a studio apartment, but that made it sound much more pleasant and sophisticated than it was. Oliver guessed it had originally been two bedrooms on the second floor of the house that had been converted into an apartment by knocking down the separating wall, converting one side into a combination bedroom/living room and the other side into a tiny kitchen and bathroom. It doesn't sound too bad, but they weren't big rooms to begin with, so calling it a kitchen was being generous and even kitchenette was pushing it. On the living room side Oliver had a twin bed pushed against the far wall with its foot in one corner and its head against a narrow, somewhat rickety wardrobe that served as his closet and dresser. Between the bed and the kitchen table Oliver had squeezed in what was either a smallish couch or a largish chair depending on how you measured that sort of thing, and on the opposite wall hung a small flat screen television. It happened to be the cheapest refurbished model Oliver could find when his old tube style one finally died. The television was roughly centered between the wardrobe and the front door. The coffee table occupied what little was left of the precious open space in the room. Open space wasn't plentiful on the other side of the apartment either. Taking what was a smallish bedroom and then throwing up a wall plus appliances and fixtures for both a kitchen and bathroom tended to fill things up pretty quickly. Basically Oliver had a hallway's worth of space with a sink and appliances along one wall to serve as the kitchen. It could conceivably be called a galley kitchen but that implies some kind of style or planning. All this remodeling had been done long ago, too, so the appliances weren't space age miracles of compact manufacturing, just old eccentricities that probably didn't last for very long on the market. A two-burner stove and toaster oven combination? Who knew? The bathroom had its own inadequacies, the main one being that it contained only an extraordinarily small bathtub with no shower option, which is why Oliver took advantage of the gym showers after basketball as often as possible despite the dangers of weird foot fungi.

Grabbing the remote off the coffee table, Oliver turned on the television as he headed into the kitchen to discover if he had anything to eat. He passed his newly purchased meds on the counter and thought about whether he should get some into his system, but realized he didn't think he needed it. In fact, since he had really felt the sickness starting to come on about lunchtime, it hadn't gotten any worse, and now he actually felt fine. It was probably just the calm before the storm, and the cold or whatever it was would hit as soon as he sat down later to work so that already punishing experience could be made more dreadful, but at least Oliver had managed to sneak in some exercise at basketball first. From the television, Oliver could hear the familiar theme music of one of the many entertainment news shows on at that time of night. As he was combing the cupboards and refrigerator for something other than cereal and milk—he was so very tired of corn flakes—he heard some coverage of one of the Los Angeles area heroes, Golden Gal. He resisted the temptation to run in and see some of the video. Golden Gal was known for her costume, which really was very golden, but mostly showed a lot of gal.

"Doesn't she look good?" gushed a female co-host. "She's so stylish." Oliver wondered if she was fighting someone or attending a movie premiere. It was hard to tell with these shows.

"Yes," agreed the male co-host, "Even after battling a supervillain, she still looks fantastic. Truly stunning."

"I just love her boots," said the female co-host. The theme music picked up again. "We'll be right back, but first we're going to leave you with a preview of our next segment of the rest of the interview we showed you yesterday from our exclusive talk last week with the legendary superhero, Metallion."

With no other viable options, Oliver settled on cereal once again and carried it into the living room. He pulled his phone out of his pocket as he sat down on the couch and noticed he had two messages. They must have come during basketball. He muted the television and called up the messages, putting the phone on speaker so he could start eating as he listened. The first message was from his mother, mostly just checking in but also complaining about one of her friends. She was retired and living in Arizona and spent most of her time doing various activities with women she seemed not to like much. Maybe it just reminded her of Oliver's dad, who had died a few years before of a heart attack, and who she also seemed not to like much. Oliver had liked him just fine and missed him but couldn't begrudge him getting some peace and quiet. The second message was from Kate. Oliver had called her to cancel their plans earlier in the day but she didn't answer so he was only able to leave a message on her phone.

"Oliver, I got your message. (Pause) Well, I sort of felt like I should do this in person, but...Look, I don't want to see you anymore. I just don't think it's going to work out...that we're compatible in the long run. (Pause) I mean, this is the third time in two weeks you've cancelled something because of work. And well...that would be fine if you were a lawyer or doctor or something important...if you made money. But I deserve better. Look, don't call me. (Pause) I've got a date anyway. Bye."

Oliver sat with a spoonful of corn flakes halfway to his mouth. What amazing timing this was. He had a ton of useless work to do, a sleepless night ahead of him, some kind of sickness most likely coming on and Kate picked just that time to dump him. So much for the good karma. Perhaps he should have recognized the good for what it was, just a little something to throw him off before the other shoe dropped.

"Sure," Oliver said to himself mockingly, "Go ahead, have a good game or two of basketball, make a nice pass, block a shot, be the big man on campus, we'll straighten you out when we get home." Oliver closed his eyes and waited for it. He knew the depression would begin at any moment. He usually got pretty down in the dumps when his relationships ended, and the dumps seemed to be getting significantly lower as he got older, in keeping with impending old maid status. With this news, Oliver knew there was no way he'd be able to get any work done tonight, although he wasn't too worried about that. Undoubtedly Sergeant Przybylinski wasn't really counting on having the data by tomorrow morning. In keeping with past experience, it would turn out not to be needed for that meeting, or he actually did need the original data and he was awful sorry for the mix-up or something along those lines, but even after Oliver had noticed the pattern, he had always done the work anyway. What choice did he have? He just couldn't take the chance the Sergeant would surprise him. No matter what, Oliver had always just done the work. Only this time he wasn't sure he could. He envisioned the depression hitting him soon and coupled with his sickness the only logical response was to fight back with his newly purchased stash of cold and flu meds. They should sufficiently knock him out so he wouldn't feel the pain of the depression or illness. Sort of like his own medically induced coma. He was pretty sure he would be calling in sick tomorrow. Screw Przybylinski, the work, Kate, all of it.

Oliver sat there waiting for the first wave of depression. And waiting. It should be rolling in any second. Still waiting. He didn't feel horrible, neither physically nor emotionally. That was…different. Surprising. He thought about Kate. He waited. The more he thought about it, the more he realized maybe it wasn't a bad thing Kate had broken up with him. Small epiphany. She wasn't that great a girl. It seemed very clear to Oliver now, with numerous incidents from their various dates popping up in his head that were obvious red flags. So very obvious. Incompatible in an extraordinary number of ways. What the hell had he been thinking? He should have dumped her. But maybe this was better. At least this way Oliver didn't have to do the actual dumping or even deal with her in person. Really kind of convenient. Instead of depressed, Oliver felt good, even sort of optimistic. The future was full of possibilities, and he was free to pursue every single one. There was clarity. Why wasn't it always this easy? Oliver shrugged and stuck the spoonful of corn flakes into his mouth that had been waiting throughout this tiny epiphany. He loved corn flakes. That bit not so much an epiphany as just a simple truth.

To round out Oliver's surprising evening, the sickness that had seemed such a sure thing earlier in the day failed to show up and make him the miserable wreck he had expected to become. This allowed him to avoid taking all the knock-out medications and get the revised data work done despite his thinking it wouldn't get done at all. Oliver was even finished by 11:30 after expecting it would take all night. He didn't think such a thing was possible, but he was in the zone work-wise and just pounded it out like it was nothing. After packing the finished work into his backpack, Oliver wasn't even feeling tired yet, perhaps because he had mentally prepared himself to be up all night, so he watched a little late night television and finally went to bed around two in the morning. As he closed his eyes, he thought he would surely regret staying up that late when his alarm went off in the morning.

Surprisingly, the morning proved him wrong. He awoke early, well before his alarm, and didn't feel at all tired. The sun was shining in through his only window, bathing everything in such an amazing light that Oliver stepped out on his landing to watch it rise for a while. Then he cooked himself a nice breakfast and ate leisurely in front of the morning shows on television, learning about the coolest new gadgets he couldn't afford and what uncommon meats you could barbecue. He never got to eat breakfast leisurely or learn useless things. Usually it was pretty much a sprint out the door in the morning.

After breakfast Oliver started dressing for work, leaving the television on for company. It was a little loud, but he knew it wouldn't bother Mrs. Lundquist downstairs because she was pretty hard of hearing. That was possibly the one and only bonus to his apartment. Mrs. Lundquist was a bit on the nosy side and strangely suspicious of Oliver even though he had never given her any reason to be. Her poor hearing made it a little easier because she wasn't bothering him about each little bump she heard, but on the other hand there were some things she misheard or just imagined that tended to lead to some bizarre misunderstandings. Oliver usually managed to get those straightened out, once he figured out what they were about, and life went on normally. Of course normal meant Mrs. Lundquist smiled strangely when Oliver handed her his rent check and routinely watched him through a crack in the curtains whenever she could. It was creepy, but it was normal.

As Oliver began dressing, the regular network morning show had given way to the local news update and the newswoman reporting said, "In a bit of a surprise move late in the afternoon yesterday, the Mayor's office announced they had filled the superhero position that had been vacant since it was created with the Mayor's first budget after taking office. No further information was given on the appointed superhero, although they said there would be a formal introduction next week."

Oliver pulled off his t-shirt and reached into the wardrobe for a work shirt. The first one he tried on was a little tight across his chest and shoulders, so he set it aside and tried another, only to get the same result.

"...and many think this is a political move by the Mayor due to the upcoming election and his sagging numbers..." continued the voice from the television.

Oliver stood looking at his shirts. They were both fairly new and he feared he had done something drastically wrong with the laundry and managed to shrink them. This was not good. He didn't have a lot of good work shirts, and if he had screwed them up it might mean a trip to the store to buy replacements with money he didn't really have. For now he delved into the wardrobe for something older, finding a shirt he knew had always been a little big. Oddly enough it fit perfectly. Oliver guessed he might have managed to shrink it with the others, although he was fairly certain he hadn't worn it for a long time and therefore hadn't washed it. He was a little mystified but he didn't have the time to figure out the problem right then.

"...little is known about the hero at this moment, other than what is specified in the budget, which we are told is a low level hero position, the minimum for a metropolitan area of this size."

Stopping in the bathroom to wash up, Oliver decided that if the shrinking clothes were the bad side of things this morning, then the good side was his hair. As Oliver wet it down and ran a comb through it, he could swear it looked better than it had in a long time. He couldn't quite put a finger on it, but maybe it looked a little fuller, or the receding hairline had somehow managed to gain back some ground. Regardless, the balding that bugged him to a certain degree seemed not so bad as he remembered. He wasn't doing anything special, not smothering any late night television advertised miracle stuff on his head or any home brew remedies. He wondered if he had eaten something bizarre lately that happened to be some particularly potent natural form of Rogaine. Perhaps something in the tofu no-egg salad or mango carrot mocha he'd had at that new overpriced-sandwich-and-strange-drink place he went to with Roger a couple of days ago. That was bizarre enough to have done something to his hair. He'd hate to have to frequent the place, even if it did help his hair grow. It was something else he'd have to check into more closely that night. Grabbing his gym bag and backpack, Oliver turned off the television and headed out the door.

6

A couple days later, on Thursday morning, Sergeant Przybylinski was holding court in the break room, entertaining a few of his buddies as they waited for Oliver to complete the task he had been given by the sergeant. Oliver wasn't in the room with them, he was currently a couple of floors below, busy lugging an ancient overhead projector up the seven flights of stairs from a basement storage room. Oliver had to use the stairs because the elevators were currently out of commission. Sergeant Przybylinski knew this, which is precisely why he had asked Oliver to retrieve the projector from storage in the first place. Sergeant Przybylinski also knew that the projector, while not all that big, was surprisingly heavy, almost as if the manufacturer had filled the inside with cement, which could have actually been the case since the machine didn't work at all. But Sergeant Przybylinski didn't want to use the projector, he just wanted to entertain himself by having Oliver get it, as he had done with many of the previous interns. The elevators tended to break down quite a bit, which made this task a ritual for any untested intern. Many of the previous victims had barely survived those seven floors if they made it all the way up at all, and Sergeant Przybylinski didn't think Oliver was a threat to break the record time. That record was held by a young man named Tim, although there was some dispute whether it should count since it was suspected he used the elevator for the last three floors when they inconveniently started working again.

Currently Sergeant Przybylinski and his pals were reminiscing about the efforts of other past contestants and making wagers on where Oliver would place. He was a twenty to one long shot to make the best time, which is why the group went dead silent when Oliver walked into the room carrying the projector a full thirteen minutes ahead of the current record. Dead silent that is except for Ted from Administration who had put ten dollars on Oliver to break the record and was now making small squeaking noises and moving about as if he had a bug infestation in his pants.

"There you go, Sergeant Przybylinski," said Oliver, as he set the projector on one of the small tables in the break room. He noticed that Sergeant Przybylinski and the rest of the people there were all staring at him a bit oddly—except for the one short, bald-headed guy kind of dancing a jig in the background—and wondered if he had walked in on them talking about him. But that would be silly and paranoid, Oliver decided, so he just shrugged and turned to leave.

"Uh, hold on, Olson," said Sergeant Przybylinski. "You're back, huh?" He was looking more at the projector than at Oliver.

"Yeah, sorry it took so long, but the elevators were out so I had to use the stairs."

"The elevators were out?" asked the sergeant, still looking at the projector.

"Yes."

"And you used the stairs?"

"Yes."

"All seven floors?"

"Yes."

Sergeant Przybylinski stepped over to where the projector sat on the table and touched it with an outstretched finger. "And this is the projector?" he said, poking it with his finger a couple more times. Then he took it in both hands and lifted it off the table a couple of inches before setting it back in place. "Yeah, that's the one," he said, mostly to himself.

"Okay, great," said Oliver, edging closer to the door. Everyone was acting so odd, especially Sergeant Przybylinski, that Oliver was tempted to wait around and see why, but his instinct was to get away from the sergeant as fast as possible before some other idiotic task was dropped on him. He paused for one more split second at the door, then said, "See ya," and slipped out. Oliver could hear someone yelling about odds and people paying up as he walked away from the door. He was focused on it so much he didn't see Joan standing in his path until her voice stopped him short.

"Oliver? It is Oliver, isn't it?"

Oliver was composed enough to nod. If the break room scene wasn't strange enough, it seemed he had stepped out of that and into a Dali-ish melting clocks flavor of odd. He could swear Joan—she of the long perfect legs and silky black hair—was speaking to him, and nuttier still, apparently knew his name.

"Oliver, I hear you know something about computers, is that right?" she said with a smile while twisting some of her hair around her finger. It seemed a very blatant and stereotypical move with the hair but somehow she managed to make it sublime. Oliver managed another nod. "Well, I've been having a little trouble with mine and was wondering if you could maybe stop by my office and have a little look at it. I know it's not your job or anything, but I thought you might be able to help me. I could call the computer tech people, but they seem so busy and you're right down the hall."

"S-Sure," Oliver stammered, finally managing speech.

"Great," said Joan. "Maybe you could come by later this afternoon. After four?" She flashed another big smile and gave her hair an extra twist. "You know where my office is?" Oliver nodded, stuck back on mute. "Good," said Joan, "I'll owe you." The way she said that last bit made Oliver's insides drop down and bounce on the floor. Joan turned and walked off down the hallway, leaving Oliver stunned in her wake. Stunned, but not out of it enough to miss watching her walk away, short skirt, long legs and all. She was gone from view for a while before Oliver could get himself moving again toward his cubicle. He found Roger waiting for him when he got there.

"Was it me hallucinating or were you just talking to Joan?" he asked as Oliver slipped past him into the cubicle.

"So you saw it too, right?" Oliver asked.

"Yeah, that's what I saw."

"Then it did happen," said Oliver, dropping into his chair. "I wasn't exactly sure myself."

"What did she want?"

"Help with...something," improvised Oliver, rather poorly. He felt it would be rubbing it in if Roger knew it was computer related. "Didn't really follow what she was talking about too closely. Bit of a deer caught in the headlights situation, if you know what I mean."

"Couldn't work your slick talking magic on her?" asked Roger with a chuckle.

Oliver smiled. "Well, I didn't want to come on too strong. If I dazzle her too early, she'll just be intimidated. That and I seemed to have trouble speaking. I might have managed a grunt or two."

"That's right, you know how to play it. Sort of a different take on the strong, silent type. The Frankenstein's monster technique." Roger eased down into the other chair and set his computer bag aside. He sat there a moment, rubbing his hands together and looking mostly down at the floor. Eventually he said, "Look, I don't know how to broach this topic so I'm just going to jump in with both feet. What's up with the hair?"

"The hair?"

"Yeah, the hair. Are you using some kind of enhancer or something? Rogaine maybe?" asked Roger. He held his hands up in front of him in a non-accusatory fashion. "I'm not against that or anything, I just thought you might have told me. You know, other guys are talking about it and they asked me because I know you, and I didn't know what to say. Whatever it is, it seems to be working great. Hell, I swear I didn't notice anything until yesterday, but it even looks better today."

"Well, I don't know...I—"

"And while we're on the subject, it seems the stuff you're taking for your hair is having a side effect on your basketball game. You've been unstoppable at the gym the last couple of nights. I know our group isn't exactly all-star competition, but I don't think I've seen you miss a shot since last week. And now Joan is talking to you. I don't know if you were informed, but she doesn't talk to guys like us. What the hell is going on? I mean, one of these things is an anomaly, two's a coincidence, but three's a pattern, maybe even a conspiracy. Am I in the wrong universe?" Roger looked around at the cubicle and the lights above, then back at Oliver. "Tell me you've noticed something too. I can't be crazy."

Oliver knew what Roger was talking about, was aware of the same weird things, but so far he hadn't been able to bring himself to confront it. Or rather, he hadn't felt like he needed to confront it. He had been feeling strangely calm about everything. The hair, the basketball, he knew something wasn't normal but every time he had even the slightest thought of self-examination, he gave up after a few seconds because he just wasn't worried about it. So instead of questioning things more as the weirdness mounted over the past two days, Oliver wrote it off as a streak of good luck. But now there was Joan. He couldn't explain Joan. She intersected his world in a place where there was no luck, so it kind of killed his theory.

"I don't know," said Oliver simply.

"You don't?"

"No. Well, actually, I'm kind of relieved right now because I thought I might have been doing some kind of delusional thing in regards to the hair, but you see it too, huh?" Oliver looked questioningly at Roger while tilting his head around at varying angles.

"Yeah, I see it. But what do you mean, delusional? You're using Rogaine or some other miracle hair growth stuff, right?"

"No, nothing. I thought it was just a fluke, like I was accidentally doing something different than usual and it just looked better. Heck, yesterday I realized I bought the shampoo plus conditioner version of my regular stuff by mistake, and I thought maybe the conditioner was making it look more full, but this morning...well, I swear there's more actual hair. It's like I'm in high school again. Maybe it's some hormone thing..."

"A hormone thing? Spontaneously re-growing your hair? Yeah, that's plausible. You sure you're not using Rogaine? It's okay, there's nothing to be embarrassed about."

"Unless the elves who make my shoes at night have signed a pharmaceutical deal, I'm not using Rogaine."

"Well, you gotta be doing something...What about PED's? Are you juicing to be better at basketball? You know that's against pick-up league rules."

"No, no steroids or human growth hormone. At least I've never failed a drug test administered by the league, and if I did it would obviously be because I drank something that was tainted."

"Of course," said Roger. He stared at Oliver's hair for a moment, then snapped his fingers. "Well, you might not be doing something, but what if something is being done to you," he said, nodding his head at the idea.

"Being done to me?"

"Yes," said Roger. "I'm not going to go all crazy conspiracy theorist on you here, like I'm going to assume you weren't abducted by aliens because the shoe elves would never let that happen, but maybe it's something more rational. You said you suspected your shampoo, so maybe it's something simple like that. Like an accident at the shampoo factory where the conditioner portion was replaced by some hair growth formula."

"Accident at the shampoo factory? That's more rational?"

"They gotta make it somewhere, right? Okay, maybe not that. Maybe something new you've been using or eating. Or where you've been. Or where you live. Maybe your apartment is on top of a toxic waste dump or sacred burial ground?"

"I have to admit I haven't considered the sacred burial ground theory, but as far as I know there's just Mrs. Lundquist below me and while she's old, she's neither dead nor sacred," answered Oliver. "It's an old house, maybe lead paint?"

"Are you eating it?"

"Not usually."

"Then doubtful," said Roger. "Besides, all of these things should be bad for you, not growing new hair—wait, is it just on your head or are you going full gorilla?"

"Just on my head. In fact, you know how we were talking about the long hairs I found that were starting to grow out of my ears?" asked Oliver.

"Sadly, I do," said Roger.

"Gone. I checked. Look," Oliver said, leaning forward and displaying an ear. "Pristine. Not a single old man hair, just peach fuzz like a baby."

Roger waved him off. "I'll take your word for it," he said. "But what about you? I mean, shouldn't you be freaking out? This is capital W weird stuff."

Oliver nodded. "Yeah, yeah. It's weird. All caps weird. But for some reason I don't feel freaked out." He paused, searching for the words. "I feel...normal," he said with a shrug.

"Normal?" said Roger.

"Normal."

"This is not normal."

"Agreed."

"You know, it's not just the hair either, you're also playing basketball three times better than before. It's one thing to have a couple good nights, probably not consecutive, but you're suddenly on a whole new level."

Oliver rubbed at the carpet with his foot. "Yeah, I've thought about that too," he said, looking up at Roger. "You want to know something else?"

"I'm not sure. It's not more about where hair may or may not be growing, is it?"

"Last night after the games were done and everybody cleared out, I... Well, you know there was that one time I got a steal and a breakaway? I was going in for the layup and I swear it went through my mind to dunk it. And not just a fleeting thought of wishing I could dunk it, but a calculated what kind of dunk should I do sort of thought. I don't do that sort of thing on a breakaway, I just concentrate on not dribbling the ball off my foot before the layup. But for some reason the hoop looked low to me and I just had this feeling I could go up and dunk it. Obviously I didn't do it. Heck, I've never even tried before because I can barely touch the rim on my best day. I'd need another foot of vertical. But then…" Oliver sort of shrugged. Roger motioned for him to continue, so he did. "Well, afterwards I stayed around shooting until everybody left, and then I tried to dunk and…I did it. It wasn't even hard. I couldn't believe it, and I thought maybe the hoop was a little low because they sometimes lower them for the kids to play on and hadn't raised it all the way back to the regular height. But that would be just an inch or two because we'd notice any more than that while we were playing, and I'd still need more than a couple of inches to dunk. Then I got paranoid someone was playing a trick on me, got me on video or something. Funniest dumb jock wannabes or something. So I just left. But…" Oliver shook his head slowly.

"But what?"

"I was thinking about it all night, so I stopped by this morning before work to try again…"

"And?"

"I could dunk. I could do everything. Two hands, a reverse, whatever—I could dunk. Can dunk. I can dunk. I even brought my tape measure with me to check the height of the hoops and they were all ten feet. I could dunk on any of them. And it's so bizarrely weird, I should be freaking out, but I'm not. I feel like I should be able to do it. That it's not a surprise. It's just normal."

"This is not normal, no way," said Roger.

Oliver nodded. "I agree, but it kinda feels that way."

"Seriously, you're making fun of me now, aren't you? You're mad about me mentioning the hair so you're tuning me up. I suppose you can throw a football a hundred yards and hit a baseball five hundred feet too."

"Haven't tried," said Oliver, "but for some reason I can dunk."

"Truth?" said Roger, waiting for a smile to crack Oliver's face and reveal all this to be a joke. It didn't come. Roger sat there for a moment longer, trying to get his mind around it. Finally he said, "Okay, so more hair and you're suddenly a basketball stud. Anything else bizarrely weird?"

"Well, and maybe this is responsible for the dunking, but I think I might be growing."

Roger stared at him for a moment. "Growing? Seriously?" asked Roger, looking Oliver up and down. "Stand up." Oliver did and they stood back to back. Oliver had always been the taller of the two, but only by half an inch, and today it was closer to two. They both removed their shoes and checked again, getting the same result. "You are taller," said Roger, incredulous. "Okay, I'm definitely going back to my nuclear waste theory now. Any third eyes? Or third anythings for that matter?"

"No, nothing I've noticed. But it's not just getting taller, a couple of days ago I tried on some of my shirts and they were a bit tight. I thought I might have shrunk them when doing the laundry, but since then almost everything seems small. I've had to buy a bunch of new clothes and even shoes. I don't know exactly what I usually weigh but on the scale at the gym this morning I was almost fifteen pounds more than I thought I should be. I've been around 170 since high school and this morning I was 185."

"Are you sure you're not taking steroids? HGH? Maybe those vitamin powders from GNC?"

"You think I wouldn't have mentioned that? No to all those. The only unusual thing I've done lately is go to a couple of those new Pilates classes at the gym."

"Really?"

"Well, mostly because there are lots of women in the classes." Oliver shrugged. "I'm weak."

"I hear you," said Roger. "That all?"

"No weight lifting or anything, just the occasional sit-ups and push-ups. I've even run a billion searches on the web trying to find anything about growth spurts at my age and I haven't found anything to explain this."

"Okay," said Roger, rubbing his head. "I don't know. This is all really, really, really weird. Really."

"Yeah, I know," agreed Oliver. "This isn't quite as bizarre, and maybe it's because there's so much weirdness to think about, but I haven't been able to sleep much the past few nights. Really not at all. I just don't feel tired. I stay up really late, and, even when I go to bed, I'm back up in an hour. I maybe drift off a little, but for the most part I just lay there awake. I've seen every infomercial ever made, and I've had time to search every inch of the web for something medically relevant. Funny thing is, I feel fine. I'm not walking around here half dead despite never sleeping. In fact, I have a ton of energy and, I'll say it again, I feel like it's all normal even though it's as weird as hell."

"Sure you're not taking any drugs? Any new prescription meds or anything? Uppers? Speed? Copious amounts of Pepto?" asked Roger.

"Nothing."

"The trouble sleeping or the weight gain sound like they could be the effects or side effects of drugs," said Roger. "Think Mrs. Lundquist is trying to poison you?"

"No real point, is there? She's not exactly in my will."

"Well, maybe she's just like that."

Both men became silent after that, each thinking on the topic. Oliver, not finding it very constructive, heeded the call of the blinking light on his office phone and lifted the receiver to check his messages. Roger picked up his computer bag and set it on the desk, pushing aside a stack of files to give himself some more room. In the process, the stack of files fell over, spreading out across the desk. He opened his case and began digging inside, but stopped when he noticed something on the desk. It was a metal folder with an insignia he recognized. He picked it up, checked the initials to make sure he was seeing it right and then looked inside. Meanwhile, Oliver deleted his last message and hung up the phone.

"I tell you, that's the third message in two days I've gotten from this Emma in Human Resources about me picking up stuff for some contract or project or something. Is this the thing you sent over, because she's acting like it's a rush, despite what you said."

Roger ignored Oliver's question and asked, "What's this?"

"That? That's what I'm talking about," said Oliver. "The project you had some guy drop off on Monday. Remember? For the 'consultant'?" Oliver made air quotes. "That's what the woman from HR keeps referring to in her messages. She says there's stuff I have to pick up and complains about having to do extra work because of it. Not as much of a non-priority as you said it was, at least not to this person."

Roger was still not really listening to Oliver, he was busy skimming, and then going back to closely read, the first couple of pages from inside the metal folder marked with the letters DSF. He stopped reading and shuffled through the stack of papers he had pulled out of it. Then he picked up the folder itself and shook it, spilling out the shiny cylinder Oliver remembered from the conference room the other day. Roger picked the cylinder up and looked at it closely. "It's been used," he said. A person could tell this because a small graphic on the side of the cylinder said just that. Used. "Whoa. Oliver?" asked Roger.

"Yes?"

"Did you use this?"

"I don't know. I put it on my finger like it said, but I didn't really know how to use it, so that's all I did. What is it? My guess was some kind of fancy new wireless pointer for presentations," said Oliver.

"No, no. Not even close," said Roger, shaking his head as he stared at the small device.

"Well, I didn't have the time to do anything else. I figured I'd get back to it later when I could read the documentation, see if that explained it. Maybe ask you if the language was too thick."

"Oh, the docs will explain it," said Roger, staring at the metal cylinder. "Wow. Actually, this explains everything."

7

"**WHAT** do you mean, it explains everything?" asked Oliver.

"Okay, first just let me verify something," answered Roger. He started rummaging through his computer bag, which held not only his laptop but just about every kind of disk, cord, wire or small tool you could imagine. He stopped with his hand still inside the bag and said, "Close your eyes. Close your eyes and set one of your hands flat on the desk."

"What for?"

"Just shut up and do it," said Roger.

"Fine," said Oliver, closing his eyes and putting his hand on the desk, "but I don't see how this helps anything. Are you sure you don't want me to stand on one leg and touch my no—AAAGGGHHH!" screamed Oliver. He opened his eyes to see Roger recoiling after hitting his hand with a small hammer. Oliver pulled his hand to his chest, cradling it while staring in horror at Roger. "What the hell are you doing? Are you crazy?" Roger didn't answer, but simply watched his friend with great interest, which Oliver found quite disconcerting. "Hello? I said, what the hell did you do that for?" asked Oliver again, shaking his hand and taking his eyes off Roger for a second to see how much damage the hammer had done.

"There's nothing, is there?" asked Roger, his eagerness barely controlled. The guy from the next cubicle popped his head over the wall to see what was causing all the commotion. Roger looked at the guy and waved his hammer. "New motivational policy," he said, "Go back to work." The guy quickly disappeared behind the wall. Roger looked back at Oliver. "I'm right, aren't I?"

"What?"

"There's nothing, right? No blood, no bruise, not even a mark, is there?" asked Roger, his eyes filled with a kind of fiendish excitement. It gave Oliver the creeps, but he looked more closely at his hand.

"Um…no," said Oliver, rubbing a finger over the spot on the back of his hand while beginning to understand that something here was very, very strange—and it wasn't simply Roger and his sudden love for small hand tool violence. "Nothing, nothing at all," confirmed Oliver, his voice showing his surprise.

"I knew it! Nothing." Roger reached forward and grabbed Oliver's hand to look for himself. "Totally clear. Not even a spot."

"No, not nothing," complained Oliver. "There was pain. I distinctly recall pain. Did you hear the yell? That was me. That was pain." Oliver pulled his hand back and held it protectively on the side of his body away from Roger. He wasn't sure this little hammer episode was over.

"Of course there was pain," said Roger, "there's bound to be a little pain this soon after, but as hard as I hit you, that hand should be broken. Swollen and red at the very least. But yet, there's nothing, just a bit of pain."

"More than a *bit*," corrected Oliver.

"Yeah, yeah, but even that's probably gone now, isn't it?" asked Roger, still plainly excited. Oliver didn't say anything, so Roger prompted, "Well?" After a second Oliver reluctantly nodded and Roger threw both hands in the air. "I knew it. That explains everything."

"You keep saying that—what explains everything? And does that explanation include your rather crappy behavior for someone who's supposed to be a good friend of mine?" asked Oliver, still rubbing his hand despite the fact that Roger was right and it no longer hurt. "I'm definitely rethinking the requirements I have for friends. No hammering is going right to the top of the list."

"*This* explains everything," said Roger, picking up the cylinder and metal folder. "You, my friend, are a superhero."

Pause. A significant one.

"Come again?"

"A superhero. You. Are one."

Oliver stared at Roger for a short moment. "You know Roger, having a healthy respect for a friend, even looking up to them is okay, but you might be pushing it a little bit now. The consultant thing you whipped up the other day was awfully nice, and I appreciate your trying to keep me optimistic about my job and feeling like I'm needed, but I think this is a step too far. I mean, hero worship? At a point it gets a little creepy."

"I'm not whipping anything up, Oliver. You're a superhero. I don't know how it happened, and I certainly didn't have anything to do with it, but you're a superhero. A real superhero." Roger paused, but the look on Oliver's face told him he had not yet gotten through, which was perfectly reasonable considering Roger felt he hadn't had nearly enough of a stunned into silence phase himself. "Haven't you seen the news lately? The Mayor appointed someone to the superhero position for the city. These…" Roger raised the metal folder and cylinder again, "These *are* the superhero position. You see, DSF?" Using the cylinder, Roger pointed at the initials on the folder. "Department of Superhero Funding. I don't know how you ended up with it, but when you stuck this on your finger," he held up the cylinder, "you were injected with the super serum that gives you the abilities of the superhero specified in the position description in this file. That explains why you're growing, why you're suddenly great at ball, why your hand didn't break when I hit it with the hammer, why your hair is growing back—specifically on your head and not out of your ears...Hell, now that I look at you, I swear your jaw's gotten more square."

"My jaw?" Oliver felt it with his hand.

"It's a standard part of the super serum," answered Roger. "Along with getting the typical super muscular hero body, you also get a prettier face and a full head of hair. All physical characteristics are improved. I don't think the face thing is a primary focus, but it just kind of happens along with all the rest. And that energy thing, the no sleeping, that's part of it too. Nobody wants to fund a superhero if they can't have access to him twenty-four seven. Can't have him off taking a nap while some big meanie is knocking over buildings downtown, so that's part of the serum. There's no down time. You don't need sleep. I think you can sleep if you want to, but you don't need it. Heck, you don't need a lot of things anymore, like air, or food, or water. You can still use them, but you can also go without them indefinitely. That's part of the standard hero serum." Roger paused to catch his breath and shook his head. "Wow, this is so cool."

"Cool? Cool for you maybe, but I didn't sign up for this," said Oliver. He thought for a second. "Well, I guess

I did sign something…but I didn't know what it was. I didn't want to be a superhero."

"Didn't want to be a superhero? Who doesn't want to be a superhero? What kind of childhood did you have? Anyway, maybe you didn't before, but do you want to be a superhero *now*?" asked Roger.

"Heck yes. I mean, yes. I mean—" Oliver stopped himself short. He thought he had meant to say no, or at the very least hedge a bit with an 'I don't know' or 'maybe'. He tried again. "I mean…" he paused, "Yes." He smiled with satisfaction, then closed his eyes and slumped in his chair. "Did I just say yes again?"

"Yes," said Roger.

"Okay."

"Don't worry, it's because you mean it. That's part of the serum too—it makes you want to be a superhero, to help people, to protect them. Sure, you may actually be that kind of guy to some degree anyway, but in case you aren't, they make sure. Can't really give a guy a job as a superhero and then have him decide after the fact he'd rather be a pharmacist. Think about it," said Roger. "You really do want to be a superhero now, don't you?"

Oliver thought about it. He didn't know for certain if he had wanted to be a superhero before, although it seemed reasonable. Every little kid wanted to be a superhero at some point, and adults probably did too given the chance, at least the normal ones. He hadn't really thought about it before, but, as he did now, there was no doubt. "Yes, I want to be a superhero," said Oliver, slowly nodding his head in amazement. "Wow."

"Wow, indeed."

"So…" started Oliver, waving a hand slightly in the air in front of him as if it would help to get his brain moving, "How is it that you seem to be an expert on all this stuff?"

"I've always been into the tech side of it," answered Roger. "You know, the powers, abilities and such. Some people follow the celebrity of it, but I'm not really into that. That's more like if you're a fan of your hometown baseball team but can't be objective about it. I'm the kind of guy who just likes the game for what it is, no favorite team, just want to see a good game, follow the stats and the trades and all that. Kind of a nerd, I guess, surprisingly enough. I'm a member of *HeroTech.com*, the only real scientific website on the subject. The rest are all fluff or tabloid-like." Roger reached into the DSF folder and pulled out the bundle of papers inside. He scanned the first page as he continued, "I've seen several of these position descriptions before, or at least mock forms of them. They don't give out the complete descriptions for real heroes because some villain might get hold of it and find a weakness to exploit, but I have seen enough of them to know what the terms and jargon mean. I can see just what level of hero you are, what special abilities you have or will have—flying, energy pulses, super vision—or allocations for equipment, cars, planes, whatever. You could even have funding for a sidekick or a secret headquarters. This is so cool." Roger paged further through the documentation.

"A sidekick?"

"Yeah, although you don't really want one. They can be a pain in the ass and it just pulls money away from other, more useful things," said Roger. "Who wouldn't rather have a cool car?"

"Okay, good to know," said Oliver, still a bit in shock, although not quite as much as he thought he would be after hearing what he had just heard. In fact, he thought it was strange that he could think clearly enough to think it was strange that he could think clearly. Or that he could even follow that thought, if it was indeed logical. He decided it was just strange enough to ask about. "So why am I not just floored by this right now? I don't understand how I'm still standing after hearing all this. This is the biggest curve ball of all curve balls. Who in their right mind even leaves the house after discovering they've grown two inches in the past two days at the age of 29? Instead, I'm off to the gym to see if I can dunk, like that's a normal thing to do in the morning. I should be hunkered down in my bed with the covers over my head. But I feel...calm."

"Well, I'm betting the calm is another part of the serum," said Roger, not looking up from the papers. "It's probably not specifically for this, since most folks actually know they take the serum, but it's there to help the heroes do their jobs. Clears the head, as they say. As a superhero you have to be able to make snap judgments under great pressure, or not be taken too much by surprise so you can react or recover quickly, and that's part of the serum. Costume, what about the costume?" he muttered, flipping through pages.

"Costume?"

"Yeah, I'm just trying to find out what your costume looks like. Oh, and your name. How could I forget? We don't know what your name is."

"I have to wear a costume?" Images of Golden Gal's costume raced through Oliver's head. So much exposed flesh. Oliver had no tan at all, he lived in Wisconsin.

"Duh, you're a superhero. And it's the law, of course. It has to be obvious you're a superhero. In fact, you aren't supposed to do anything out of costume ever because— and this is a shining example of our judicial system—the criminals can sue you for not making it known that you're a superhero. Something about fighting under false pretenses or entrapment or...I don't really know what they call it. Anyway, you have to wear a costume at all times."

"Costume? But why not just a, a uniform, like a cop's uniform? That seems much better than a costume. Not all shiny and...small and such."

"Well, you can't wear a regular police officer's uniform for the same reason you have to wear a costume in the first place; you have to be identifiable to the bad guys. And that means they must be able to easily tell you apart from citizens and regular cops as well. Once again it's all about lawsuits."

"But...a *costume*? Can I at least call it a uniform?"

Roger was still skimming the papers in his hand. "Call it whatever you want, it's still a costume," he said, finally looking up. "Hey, that woman you said was calling from Human Resources, she has stuff for you?"

"That's what she said."

"That must be your costume. Probably other gear too. Maybe extra costumes. You should go get them. Heck, go get them and take them home. I'll take this paperwork and look it over to see what all you have, and I'll meet you at your place as soon as I'm off work. No ball for me tonight," said Roger, diving back into the papers on his lap.

"Take them home?" asked Oliver. "What about...?" He gestured vaguely at his computer, meaning his work.

"Screw that," said Roger. "That's not your job anymore. You're not an intern or a consultant or anything else. You're something totally different. You're a superhero now."

8

"EXCUSE me, I'm looking for Emma?" Oliver asked a woman near the front of the Human Resources Department. The large, fluorescent lit room was laid out similarly to the area in which he worked, with cubicles filling the interior of the space and offices along the outside, but this room was painted a much more daring shade of beige. The woman was wearing a telephone headset and Oliver realized she was on a call as she covered the mouthpiece and said, "That way," while pointing toward one of the aisles running between the cubicles. Oliver mouthed a 'Thank you' and headed down the aisle she had indicated, checking nameplates as he went. The third cubicle on the left belonged to Emma

Simms. Oliver stepped into the opening and knocked lightly on the wall of the cubicle.

A young woman with shoulder length, slightly wavy blond hair was sitting mostly with her back to Oliver, talking on the telephone. She swiveled partially around in her chair and held up a hand as she said into the phone, "—So if you could call me back, that would be great. Thanks." She hung up, scribbled something on a pad of paper and turned to face Oliver while pushing some stray strands of hair behind her left ear. She looked to be about Oliver's age, maybe a year or two younger, and had a nice smile and friendly blue eyes. Friendly, at least right up until Oliver introduced himself.

"So you're Oliver Olson," she stated. Suddenly, the nice smile he had been admiring didn't seem to possess the emotion you normally associate with a smile, but Oliver couldn't quite place what it was he was detecting. "I was just leaving you yet another message. That must be somewhere close to five now. Possibly a record for an employee who I didn't find out later was actually dead. But maybe you folks just have the phones without buttons over in your department," she said, the smile still fixed in place. "Or is dialing just too complicated a concept for you to handle? No, I bet you didn't even get that far. Probably so confused by which end to speak into that you just threw in the towel, right?" Oliver was definitely detecting sarcasm, that much was obvious, but the woman was also conveying a nice hint of outright hostility too, if it were possible to hint something outright. It seemed a contradiction, but Oliver was fairly certain she was achieving the effect quite well. At least in her voice. Oliver called upon his incredibly weak social skills involving women to investigate further. He searched for clues. The smile. That nice smile he had noticed straightaway wasn't the same. It had taken on a somewhat demonic dimension. Oliver checked her eyes again. Blue and friendly before, still blue but not at all friendly now. Hostile. Definitely hostile. But she was smiling. How did she do that? It was very unsettling. Oliver fought the urge to flee.

"Yes, um...I'm very sorry about that. I've just been really busy the last couple of days and I didn't realize—"

"Spare me," said the woman, holding up a hand. She closed her eyes and rubbed her temples as if she were trying to fend off a headache. Oliver just waited quietly, feeling that was the best thing to do. Ironically, on the walk over he had been thinking about all the possible bonuses of the hero thing, one of which seemed to be a sort of charisma. Joan had suddenly noticed him, so he was more...noticeable at least. So, being Oliver, he figured maybe it meant he might be able to get a date. Funny how, as a brand new bonafide hero, some guys might be daydreaming about the chance to stop some nefarious crime or save the world, yet Oliver had settled on dinner and a movie. Regardless, he was concentrating on the possible good in his situation when he should have realized he was still Oliver Olson, and the bad was always right around the corner. And in this case, sitting right in this very cubicle. Here was an attractive woman his age, possibly unattached—he quickly looked for any kind of ring on her finger and saw none—and she already hated him because of the superhero thing. Dinner and a movie was probably out of the question. Oliver would be lucky to pull her back to the status of ambivalent coworker at this point. The woman finally stopping rubbing her temples and opened her eyes. "Doesn't matter," she said. "At least you're here now. But I would very much appreciate it if you got back to me more quickly in the future since the Mayor's office is hounding me about you."

"Why are they...?"

"Because they want everything pertaining to them done yesterday if not before, and it only gets worse at the end of the budget year or near an election. And for some reason this time around they've decided to go that extra mile and ruin my life specifically just for the fun of it." The smile had backed off to sarcasm now. She motioned to an extra chair. "Please sit down. I'm Emma, by the way." She held out her hand.

"Oliver," said Oliver, introducing himself again and shaking her hand. Emma seemed less angry now, at least directly at him. Maybe this relationship, whether ambivalent or even potentially friendly, could still be salvaged if Oliver could steer her anger toward the Mayor's office. Maybe if he did it right even dating was still a possibility. As he sat down, he said, "Yeah, the

Mayor's office. I feel your pain. How are they ruining your life?"

"With you," said Emma simply. She rolled over to the other side of her cubicle and grabbed a large folder off a shelf.

"Oh, well…I'm sorry," said Oliver, seeing his ability to steer a conversation was crap, but impressed with her ability to be hostile so matter-of-factly. She had a lot of range with that emotion. He wondered if Emma was really the right type of person to be working in the Human Resources Department, although he still hadn't ruled out dating her. "Okay, exactly how are they ruining your life using me? As a pawn, I might add."

"Oh, it's simple. On top of my current job, I now have to be your liaison because they didn't bother to write that into the budget even though it's pretty much a full time position. They won't have anyone over in the Mayor's office do it because they can't spare the people, nor do they want to be that closely associated with you. It's the same with the Police Department. They'll want things too, but they aren't going to call you or give you a contact in their office, even though that would make a whole hell of a lot of sense. Instead, they'll go through me. I have to carry around a special cell phone all the time just because of you, and forget it if it's the middle of the night or a weekend, I'm still working. I googled 'hero liaisons' and there are message boards galore of people in the same position as me posting how much it blows. But on the good side, at least they're not paying me extra for the pleasure of doing it all."

"Yes, that's lucky," said Oliver, trying some humor. Emma didn't crack a smile, not even a hostile one. "Okay, back to the Mayor's office. Don't I *have* to be associated with them? They gave me the job."

"You'd think, wouldn't you?" said Emma, then shook her head, "But no, that's not how it works. In politics you can distance yourself from anything, but it's easier if you do it right from the start, especially if there's strong potential for failure."

"Strong potential for fail—?"

"Regardless, I figure that when you eventually screw something up, I'll be the one they fire, since they obviously can't fire you." Emma looked up toward the ceiling and sighed. "God, this is going to suck."

Oliver sat there. Based on the last couple of minutes, he had an inkling that his chances of dating Emma were slim. He would be lucky to hold onto this thing at a level of comfortable ambivalence. Friendship might even be a pipe dream. He decided to drop it for the time being and focus on the job, especially since he couldn't devise a subtle way to find out if she had a boyfriend. "Um, I don't really know what to say, since this is all new to me and I don't have a clue as to what's going on, but I will try very hard not to screw anything up and get you fired."

"Well, that's reassuring," said Emma, still staring at the ceiling.

"I'm sorry, I really can't offer more than that."

"Okay, fine," she said, looking at him, "then let's just make sure of one thing. When I call, you come running—or flying, or whatever it is you do fastest. If I ever have to leave another message, you might as well leave town and never come back. Okay?"

"Okay."

Emma sighed. "Well, to that end, this is for you." Emma pulled a thick file card out of the folder, peeled back a plastic coating and then pulled off what looked to be a small round sticker. "Lean forward and turn your head."

"And cough?" asked Oliver, trying the humor once more.

Emma stared at him. "You really just want to keep your mouth shut," she said. She pulled Oliver's left ear forward and placed the small sticker behind his earlobe. Leaning back, she said, "Leave that there for at least five hours, then you can take it off. I don't know exactly how it works, but there's a microscopic communication device that will migrate to a position on the inside of your ear." Oliver resisted the temptation to say how cool that was as Emma continued, "I'll be able to contact you instantly wherever you are if I need to talk to you. From the material I read, you should hear a beep or a tone announcing a call, and a voice will tell you who's calling. Like caller ID. To answer you say, 'Answer call' out loud—just speak normally, the device will pick it up—and you should be able to hear me. Another slightly different tone will sound to indicate when the call has ended. In

order for you to initiate a call, you need to say, 'Comm,'
which is short for communicator, and it will beep to let
you know it's ready. Then, to call me for example, you
just say, 'Call Emma,' and you'll be connected. 'Comm,
end call' cuts the connection. I use a special cell phone to
talk to you, but you can use the communicator to call any
number or even tie into other systems, like the police
band, based on the commands you use. There's a list of
those in the manual. You also have a number you can
give out for others to contact you, but my calls have
priority and will cut in on anything else. That's as far as
I've gotten in my copy of the manual. Here's your copy.
You'll need to read through it so you know what all you
can do and how to not accidentally call China or me in
the middle of the night. I've got my new phone right
here, which of course I have to keep with me at all
times." She held up what looked like any other cell phone
except for being that same shiny silver color as the
original file. "Got all that?"

"Got it." Oliver kept it short. Making nice here was
going to take more time. For the moment he would stick
with being the model employee who also happens to be a
superhero approach.

"Okay, then for now I only have a couple more
things. First, here's a box of stuff for you, uniforms and
whatever else." She reached under the desk, pulled out a
cardboard box and kicked it toward Oliver with her foot.
"Take that with you." Pulling a couple of sheets of paper
from the same folder as the communication device, she

said, "Here's the itinerary for Monday's unveiling and press conference. Don't be late, and be in costume. From that day on you are the official superhero of Milwaukee. Next, here is your ticket, itinerary and other information for your Hero Orientation in Washington, DC. You'll leave after the press conference and be attending the orientation for the rest of the week. Personally, I don't think it's the best idea to introduce the new superhero and then ship him off for a week, but maybe they want to give the criminals one last chance to go nuts. That's politics, I guess. Any questions?"

"Will you be at the press conference?" asked Oliver.

"Yes, I will," replied Emma. "Unfortunately, I have to attend any public appearance with you because I'm your official liaison. Just something more to take up my time."

"Oh…uh, sorry."

"Oh, don't be, we can even some of that up right now," she said, standing. "Grab your box and follow me." She led Oliver out of the cubicle, down the aisle and into a small conference room with a table, a few chairs and some miscellaneous equipment on carts along one side. On the table was a laptop attached to a projector which was aimed at a blank white wall. "Sit down," she said, pointing to a chair that faced the blank wall. She pressed a switch on the projector and it hummed to life, showing the laptop's screen up on the wall. Emma sat down in front of the laptop, opened a folder, and searched through some file names before double clicking on one of them. "Here's a little payback for you—A sexual harassment video anyone starting a new position has to watch. It's policy. I also hear it's somewhat unbearable. After that, you're free to go. Oh, and I'll be calling in about five hours to make sure my phone and your communication device are working correctly. Have fun," said Emma with a smile. It was the sarcastic version of her smile which made Oliver long for the nice one he had experienced right before she found out who he was. But at least it was no longer hostile. That was progress. As Emma left, closing the door behind her, Oliver turned his attention to the video as it got past the opening credits.

"Hello, I'm Quentin Drew, your host for the next four hours..."

Oliver groaned and tuned the video out instantly, but he thought about the name. It was kind of an unusual name—Quentin—and it got Oliver to thinking. "Speaking of names, I wonder what mine is?" he said aloud.

9

"SUPERGUY?" asked Oliver.

"Right," confirmed Roger.

"SuperGuy. One word?"

"Yep, but with a capital 'G'on Guy."

"That's kind of…plain, don't you think? The bit about the capital 'G' aside."

"Generic is probably the more accurate term, but I think I've figured out why," said Roger. They were in Oliver's apartment sharing a pizza as they sifted through all the material they had on the superhero position. Roger had shown up with the pizza and a six pack shortly after he got off work, but Oliver hadn't exactly been sitting around home all afternoon waiting for him to arrive. In fact, he had only beaten Roger there by ten minutes because his trip to see Emma in Human Resources had proved to be much more involved than expected. Then, as he finally finished with the sexual harassment video and was returning to his cubicle to get his stuff for home, he ran into Joan outside her office. Subsequently he spent the better part of the next two hours helping her with her computer, then moving a large potted plant around the room a few times, and finally hanging a picture. Actually Joan hung the picture, Oliver simply steadied the short ladder, which was the better job considering who had the great legs. All the while, Joan was *very* friendly, although never out of line, as Oliver knew from his very recent viewing of the sexual harassment video. He finally made it out of her office, but not before promising to come back and help her with some other vague issues she had. Oliver, while very intrigued by the vagueness of Joan's issues, was desperate to get home and find out what the hell was happening to him. The only other delay came when Oliver was starting his car in the parking garage, and he heard an unfamiliar beep. After five minutes of checking his dashboard warning lights, unbuckling and buckling his seatbelt, and opening and shutting every door at least twice, he figured out it was the new communication device. He answered and found Emma once again not very happy with his slow response. Despite Oliver's protests that it was brand new and he didn't realize what it was at first, she still called it a disturbing pattern. But eventually he made it home.

"Well, don't keep *SuperGuy* in suspense," said Oliver with a touch of sarcasm. "Why the generic name?"

"What I think happened is that when the Mayor's office filled out the hero application, they didn't give any specifics on the name or the costume. You can see it here on the copy of the original application," said Roger, pointing to a specific page where it sat among many others, all of them spread out on the floor of Oliver's living room. The pages were relegated to the floor because the pizza occupied the place of honor on the coffee table, a table actually made up of two milk crates and a found piece of countertop. "Back when this hero thing first came up, a lot of people on the other side said it was just a political move by the Mayor to get elected. Seeing as we've never gotten our hero, I'd say that's right. He created the position as a part of the budget, sure, but that was just keeping a campaign promise. Since the position wasn't filled, they've been able to use the extra money to fund other things in the budget when it was needed. Essentially a slush fund, which is a pretty standard practice."

"So they get me instead of a slush fund," said Oliver, mostly to himself.

"Anyway, the application looks as if they didn't even give the hero much thought, probably because they never actually intended to fill the position. The funding is pretty much at the minimum for abilities, with nothing special at all, no real super powers I mean. So no flying, no teleporting, no cool mechanized suit or energy beams, no fire or ice control. Really nothing fun. And the name and the costume were not specified in the application either. Those things don't have to be specified if you don't want them to be, but most of the time they are. For example, a lot of cities and states will specify the name and costume because the hero is representing them, so they'll match the state bird or rock or something. Like Longhorn from Texas, for example. But if those particular things are not specified, the DSF will look at the application, and, taking into consideration any powers requested, they will assign an appropriate name and costume. They're really pretty good at that, usually coming up with good names and cool costumes. However, you seem to be the exception. Maybe someone was making a joke, or maybe because they didn't have anything to work with due to no super powers or special abilities, they went with the generic theme. Actually, considering it is all the bare minimum funding, maybe it is an appropriate name and costume." Roger shrugged, taking a bite of pizza.

"So that explains this," said Oliver, pointing at one of his costumes laying on top of the cardboard box he had gotten from Emma. It was a simple suit of all white with black accessories: a mask, gloves and boots. All of the items were made of a strong but unfamiliar material, not too shiny, and the suit had a large black barcode across the chest. The addition of a mask was a bit of a throwback since most hero identities were not secret and they had no reason to live double lives, but the public still thought they were cool[2].

"Yeah," said Roger, the disappointment clear on his face. "I ran across the design in the paperwork earlier. Pretty lame. Got a mask at least."

"For a while I thought maybe this might be how all the costumes come at first, that I might have to have it scanned or something to officially activate it, to make it somehow transform into the real costume." Oliver picked up the costume and stared at the barcode. "But this seems to be it."

"Afraid so," said Roger. "At least it's not really flashy or obnoxious or any pastel color. Maybe you'll always get the drop on the bad guys because they're laughing. Could be an advantage."

"And the barcode lines are vertical, that's slimming," said Oliver, tossing the suit back on the cardboard box. There were a total of five suits in the box in case one or more were damaged, along with five pairs each of the boots and gloves. "Okay, so forget this stuff for now, what about the powers? You said no super powers?"

"No, nothing special," answered Roger, taking another bite of pizza and sitting back with a copy of the position description. He chewed for a moment and took a drink of beer. "Okay, with heroes, there's a standard level

[2]In surveys and focus groups, masks received a 74% overall approval rating, while only 18% found them confusing, in a Lone Ranger kind of way. —*The Department of Superhero Funding*

of power everyone gets, then you can be funded above and beyond that for specific special abilities or super powers or equipment. Part of the problem is even getting the standard level is not cheap, so going beyond to any great degree is tough for smaller positions, like for just a city, as in your case, or some smaller state or region. But the heroes from big cities, like New York or L.A., they have plenty of money behind them, as do the federal level heroes, so they can all fly or emit energy bursts or shoot lightning or fire, or combinations of those. Whatever. Those are usually referred to as the super powers, whereas the standard abilities are just called supra powers."

"So I'm just a suprahero."

"Yeah, I suppose so, technically. But that's nothing to laugh at. First of all, you're invulnerable," said Roger. Then he shrugged. "Or at least nearly."

"At least near—Why do I not like that last bit?"

"Well, you're made to take a ton of punishment, but there are always limits. Like if you ran up against a supervillain who had an incredible amount of super strength, then maybe he'd do enough damage to take you out, but that's only a slim chance. The invulnerability is really pretty good, I think."

"Technically not *in*vulnerability if it can be labeled as just *pretty* good."

"Okay, let's say near invulnerability," conceded Roger. "Anyway, that's a standard power because nobody wants the hero they just funded to get killed off right away in some fluke accident. You know, like getting hit by a bus while crossing the street on their first day of work, especially since there's a high chance that bus was thrown by a supervillain. Kinda makes it a bad investment. That near invulnerability pertains to the brainiac heroes and villains too, even though they look like skinny geeks with big heads. They don't have all the muscles and can't dish out physical punishment in the same way, but if you do drop a bus on them, they'll survive. Kind of cockroach-like." Roger tapped on his beer bottle as he read down through a page. "Okay, let me see…what other standard stuff? All the basics really. You'll be much stronger than the average person, much quicker, you can run way faster, jump higher and farther…you get the idea. Now, so far you've seen a slight increase in these abilities, but they tend to increase exponentially as the serum kicks in, so in a couple of days you'll be more than able to dunk a basketball. In fact, the process should be complete by this weekend, probably Sunday, which is why the Mayor's office is set to unveil you to the public on Monday. That was the lead story on the early news, by the way."

"Yeah, I already have an itinerary for the event. Got it from Emma along with all the other stuff. Now she's someone in this town who's decidedly not happy about having a superhero. There was a bit of hostility. Kind of cute, but not very happy at all."

"Really? Why not?"

"Let's just call it the Oliver Olson factor. My involvement makes anyone's life better, right?" Oliver waved a hand and said, "Let's not get into that right now, I'll tell you all about it later. Let's stick with the powers and stuff."

"Gotcha. Well, so there's the basic increase in everything across the board. That includes hearing and sight, so if you did wear glasses—you don't—but if you did, your eyes would get better and actually keep improving until they were much better than normal, as will your hearing and even your sense of smell to some degree. That overall increase also accounts for your brand new full head of hair and the nice square jaw, and probably a boost to your charisma, however they manage that. Since you're a hero, you have to be attractive and well liked by the public." Roger continued to scan down the page. "You already know about your high energy level and not having to sleep or eat, although you can if you want. Oh, you will essentially have a compulsion to do good too."

"Are we talking clinically diagnosable compulsion?"

"Yeah, but it's a good thing. It's kind of a built in safety so someone can't take advantage of the hero system. Like if some corrupt politician created a hero to use for his own personal gain. While the hero does have a loyalty to his city or region, or Mayor in your case, he's not going to blindly follow orders if they're evil. Of course a hero can be given the wrong information and then what he thinks is right obviously isn't, so it can get complicated. This works on a smaller level too, like you won't cheat on your taxes or pretend not to notice when some clerk gives you too much change. But I think you can still tell some white lies, if it's best for the overall good."

"So if there's this compulsion for good, where do supervillains come from?" asked Oliver while reaching for another piece of pizza. He knew he didn't need to eat now, or ever apparently, but it still tasted good.

"It varies. One is the super serum itself. A certain percentage of serums produced are flawed, but aren't always easy to detect, and the hero who injects it essentially gets all the powers but with the addition of a really messed up head, usually wanting to do bad or take over the world, instead of the standard good stuff."

"How high of a percentage?" asked Oliver, suddenly nervous. "And when do you know?"

"Oh, don't worry, it happens almost right away in those cases. The person just goes nuts. The percentage isn't that high anymore, and it drops every year because they keep refining the super serum formula and its production, but the bulk of the supervillains you've heard of are from those early years of the program when detection wasn't as good. Still, those are accidents. They don't account for the ones who take a bad serum on purpose."

"On purpose?"

"Yep. Nutty folks. Even with all the modern improvements in the serum creation process, flawed serums are still occasionally produced and they can end up being sold on the black market for the express purpose of making bad guys. It's extremely rare for a bad serum to make it all the way through the creation process without being discovered. Those that are detected are supposed to be destroyed. However, it seems certain people will pay a lot for a bad serum, and therefore some of these mistakes survive to be sold to the highest bidder. Maybe to a rogue nation or an oil company or a major corporation for example, so they can create a supervillain to do their dirty work. So those bad serum guys are the most common villains, but there's also a small percentage who are actually former heroes. Usually their funding was cut or they were booted out for some reason. Normally, the hero has that compulsion to do good, but if they get screwed—which isn't uncommon in politics—that compulsion can be overcome. Some people believe it's tied to the loyalty the hero has for the city or state, and when that city or state screws them, something vital breaks and all bets are off. They can become bitter or disillusioned and eventually even turn into a villain if they don't find another sponsor, although they're usually not very evil, mostly they just steal money and get revenge. One example of that is the Stone Hand. He retired as a hero about six years ago, but then Florida had a huge budget problem a couple years later and cut out his pension and retirement benefits as part of the solution, so he came out of retirement as a villain. Focusing on Florida of course. Doing pretty well too, so I hear."

"Well, good for him," said Oliver, "Although…I say that but I also feel as if I should do something about it."

"That's just the 'doing good' thing kicking in. You're literally made to fight supervillains so that's what you should be feeling," said Roger. "But don't worry about him, he's in Florida, and you only have to think about this city. Not to mention he has a lot more than just the basic powers. Probably not the first bad guy you want to tackle when you're still reading the manual of how to be a superhero."

"Okay. No super powers, we've established that, but what about the equipment possibility? Maybe a mechanical arm or arms? Or a flying motorcycle, possibly flaming? Trident?"

Yeah, I looked at that section in the description, but not much there," said Roger. "And if the woman in HR didn't give you anything, then I'm guessing there's nothing. But let me double check." He took a minute to look through a couple more pages so Oliver cleaned up some of the mess, disposing of the pizza box and putting the empty bottles in recycling. "Here's something," said Roger as Oliver sat back down. "There does seem to be one thing…Are you sure they didn't give you anything else at HR? Anything else in that box?" asked Roger.

"What? You think I'd miss a trident?" asked Oliver, digging through the box of costumes again. It also contained the certificate of his hero status and some various manuals.

"Wait," said Roger, "here's something…it's only referred to as 'transportation'. It says to see Appendix F, attached. Hey, maybe it's a jet or helicopter. Guess they can't toss that in a cardboard box for you to take home."

"A jet or a helicopter? Now that would be cool, only I don't know how to fly either of those things. Is there a superhero version of a kite?"

"Don't worry, flying whatever it is would have been part of the serum," said Roger, paging back, looking for the appendix. "You'd just be able to do it."

"Very cool," said Oliver, nodding to himself. "That I could like." Still fishing around in the box, Oliver felt an envelope at the bottom and pulled it out. On the outside of the envelope was a number corresponding to a parking space in one of the city government parking lots downtown and inside was a set of keys. "Hey, it looks like it's a car," said Oliver, getting a little excited. "Maybe it's really over powered, like a James Bond car with missiles and ejection seats. Or it can fly or go under water—we are on Lake Michigan after all—or it's bullet proof, or a rocket car, or really smart like the Knightrider car—"

"Or it's a Taurus," interrupted Roger.

"What?"

"Taurus, Ford Taurus. That's what it is. Just a regular city government vehicle."

"Not bullet proof?"

"Nope."

"Not even a little bit?"

"You mean like bullet resistant? Nope."

"Well, that's crap," said Oliver, staring at the keys. He shrugged. "Still better than the Omni, though."

"Yeah," agreed Roger. "And they'll pay for gas."

10

MOST everything physically about Raymond Joyce was small. He was a bit under five feet four inches (like about two inches), with small feet, small hands and predictably small, beady blue eyes. Just about the only physically big thing about Mr. Joyce was his bright white hair, but only if he allowed it to be, which he did not. If he didn't keep it flattened down with a copious amount of gel, it would rise up out of control like it had a mind of its own, making it way too easy to compare him to Albert Einstein. This was too much of a cliche for Mr. Joyce to handle. Not to mention Mr Joyce was, in his own estimation, three to four times smarter than that wacky haired simpleton. But not in a good way.

Mr. Joyce was the founder and CEO of Joyce Industries, a billion dollar conglomerate that had a piece of almost every type of business a person could think of and even a few many people preferred to believe could not and did not exist. However, Mr. Joyce was not content with the large piece of the pie he had. He still wanted more. Much more. Specifically, he wanted to rule the world. Another cliche, like the hair, but true. To that end, a couple years earlier he had paid handsomely for a special dose of black market super serum. This serum was one of many that had been specifically designed to enhance the brain capacity and intelligence of the subject. However, since this particular focus of super serum production has such a delicate relationship to the brain, there is a much higher incidence of faulty serums. One correlation in the serums was the higher the level of intelligence pushed for, the higher the chance of the serum being faulty. Mr. Joyce's particular serum possessed one of the highest intelligence quotients ever attempted in the lab and, like many of the serums before it, this one had been detected as faulty and designated for destruction. Mr. Joyce paid a lot of people a lot of money to make sure that serum wasn't destroyed. Instead, it was delivered to him.

It's not like Mr. Joyce was a mouth-breathing knuckle dragger before the serum. He had already built his company into one of the largest and most wealthy organizations in the world, as well as building his own legend as an amazing corporate mogul. In addition to his brilliant business acumen, he was also a bit of a jerk. Mr. Joyce took great delight in squashing whoever or whatever he could during the average work day, but even with all his success he really felt he could step it up to yet another level in both the evil and genius departments. He was close, he just needed that little extra boost. At the time, Mr. Joyce didn't feel like any kind of motivational book or online course was going to be enough to help him do it (they were littered with positive thinking anyway), so he opted for the brainiac super serum a little past its Use By date. If it happened to curdle his brain a bit in the process, he figured it was worth it.

With that step was born Gray Matter, one of the most intelligent and ruthless supervillains ever to have existed. Not that anyone really knew he existed. Unlike many of the supervillains who ran amuck these days, Gray Matter wasn't flashy or bombastic. He didn't wear a costume, choosing instead to dress in a nice double-breasted gray pinstripe suit with matching gray shoes, socks, shirt and tie, and he didn't go on and on about how he was going to take over the world and force its inhabitants to fulfill his every whim—blah, blah, blah—although that was the gist of his plan. Gray Matter chose to keep his schemes more secretive, slowly building up his business over the past couple of years in an effort to position himself well before putting his final plan into action. And now it seemed the time had come to take some more decisive steps, ones that would inevitably attract attention and finally make his presence known, but that wouldn't matter because it was almost certainly too late to stop him from achieving his ultimate goal of world domination.

Well, maybe ultimate is too strong a word. Certainly it was a goal, and probably the biggie, or at least in the top three, but things had been muddied a bit lately by something else that had captured Gray Matter's attention. Alice. She was a waitress. Gray Matter thought she looked like Audrey Hepburn playing a waitress, or maybe some actress playing Audrey Hepburn playing a waitress in a made for TV biopic. He had many theories on waitresses, Audrey Hepburn, and method acting/psychic channeling, but he generally kept them to himself since he found most people couldn't follow his undeniably genius train of thought. And they tended to look at him funny.

Alice was a good example of what many so-called experts thought plagued the typical evil genius. It wasn't because she was a woman, although there were a few proponents of that particular theory (dubbed the "Yoko Syndrome" theory), it was because she was a distraction. Some small element that didn't necessarily have anything to do with the grand scheme, but that the supervillain often let disrupt his or her efforts toward the greater goal, perhaps purposely on some level. In other words, somewhere deep down in the psyche, the evil genius knew that actually accomplishing the goal of taking over the world would eliminate their reason for being. Because of this, it has been put forward that they might subconsciously torpedo their own efforts. This theory was explored most successfully by Jonathan Kelp, Ph.D., in his book, *What's That Shiny Thing?: How the Black Bard Failed to Conquer the World*, and in the equally successful sequel, *Don't Worry World, There Are Lots of Shiny Things*. Another closely related theory is that it's more about the *plan* for the supervillain than the end goal, more about the journey than the destination. They tend to create epic, overly complicated schemes that actually put the goal farther from reach and allow for plenty of opportunities for the good guys to foil them. Subconsciously this is what they want, because whatever setbacks or opposition they have allow them to create other convoluted mini plans within the epic plan to counter any hero's attempts to stop them. There have been plenty of books written on this theory as well, most notably Dr. Angela Larson's, *The Red Crossbow: How the Evil Achilles Shot Himself in the Heel*, and Herm Denham's masterpiece, *The Ass in Assumption: Don't Start the Rube Goldberg Machine of Death and Just Leave the Room*. In fact, the supervillain self-help section in your typical bookstore or online retailer is huge, usually the second largest nonfiction one next to regular self-help. There aren't nearly as many self-help titles for superheroes, probably because they tend to win. Lots of self-aggrandizing memoirs, though. Too many to count. Seriously, it's not like any of them overcame incredible challenges or prevailed over really difficult odds in childhood. They just stuck something shiny on the end of their finger.

Gray Matter's personal torpedo, Alice, worked in a small diner across the street from his office, which was the penthouse floor of the tallest building in Milwaukee, and he tried to make the trip across the street at least once a day. When he couldn't make it, he often sent several employees to eat there, during which he insisted they subtly try to discover whether or not Alice liked him. They were to casually mention his name in her presence, see how she reacted, and report back. There usually wasn't much to report back since the employees had taken to being extremely subtle in their inquiries, if they inquired at all. It was generally deemed better to come back empty handed than to risk doing something wrong like Bob from Accounting. He had managed to strike up a very engaging conversation with Alice one day and had foolishly gotten her number. Needless to say he didn't make that call, or any other call, nor was he ever seen in the Accounting Department again. One of the rumors floating around Joyce Industries had Bob being transferred to the Murmansk branch and being killed in a glacier collapse shortly thereafter. That's one of the more optimistic rumors. Very optimistic considering the truth.

At the moment Gray Matter was seated at his huge mahogany desk inside his cavernous penthouse office. The size of the office and its furnishings were interesting choices by Gray Matter since they seemed to accent his diminutive size even more, but he considered it a challenge, a reminder of what he was up against. Others might say this was just another example of how supervillains get sidetracked with meaningless trivialities. Gray Matter would no doubt dispute that assertion and would try to have those said 'others' eliminated in devious and overly complicated ways that undoubtedly had to be completed before the next phase of his plan could continue. Irony, schmi-rony. There was a knock at the door and Gray Matter's chief assistant entered, walked the rather long distance over to the desk, and stood waiting.

"What is it, Alex?" asked Gray Matter, without looking up from the papers he studied.

"Sir, the Mayor's press conference will be starting in less than an hour. We need to notify our operative whether or not to proceed."

Gray Matter set his papers down and looked over at one of the far windows in thought. "Well, we've done our best to confuse the powers that be, and, while they may not know exactly what's happening, they are suspicious. I didn't want it to come to this so early, but we have no choice. He has to be eliminated. And conveniently, by the time they replace him, it will be too late. Tell our man to proceed."

"Yes, sir," said Alex, turning and heading for the door. He only got a few steps away.

"Alex?"

Alex turned back. "Sir?"

"Did you go to lunch today?" asked Gray Matter, although he knew the answer since he had ordered Alex to eat at the diner.

"Yes, I did, sir."

"Was Alice working?" Another question to which he already knew the answer since he'd had cameras installed to watch the diner, besides having memorized Alice's hours.

"Yes, she was, sir."

"Did she…? I mean, did…by any chance did I…my name come up at all?" He asked. He didn't know the answer to that. He had stopped short of putting listening devices inside the diner because he thought that might seem creepy.

"No, I'm afraid not, sir," replied Alex. "Although it was fairly crowded in the diner today, and she was rather busy. Hard to make extraneous conversation considering the circumstances, and I didn't want to seem obvious."

"Yes, I see. Absolutely."

"However, it did seem that Grace had some extended interaction with her. Perhaps she has something more useful for you." Grace worked in Legal and had turned Alex down for a date. She had been at lunch but hadn't spent any more time than anyone else talking to Alice. Still, she did turn him down. "I was a few tables away so I don't know what they were talking about, but it seemed like more than just an order for a salad with dressing on the side."

"Really? Grace, you say?"

"Yes, sir. From Legal."

"Excellent."

"If that is all, sir, I'll go give the order for the Mayor's press conference."

"Yes, yes. That's all. Thank you. Oh, can you have someone from Legal stop by? I want to go over some...contracts. Perhaps Grace?"

"Yes, sir, right away," said Alex. He turned and left the room with a smile.

11

OLIVER pulled his official city government Ford Taurus into his newly assigned space in the underground parking structure and shut off the engine. Initially he had been disappointed upon hearing his cool superhero car was actually just a regular car, but it was still better than his Omni in a myriad of ways, especially roominess. That made a huge difference now that Oliver had grown a few inches. It had been a little tight in the Omni before the serum, now it would just be cartoonish. His only real gripe with the Taurus was that it was white, which was a pain to keep clean, but it did fit with the generic theme so it made sense. Roger was waiting beside the next car, having arranged to meet Oliver so they could go to the press conference together.

"Okay, here is one thing I don't get," said Roger, talking to Oliver as he got out of the Taurus. "You, the superhero, get your own space near the stairs like the other big hitters, but you're also the guy who could run from your apartment to here faster than I can walk from the far side of the garage. Seems a bit unfair doesn't it? Not to mention silly."

"So, with all the benefits of this whole superhero thing, like the strength, the speed, the invulnerability, the hair—especially the hair—it's the parking spot you're jealous of?" said Oliver as he dropped his keys into the pocket of his long black raincoat. It wasn't raining today but Oliver felt a little too weird walking around in his costume.

"Yeah, pretty much the parking," said Roger. "That and the fact you no longer have to exercise. For us non-superheroes, that sucks. I will probably curse your name every time I run up and down a basketball court from now on. Not to mention when I skip dessert."

"Can't blame you," said Oliver with a shrug. He grabbed his gloves and mask out of the car and shut the door.

"Wow, look at you," said Roger. "You're huge." Roger had left town the previous Friday morning to attend a family event over the weekend he couldn't get out of, which caused him to miss the days where Oliver's growth really jumped. "What are you, six-five, six-six now?"

"Six-seven last I checked. About 245 or so. Bizarre, isn't it?"

"Nothing but. That's like seven inches and 70 pounds in three days. Amazing. And the hair, check out the hair. That's definitely superhero quality," said Roger. Oliver's hair was a thick, shiny blond, and perfectly styled as if he had just walked out of a salon.

"Yeah, and I don't even have to wash it. It's actually less maintenance than that shaved head of yours."

"Must be rough." Roger shook his head in wonder, and then gestured at Oliver's chest. "Hey, let's see it."

Oliver opened the raincoat to reveal his costume. The first time he had tried it on was the night he had gotten his box from Emma. That was before he had gained all the height and weight he now had, so it had hung loosely on his body then. Now was a very different story after Oliver had filled out. The black and white costume was perfectly snug. To a fault in Oliver's opinion.

"I feel like I'm flashing someone," said Oliver with a bit of a groan in his voice.

"Well, cripes, you practically are. Doesn't leave much to the imagination, does it?"

"Am I interrupting something?"

Oliver jumped at the sound of the new voice, although both his jump and the reflexive closing of his raincoat were too fast for anyone to see, even Roger who was looking right at him as it happened.

Emma walked up from behind Oliver. "Sorry, I couldn't resist when I saw you whip open the raincoat.

Made me think they got the name wrong and your real superpower is flashing people."

"No problem," said Oliver, choosing to keep things civil despite his embarrassment, at least until his next sentence. "Roger, this is the hostile woman I was telling you about from Human Resources, Emma Simms. Miss Simms, this is Roger Allen. He's a computer IT guy here."

"I don't need the crap," said Emma to Oliver, then she turned to Roger and shook his hand. "Nice to meet you. How did you get screwed into helping with the Frankenstein project?"

"Well, I guess you could say I'm a volunteer. Just a lover of horror stories."

"Oh. Must be nice to have the extra time. I could be working right now except I have to be here for this press conference," said Emma, the hostile smile making a brief appearance.

Oliver pointed at Emma as he said to Roger, "See what I was saying? Nicest girl you ever met, except for mostly having gone over to the dark side. Why doesn't the whole superhero charisma thing work on her?"

"That's not really what it's designed for," said Roger. "It's more for the general public on a large scale. Sort of a good first impression thing. I mean, if you end up sucking as a superhero, the public isn't just going to keep loving you. There'll be hate mail, or email, or tweets. Whatever type of communication comes along next. But with hate."

"Great."

"You can budget for some powers of influence, though. There's mind control, or stuff like intimidation or fear. Those can make some bad guys just take off and run. But I think flying and maybe blasting the crap out of someone with an energy bolt from your eyes would be much more personally rewarding abilities to have," said Roger. "Or a cool car."

"Yeah, a cool car," said Oliver, glancing at the Taurus.

"Um, I'm sorry to interrupt the whining session about all the things you lack as a superhero, but we should probably get going," said Emma, gesturing toward the stairwell.

"Not yet," said Roger. He nodded at Oliver. "You gotta lose the raincoat and put on the gloves and mask."

"I will…" said Oliver, nodding in the direction of the front of the city government office building, meaning that he'd do it there.

"No, you've got to do it now. It's the law. You have to be in full costume when you're on the streets as a hero, remember? That's all the time, even for a public event like this, not just when you're fighting the bad guys. You should have had it all on during the drive over. You don't have to wear it all the time, but when you're not, you can't do anything superheroish, which, since that's what you're programmed to do now, might be impossible for you to resist. Best to just always be in costume when in public. And probably most of the other time too."

"He's right," said Emma. "I haven't been able to cover all the stuff I have about your position, but I read that. We can't have anyone suing us because you aren't wearing your jammies."

"But what could possibly happen between here and the front of the building?" asked Oliver.

"Who knows, but something could and if you acted on it we could get in trouble," replied Emma.

"Yeah, you've just got to get used to it," said Roger.

Oliver looked back and forth between them and shrugged. He pulled his keys out of his pocket and handed them to Roger, along with his mask and gloves. Then he took off his raincoat and tossed it inside his car. Taking his mask back from Roger, he put it on. Made of what seemed like a metallic fabric, it was a slightly shiny black and made in the style that only covered his eyes, leaving his nice head of hair free to be appreciated. The mask was molded to fit the contours of his face and had an elastic section in back that kept it snugly in place. He slipped on his gloves next, which were also made of the same shiny black material. That black was repeated in the boots Oliver wore, as well as the slightly raised pattern of the barcode stretching across his muscular chest. After he finished, he noticed Emma staring at him.

"Sure doesn't leave much to the imagination," she said.

Roger nodded. "Yeah, I was just saying…"

Oliver dropped his hands down in front of his groin. "Okay, let's go. I don't need anymore crap." The other two started walking, but Oliver gestured quickly with one hand, waving them away from the nearby door. "No, let's go to the other stairwell, I'm not walking through all the offices like this." Roger and Emma stopped, and with a couple more insistent waves from Oliver, turned and started walking toward the door on the other side of the garage that led to the front atrium of the city government building. Oliver made sure Roger and Emma walked ahead of him. After a few steps he asked, "It's not that bad, is it? The uh…tightness, I mean."

"It makes me uncomfortable and I'm a pretty open-minded guy," said Roger.

"I'm considering it the one perk of the job so far," said Emma.

"Great," said Oliver, slowly shaking his head. "Hey, give me something to hold onto at least. Emma, let me carry your briefcase or something." Emma started to look back but Oliver blurted, "No! No. Eyes front." He waved at her with one hand while the other remained strategically placed.

Emma turned back to the front with a smile. "You could have my purse, but I think that might push things into a different realm of weird," said Emma.

"Just give me something to carry or I'm taking off and you'll have to explain why I'm not here."

"Okay, okay, relax. Take my briefcase," she said, handing it back without turning around.

"You might want to make sure he doesn't…well, hold it too tightly to anything," said Roger.

"Yeah, keep a gap," said Emma.

"Well, I'm glad to see you two get along." Oliver held the briefcase in front of him. It would do for now but he knew he definitely had to come up with something to help this situation. He didn't think he could get away with fighting evildoers while carrying a briefcase.

They rounded the corner by the other stairwell but came to a sudden stop because of several people standing in their way. The discussion among that group, a group made up entirely of police officers, stopped abruptly with their appearance. It only took a second for Oliver to realize they weren't regular cops because each of them had lots of extra stripes and gold thingies here and there, indicating they were the bosses. Then he recognized the guy with the most stripes and gold thingies to be the Police Chief, who stepped forward and stood in front of Oliver as Roger and Emma gave ground.

Oliver felt compelled to say something. "Hello sir...I'm Oliver Olson, or SuperGuy, officially." Oliver held out his gloved hand, but the Police Chief didn't reach for it. He just stared at Oliver instead. Oliver pulled his hand back and patted the briefcase in front of his groin a couple times because he didn't know what else to do. "Well, I just want to say I look forward to working side by side with you in our fight against crime," continued Oliver, fairly uncertainly. He wondered if it sounded as dumb to everyone else as he thought it did.

"Do you?" replied the Chief. He was a tall man, just a couple inches shorter than Oliver, with closely cropped white hair. His dark eyes did not hold anything that might possibly be misconstrued as kindness at the moment. "Well, I don't. And just so we get off on the right foot here and have no misunderstandings, I'll explain some things to you. You are the Mayor's pet, not mine. I won't be cleaning up after you. The Mayor wants you so he can get re-elected, despite how it makes me and my officers look. Like we can't handle the job ourselves. Let me tell you, we can and we will. There won't be any working 'side by side' at all. You stay out of our way. I don't want to see you or hear about you. Save some kittens from trees, take some pictures with the Mayor, but leave the real work to us. Do we understand each other?"

Oliver managed to nod slightly.

"Good, we'll get along great then. I guess we should go welcome you to the family," finished the Chief. He turned and walked through the door one of the junior officers opened for him, and the rest of the group followed, leaving Oliver, Roger and Emma standing there. The heavy metal door clanged shut behind them.

"That didn't go so well," said Roger. "No group hug or anything."

"No, no hugs," said Oliver.

"He's a bit of a jerk," said Emma. "Of course, if you stick to the kittens and photos as he suggested, I think my life will be easier. So I think I'm kinda on his side."

"I didn't really think about it until now, but this is something you see a lot with heroes and the police," said Roger. "It doesn't really make them look competent if they need a hero, especially in a smallish city, so often there is some...friction."

"Won't be any friction if he doesn't see or hear me."

"True."

"They should have given me invisibility as a power."

"You're anything but invisible in that suit," said Emma as she walked by and opened the door. "Come on, we're going to be late."

"Hey, you better watch out. You might be getting close to harassment," said Oliver, pointing at her. "I should know. I've watched hours of video on the subject." Roger followed Emma through the door as Oliver stood staring after them. "Seriously, hours," he yelled into the stairwell. "Hours I'm not getting back. Ever."

Roger stuck his head back out of the doorway. "You do understand that you basically don't have to eat or sleep anymore, right? And you're complaining about a little of your time being wasted. You've got nothing but time to waste now. Come on, fool," he said, disappearing again.

Oliver slowly started to nod. "The man makes a good point," he said. Then he followed the others.

12

THE press conference introducing SuperGuy was held on the front steps of the city government's main office building. The large platform used in all such events had been erected early that morning in its usual location. The long, wide expanse of steps leading up to the building from the street below was in two sections, broken up halfway to the top by a level expanse that echoed the street and the landing above in front of the main doors. The platform was erected on the bottom few steps of the upper set of stairs so the press and any spectators could stand on the level section in the middle. This created a viewing angle that made certain the columns of the building would be visible behind the speaker, especially in photos and news footage, which was judged to be very governmental and impressive looking. Today the crowd filled the level middle area in addition to the lower steps and even stretched out into the street. Many of them were members of the press, both news and entertainment in this case, but there were a large number of regular citizens as well. Those 'regular' citizens did include some rather surprisingly zealous fans of the as yet unannounced superhero. There were always leaks concerning these events so it wasn't exactly a secret what was going on, but a couple of people had been industrious enough to print up SuperGuy t-shirts and hats and were selling them on the fringes of the crowd. The street had been blocked off, keeping it empty except for several news vans and a few police cruisers. It was a slightly cool early fall morning, but the sun was out and it had the promise of becoming a warm, almost throwback summer day.

Oliver, Roger and Emma were enjoying that weather now as they stood on the landing at the top of the steps, positioned behind one of the huge columns lining the front of the building. The Police Chief and his contingent were there too, but keeping their distance while only occasionally glancing with disdain in Oliver's direction. Everyone was waiting for the Mayor to come down from his office to start the show. Oliver and Roger were occupying themselves by scanning the crowd below for faces of various pseudo famous local news people. Roger had a bit of a thing for one of the Channel 7 reporters who often covered city government events.

"So if we see her, maybe you could grant her a one-on-one interview," said Roger.

"And what would that do for you?" asked Oliver, still scanning the crowd. He was a little bugged by something he couldn't quite place and wondered if he was getting nervous about being in front of the public. He thought that sort of thing wasn't supposed to happen, being somehow covered by the super serum. His expectations of what all the super serum would cover was getting pretty high.

"Well, I'd be there too, of course. You'd introduce me. Maybe I should even have some kind of official capacity. Special liaison to Channel 7's Roberta Foxdale sounds good to me."

"Sorry, but he can't do interviews yet," said Emma, "not until after he gets back from the official hero orientation in DC. That's what the Mayor's office said, and maybe it's somewhere in all those pages and pages of information on this position, I don't know. Anyway Roger, you strike me more as a Susie Shaw from Channel 4 kind of guy."

"Susie Shaw? No way. Well, not no way, there's probably a *way*, but if I had to choose a favorite, Roberta's my girl."

Emma was about to say more but stopped when the front door opened and the Mayor appeared, followed by the Deputy Mayor and a pack of aides. The Mayor, a man of average height and slightly above average weight, walked up to the Police Chief, shook his hand and exchanged a few of words. After a moment he patted the Police Chief on the arm and walked over to where Oliver, Roger and Emma waited. Most of the aides followed while the Deputy Mayor, a tall, slim man with a beak-like nose, stayed behind with the Police Chief.

"Mr. Olson," said the Mayor with a very practiced smile. He had dark hair with some gray mixed in at the temples and slight wrinkles around his eyes. Shaking Oliver's hand, the Mayor continued to talk while throwing his smile around at Roger and Emma also. "At least I'm assuming you're Mr. Olson considering the costume, but I suppose I could be wrong. I have seen stranger things on the street in this city."

"No, you're not wrong, sir."

"Well, it's good to finally meet you, SuperGuy. That sounds a bit strange. May I call you Oliver?" the Mayor said, draping one arm over Oliver's shoulders (which was a little awkward for a 5'11" man to do to a 6'7" man, but he managed to pull it off) and guiding him a short distance away from the rest of the group. "Look, I'm damn glad to have you on our team. I know the Police Chief isn't too happy about this—they never are—but it's good for the city of Milwaukee, and eventually he'll see that. We have to put the city first. That's what's important. I have every confidence in you." The Mayor stopped and faced Oliver when he spoke that last sentence, punctuating it by tapping him on the chest. He threw his other arm over Oliver's shoulders and guided him back toward the group. "Look, you just do what you were made to do. You know, be heroic. Do that and everything will be great, but…" The Mayor slowed their pace down slightly and lowered his voice. "But if you screw something up, you know to keep your distance from my office, right? We don't want anyone else for this position, we want you, but if it doesn't work, then things have to be done. You understand, I'm sure. Nothing to worry about." The Mayor patted Oliver on the chest one more time as they got back to the rest of the group. "Okay," he said to the other people gathered there, "Let's get this thing done. I'm going to say a few words and introduce Oliver here, then he'll say something…" An aide handed Oliver a couple of note cards with remarks already written for him which were short but very strong in their praise for the Mayor. "…And then there'll be some pictures. Okay? So let's have some fun." With that, the Mayor led the group down the steps to the platform.

Once everyone was in place, which meant the Deputy Mayor, the Police Chief and Oliver were all side by side just off to the right of the podium with everyone else behind them, the Mayor stepped up to the microphones. After about ten minutes it became obvious to Oliver that the Mayor's definition of a few words was somewhat different than anybody else's on the planet who wasn't a politician, so he scanned the crowd again to see if Roger's favorite reporter, Roberta Foxdale, was present. He spotted her in the front of the crowd, just a couple people away from Susie Shaw. Oliver figured he was probably more of a Susie Shaw kind of guy and started to consider the whole Superman/Lois Lane angle. As Ms. Shaw was listening to the Mayor's comments, she looked his way and he thought about giving her a little smile when they made eye contact, except her eyes never got there. She seemed to be looking a bit lower, which made Oliver realize he had relinquished Emma's briefcase and was now standing there with nothing in front of himself. He quickly checked Roberta Foxdale to find she was looking at the same thing, as well as the majority of the rest of the people in those first couple of rows. At first Oliver found it hard to believe people could be so shameless but then realized it was kind of unavoidable. Since he was elevated a few feet on the platform, his groin happened to be right at their eye level. He quickly dropped his hands and fanned out his two note cards to cover as much as possible.

A moment or two later, something strange happened. Oliver started to move without thinking, except for the fact he knew exactly what he was doing and why. It was almost as if there were two of him, one asking why he was doing something and the other giving the answers, which then made perfect sense, as if he already knew what those answers were. Oliver stepped out in front of the Police Chief, dropped his note cards, and intercepted a cylindrical object that had been thrown from the crowd. He knew it was a bomb. He had seen the man who threw it. In fact, he had spotted him in the crowd earlier before the Mayor's arrival and had been keeping an eye on him the whole time. At least Oliver realized that now. He had kept track of the man as he had worked his way forward through the crowd and into a position close to the platform, and all the while the man kept a constant eye on the closest police officers working security for the event. Then Oliver saw the man pull the bomb from his jacket, activate it, and throw it at the stage. That same bomb which Oliver now caught with both hands and guided into his stomach as he bent over and dropped to the ground, curling around the device as completely as he could. When it exploded, as he knew it would, Oliver found himself flying upward into the air, flipping over, and dropping perfectly back down into the hole that had been created in the platform where he had been.

13

"**LOOK** at this, what am I supposed to do about this?" yelled Oliver, sort of at Roger and Emma but mostly at the world in general, all the while gesturing repeatedly at his chest. The bar code symbol of his uniform was obscured by a black stain that covered most of his upper torso and arms. "How do I clean this? I don't recall there being any tags with cleaning instructions on anything. I seriously do not want to own anything that's dry clean only. Hell, I don't even want it if it needs ironing." Oliver's yelling echoed around the parking structure where they had retreated after the explosion at the press conference. Oliver was looking at himself in the side mirror of a van. It was no longer attached to the van, since Oliver had broken it off accidentally when trying to tilt it outward.

"Maybe just some bleach," offered Roger. "I like to use a little bleach with my gym stuff." He was pacing back and forth, overflowing with adrenaline after their brush with danger.

"Okay, sure, I'll throw it in with my sweaty socks," said Oliver.

Roger paused momentarily next to Oliver and sniffed. "What is that smell?" He leaned in close to Oliver. "Is that you? Oh, that is not a good smell. A little like asparagus, only after it's been eaten. Is that bomb smell? Do bombs smell like that? Or maybe it's burnt superhero." Roger began pacing again as Oliver sniffed the air around him, then himself.

"Don't worry about it. You have extra costumes," said Emma.

"Uniforms," corrected Oliver.

"Yeah, yeah. Anyway we can get more if we need them." She was leaning against a nearby car, her briefcase at her feet. "You'd think you'd be a little more concerned with the fact someone tried to blow you up."

There had been a huge commotion after the bomb went off, with the crowd scattering, people screaming, and the police trying to get some kind of handle on it all. The Mayor had been whisked away even before Oliver had managed to climb out of the hole in the platform. The senior police officials had tried to get the Police Chief away but he stubbornly refused to leave and began directing the efforts to get control of the scene and safely clear the area. Oliver looked for the man who had thrown the bomb, but he was nowhere to be seen, lost among the fleeing crowd. After a couple of minutes standing in the middle of the chaos, Oliver decided he had better get Emma and Roger away in case anything else were to happen, so he led them back into the building and through to the parking structure. That's when he noticed the mess his uniform was now in. Being able to shake off the excitement of the explosion so quickly and think clearly was an effect of the super serum. Being pissed about the potentially ruined uniform was Oliver's own weirdness.

"No one tried to blow me up. I wasn't the target," replied Oliver. He licked his thumb and rubbed a bit on the stain. It just seemed to move the black gunk around. "Seriously, this is brand new." He shook his head sullenly and finally quit looking in the mirror, carefully setting it back in position on the van and pinching some metal to hold it in place.

"If it was the Mayor, then the bad guy didn't have the most accurate arm I've ever seen," said Roger. "Almost hit the mascot."

"No, it wasn't him either, although they didn't have to be all that accurate with how close we all were together. The Police Chief was the target."

"Really? Why?" asked Emma.

Oliver shrugged. "I don't know. I'm new to all this." They stood there for a moment, the only noise being the muffled sounds of occasional sirens.

Roger eventually broke the silence, still walking back and forth in front of the other two. "Well, before now I would have said it's nice and all to have you as a hero for the city simply because I love the hero thing, but I'm willing to admit I wasn't sure if it was really needed. I know it was a political thing and even though there's a decent amount of crime in this city, I wouldn't say it's exactly hero worthy. But when people start tossing bombs around, I'm thinking there may be a point to you after all."

"I thought the point was to ruin Emma's life," said Oliver.

"No doubt," agreed Emma, "but it's not a bad bonus to save a few lives too." She smiled at Oliver.

"Whoa, is that Emma being nice to me?" said Oliver in mock surprise. "I don't know if I can handle such a personality change."

Emma shrugged. "What can you do? Bombs start going off and attitudes will change."

Roger was still marching around in circles, working off the energy. Finally he stopped and shook his head. "What the hell was that?" he said, a grin spreading across his face. "I'll admit, I love it. Bombs, explosions, sirens. You saving the day. It's kick-ass. What a rush!" He held up a finger. "It's a bit closer to home then I'd like, and I won't be doing anymore public appearances with you ever again, but I still love it. Hell, I thought you'd be putting out fires and clearing lanes after traffic accidents, but this is the real thing. I mean, that was a bomb! That was one hundred percent, grade A, frontline real superhero stuff out there."

"Enjoying the adrenaline, Roger?" asked Emma.

"Hell, yeah!" Roger jumped up and down in place a few times, spinning in a circle. Suddenly he stopped and took a couple steps backward, staring past a couple of cars. Before Oliver could ask him what it was, the Police Chief and one of his aides came walking into view. The Chief gave Roger a long look as he walked up. His dark eyes seemed perfectly made for those types of looks. Some might call them piercing, especially if he didn't like you. The Chief seemed to come to the conclusion that Roger was harmless and turned to Oliver.

"You don't seem to listen very well. I tell you to stick to saving kittens and you disregard my advice almost immediately," said the Chief, staring intently at Oliver. "Of course, if you hadn't, I wouldn't be standing here now, so I guess I'll have to be thankful for that." He gave a very slight smile as he took off his hat. He looked to be in his fifties, although the lines of weariness around his eyes added a couple years.

"So you were the target?" asked Oliver.

"While I can't be one hundred percent certain, I believe so. Look, I don't want to spend a lot of time talking about this right now because I don't know how private this is," he gestured at the parking structure around them, "but I want to make a deal with you, my earlier behavior to the contrary."

"I'm listening."

"Put simply, crime has been rising in the city lately, but it's not been…normal. More as if there was something or someone orchestrating it all from behind the scenes. I've had some select detectives looking into it, but nothing is ever private on the force, so I don't think our efforts have gone unnoticed. This attack pretty much proves that. My suspicion is that this is something bigger than we've ever dealt with before, because there's just too much happening, too many odd connections here and there for it all to simply be coincidence. It feels big, and if they'd go so far as to try and take me out, then I think I might be on the right track. It also makes it clear to me that I could actually use a little more help. That's where you come in."

"And the kittens?"

"Screw them. I'm a dog person. Look, I gave you a bit of a show earlier, but that was for the benefit of the other men. Like I said, nothing stays secret on the force, so I'm putting on a very public face of disapproval when it comes to you. But despite my initial, very great unease at getting a hero, I think the reality is that a hero might be just what we need this time around, especially one who can work outside the department. As far as the public and most of my police force is concerned, it's my policy that you're crap, but behind the scenes we'll have a deal. We can share information privately and you'll have more latitude and secrecy with which to work than I have. That will be helpful. And if whoever ordered this hit is successful next time, at least we'll still have someone going after them." The Chief paused a second. "Besides, you just saved my life, so I owe you a little more than being a hard-ass."

"I didn't think you were that bad, maybe a little crotchety. Your hat's probably too tight," said Oliver.

The Chief ignored him. "We keep the contact between you and me to a minimum, and when we do talk, it'll be secretly. Frank here," he said, nodding his head at his aide, "is the only one in my office who'll know we have a deal. If I need to talk to you or vice versa, we make contact through your girl there." He nodded toward Emma this time. She bristled a bit at the girl part, but didn't say anything. "But you never contact me through my office, and, if we do see each other in public, we don't get along. Deal?" asked the Chief.

Oliver looked at him for a few seconds. "I want two things," he said, waiting for the Chief to object. When he didn't, Oliver continued. "I want Roger here to work with me full time. Call it technical support or whatever, but I need some help. I'm sure you've got some department money you can use to fund him and you can label it however you want so people don't make the connection. Full time with a thirty percent increase for hazardous duty. Bombs and such."

The Chief stared at Oliver. "Twenty percent. What else?"

Oliver tried to ignore Roger jumping up and down in the background and continued. "Emma. I want her workload cut down to just handling me. Seems like it's a bigger job than we all thought before." Oliver waited for an answer.

"I'll have to trade some favors, but I think I can arrange that," said the Chief. "So we have a deal?"

"Yes, sir."

"Good. I'll be in contact." The Chief replaced his hat, turned and walked away with Frank on his heels.

Once he was out of earshot, Roger squealed a little and started jumping up and down again. He grabbed Oliver and gave him a hug. "Twenty percent! Holy crap, I would have done it for room and board."

Emma fended Roger off when he bounced toward her, refusing to give him a hug. "I notice you didn't get me more money," she said to Oliver.

"I thought you were pissed about too much work, so I focused on that."

"Sure, but a raise wouldn't have hurt."

Still jumping up and down, Roger said, "Hey, let's go out somewhere and celebrate."

"I suppose I could go for a little—" started Oliver, but Emma cut him off.

"You don't have time for going out," she said. "You have to get to the airport. It's time for superhero camp."

"Hey, where there's an airport, there's an airport bar. Or maybe like a Bennigan's. At least a Cinnabon. We can celebrate there," said Roger.

Oliver smiled. "Well, I did pack spare uniforms in my carry-on and I've got to wait somewhere at the airport. Let's go."

*　　*　　*

"So that's the city's new superhero already earning his pay," came Susie Shaw's voice from the large plasma wall monitor as the footage of the bomb attack was rerun. "And I, among other reporters and innocent bystanders, owe a debt of gratitude to SuperGuy. That bomb detonated only yards away and his intervention likely saved us from injury at the very least, if not death. So thank you, SuperGuy." She spoke this last part with the utmost sincerity, her voice full of emotion, her eyes wet, and the camera framing her perfectly with the damaged platform in the background.

Gray Matter watched the ongoing local television news coverage of the attempt on the Police Chief's life from his desk. He was annoyed at the failure but it would be properly addressed, meaning certain people in his organization would be reassigned to the Murmansk branch. That branch was getting awfully big. Gray Matter might even consider another try at the Police Chief, but he wasn't sure just yet. He was mostly intrigued by this surprise twist. He knew the event was to introduce Milwaukee's newly created superhero and, like many others, he was aware the motivation behind the appointment was purely political. He had seen the superhero position description himself, he had a copy right there on his desk. This hero was bargain basement material. Yet there he was, right up on the plasma in high definition, thwarting Gray Matter's plans the very first day on the job. The villain sensed this was no fluke. The Police Chief wasn't his only obstacle. There was a new hero in town and now it seemed his plan to take over the world might actually be challenged.

"...it's good to know we have such a man protecting our city," continued the male news anchor from the television.

"And how about that costume?" asked his female co-anchor. "I saw the mock ups when they announced the position and thought it was a bit silly, but he seems to pull it off. What did you think, Susie?"

"You're right, there really seems to be an extra element to it in person..."

Gray Matter muted the television and pressed the call button on his intercom, asking for Alex to come into the office. He knew what he had in the Police Chief, but this SuperGuy was an unknown quantity. He needed more information, some kind of assessment. A formidable adversary can often push a man to even greater heights, and Gray Matter was intrigued at the thought of having such an adversary. As the door opened on the far side of the office and Alex entered, Gray Matter made his decision. He would start simply, with a test. He would bring in some outside talent to see what this SuperGuy could do.

14

IT was lunchtime on the second day of the conference and Oliver sat at one of the many round metal tables filling a large, open section of the conference center in Washington, DC. He was eating an egg salad sandwich and chips with a friend he had made named Janice, otherwise known as Stormfront. She was Thunder Bay, Ontario's fairly recently created hero. She had already been through the rookie orientation sessions six months previously, but as Oliver had discovered, the conference wasn't just limited to the orientation of new superheroes. It also catered to veteran superheroes wanting additional training and continuing education credits. On his way to the conference, Oliver had envisioned himself in a small room with six or seven newly created heroes, all sitting in a circle on metal folding chairs and talking about their childhoods. Maybe there'd be some role-playing or situation scenarios, he wasn't sure. He didn't know why he thought about it this way, but he did. Instead, there were hundreds of heroes, rookies and veterans, dozens of celebrity speakers, and all kinds of breakout sessions, educational seminars and optional trainings.

All of this was held in a convention center that was a maze of little rooms, slightly bigger rooms, even bigger than that rooms, and auditoriums. The Superhero Union, which organized the conference and which Oliver was forced to join even before he could pick up his registration packet and complimentary tote bag full of goodies, had built the convention center in conjunction with the Department of Superhero Funding several years earlier. It was conveniently located next to the DSF's main complex and eliminated the costs of renting conference space three times a year. Not to mention they could then rent it out for other conferences, which meant they were always busy since they were located in Washington, DC. The four day superhero conferences were held during the first weeks in January, May and September, and combined both the new hero orientation sessions as well as the veteran continuing education sessions. This was a format that allowed the new heroes to mix with the veterans and kept the union from having to do separate conferences.

"So what do you think of Metal's proposal?" asked Janice, between bites of her turkey and ham. She had brown eyes and long black hair that was thick and wildly out of control. She told Oliver her hair had been a little hard to tame before becoming a hero, but then it transformed into a whole new animal once she took her serum and became Stormfront. Apparently female heroes had a little more leeway in what was considered a good head of hair. When Oliver gave her a quizzical look after her question, she added, "Of us joining the new group? What do you think?"

Oliver shrugged. "You know, I had a hard time following what all he was saying. Every time he moves in the slightest it sounds like one of those car crushers in a junkyard. Doesn't help that he seems to fidget a lot. I thought he had to go to the bathroom. I know I have above average hearing, but I only caught about every fourth word."

"Yeah, like having a conversation during a car accident," said Janice with an enthusiastic nod. "I had the same problem but I'd already spoken with the Creeper, the hero from Erie, PA, so I knew what Metal was talking about."

"And the translation...?"

"It seems they want to restart the hero group from the Great Lakes area. Metal, from Detroit, and Buffalo, from Buffalo of course, were members of the original Great Lakes Area Defenders, otherwise known as GLAD." Janice paused for a second to wipe some mustard off her lip. Oliver had noticed she had nice lips, real superhero quality.

"GLAD? Sounds like some kind of really peppy outreach group for Superheroes."

"I know. Anyway, when they couldn't all get along a few years ago the group broke up, but now those two want to start it up again, except for a slight name change to distinguish it from the former group. They seem to have some ongoing issues with the other former members of GLAD, or maybe there's some kind of naming rights thing, but they want to start the Great Lakes Area *New* Defenders."

Oliver looked at her for a second. "GLAND? Really? I'm assuming BOIL or GOITER were already taken."

Janice shrugged, "Afraid so. In their defense, this was Metal and Buffalo. Their serums weren't exactly chocked full of brain food. In fact, I think restarting the group is less about the security of the Great Lakes region and more about the weekly meetings, which usually entail some kind of buffet and the viewing of a sporting event."

"So what's the point of being in it?"

"Well, I suppose you do have to consider the help they could potentially give with a supervillain or natural disaster, however unlikely those are, but mostly it just looks good to be a member of a group. It carries a bit of prestige and I'd bet your mayor or city council would recommend it. Mine did. Then they can say their hero is doing something for the greater good and such. Of course, they don't want me wasting much time on it since I'm their hero, but they still like to brag. I thought I might get stuck with membership in some Ontario or province level group since there wasn't really a regional one anymore. Something bigger, like federal, is out of the question for someone of my status, but then they approached me about this. It's regional and pretty big compared to some, so it's more than I hoped for."

"So you were actually hoping for something less than GLAND?"

"Well I guess, if you have to put it that way, but it's better than being part of the lame Ontario group. They don't even have weekly meetings. Monthly, I think. There's just not that much going on in Ontario." Janice had finished her sandwich and pulled an apple out of her complimentary tote bag.

"So who else is in it?" asked Oliver.

"Those first two, plus the Creeper said he's in, and somebody from Cleveland but I didn't get the name. If you and I say yes, that's six, the number they want if I heard Metal right. What do you think?" she asked, and then gave him a shy smile. "I'd like it if you were in."

"Were you a flirt before, or is that the serum talking?"

Janice shrugged. "Who knows? This is who I am now. Besides, don't take it as too much of a compliment, I just want someone around I know. I don't want to be stuck alone in some headquarters for a weekend with the Creeper, who absolutely lives up to his name. I mean, think of the most disturbingly creepy uncle you have and multiply him by a hundred. Seriously, really creepy. How that makes a hero I don't know. I thought serums were supposed to make you likable."

"Definitely the exception to the rule," said Oliver, tapping his fingers on the table. "Well, I can't think of a good reason not to join, besides the name, and I don't want to miss more flirting, so I'm in."

"Great, I'll tell Metal. I think he's going to be at the Bomb Disposal Methods seminar with me later. I'm sure there's some sort of paperwork we need to get started on to make it official. Maybe we'll all get together before the conference is over, depending on whether there's an appropriate game on television and some kind of buffet available," said Janice, taking another bite of her apple.

"Can I ask you something, all flirting aside?"

"Sure."

"Do you find it a little hard wearing a costume like that?" said Oliver, finally asking the question he'd been thinking about since meeting Janice. Her costume was similar to Oliver's in that it was extremely tight and, in her case, generally scant. At least she had a cape, so she could keep herself covered. "I mean, mine's tight too but at least there's more of it. But even with that small caveat, I still haven't had eye contact with a regular civilian since I put this thing on."

"I definitely thought I'd have a problem with it at first, if for no other reason than the fact that I'm basically wearing a bikini full time and live in Thunder Bay, not South Beach, but since we don't feel any normal temperature changes, it isn't really an issue. Otherwise I have the cape to keep me covered most of the time, except when I'm fighting, but even then I'm usually flying and causing a lot of havoc, like clouds and rain, so I don't think it's all that easy to see me. I'm sure I was like you when I first started, but I don't think about it anymore. I think that worry just goes away. It becomes normal. Maybe it'll be the same for you."

"Maybe."

"You could try another layer or something," said Janice, leaning forward a little and looking down at Oliver's lap as she thought. Oliver reflexively covered himself up. "Come on now," said Janice. "We're both adults here, and heroes. This is a professional discussion which, I might add, you started." She waved at him to remove his hands and he reluctantly did. Janice looked at his costume some more and nodded. "Yeah, maybe you could put something over the top," she said as she sat back down. Then a big smile spread across her face and she added, "Because you'd never get anything under it." She laughed and clapped her hands as Oliver blushed and scooted his chair in as far as it could go.

"That wasn't very professional."

"I know, but I couldn't resist. Look, there are plenty of heroes walking around here in similar suits. It's just a part of the job. You have nothing to be ashamed of, and you'll get used to it soon enough. Just relax."

"Yeah, yeah," said Oliver, waving her off. "Let's just change the topic. What are you going to next?"

Janice picked up her conference program and opened it to a marked page. "I'm going to 'Who's Your Pancho?': Choosing the Right Sidekick' at 1:30 and then it's the

'Bomb Disposal Methods: What To Do If You Don't Have the Arm To Get It Off the Planet' seminar at 3:00. We could meet for dinner around 5:30. What do you have?"

"A bunch of short ones, all orientation stuff." Oliver dug into his tote bag, searching for his schedule. He pulled out a file he had received from Emma that morning which contained all the information the Police Chief had on the strange crime problems plaguing Milwaukee. He hadn't had any time to look at it yet because he was so busy with required orientation sessions at the conference. Setting the file on the table, Oliver kept digging, finally finding his schedule and reading aloud. "First up is 'The Superhero Union: You're One of Us Now' at 1:00. I'd have to say that sounds boring and only ever so slightly different than half the other sessions I've attended since I got here. Seems they really want to get their message across."

"You gotta love all the party propaganda."

"Then it's 'Malpractice Coverage: Make Sure You Have a Hero's Worth' at 2:00, followed, pretty fittingly I might add, by 'Limiting Damage: Don't Always Throw the Bad Guy Into Stuff' at 3:00, then 'City, State and Federal: Which Hero Are You? (And How to Get Along)' at 4:00. Yeah, I should be able to meet you at 5:30 for dinner."

"Great, how about meeting right back here, then maybe we can go out somewhere?" asked Janice. "I know a good place over in Baltimore. I could fly us."

"Sounds good to me," replied Oliver, mostly just imagining how the flying would go. Not so much about the speed or heights, but more about the mechanics of holding on to Janice in her costume.

"Okay. I think I'm going to swing by the exhibition hall and check out some of the gadgets and vehicles before my session. You interested?"

"I'd like to, but I want to take a look at this file, see if there's anything interesting in it. Besides, I think looking at all the cool stuff I can't have isn't the best thing in the world for my morale."

"Okay, I'll see you later."

Oliver watched her walk off toward the exhibition hall, still somewhat thinking about the flying, then checked the clock to see how much time he had left to go through the file. There was only about a half hour, which wasn't much, but he was itching to get started on it. In fact, it was a pretty good indication of just how much the super serum programmed him to fight crime since he was choosing not to spend the extra time with Janice and was even considering opting out of dinner if the file proved interesting enough. "God, what a sad, sad superhero am I," he said quietly.

15

OLIVER was pretty certain he was clutching. The exact motivation behind the clutching was a little harder for him to establish. It could be because he was presently flying thousands of feet above the ground, not in the typical manner of a passenger jet's cramped coach seat, but rather clinging to the back of a superhero. Another possibility was that Oliver was simply letting the more instinctual part of himself take control and it knew what to do when holding on to a scantily clad female superhero, flying or not. Since he was pretty sure the super serum would have taken care of any fears of heights or flying, it was most likely the instinctual thing and Oliver was indeed clutching. In his defense, he was only human[3]. He may not have admitted to it at the time, but Oliver probably envisioned that very clutching when Janice had extended the invitation to fly him home from the conference earlier that evening and Oliver had been clutching and debating the clutching question for miles now. He decided to make some conversation so the silence wouldn't be so obvious.

"So...the guys in GLAND seem okay," he said, referring to the superhero group they were both now part of and with whom they had just held their first official meeting. Oliver had opted to miss his flight home at the end of the conference so the group could have their inaugural meeting at a Thai buffet place. Janice had made the decision easy by offering to fly him home so he didn't have to bother with getting another flight.

"All except the Creeper obviously," replied Janice. "But I guess that's kind of the point, so he's getting the job done. Oh, and Ohio Man is a little odd. I actually felt sorry for him when he introduced himself with that silly name." She had taken off her cape and stowed it in her tote bag for the flight back to the Midwest because, as she said, it just got in the way when carrying a passenger. This didn't exactly help Oliver's situation since the cape wasn't

---

[3] Apart from being chemically enhanced to the point of near invulnerability and endowed with super strength, super speed and most other super abilities and senses. Any super lust was undoubtedly present before we got there. —*Department of Superhero Funding*

there as a buffer between them. Oliver was laying on Janice's back with both arms wrapped as tactfully around her chest as he could manage, but the question of clutching still came immediately to mind. To his credit, Oliver's positioning strictly adhered to Janice's own instructions, who had told him how to hold on once they were in the air because it was the most comfortable position for her during a long flight. Oliver didn't argue, since she was the expert on flying. He had merely gotten on with tying both their tote bags to his waist for the trip and thinking about baseball.

"You think Ohio Man's name is silly, what about SuperGuy?"

"Well, at least SuperGuy's a bit imaginative. I mean, sort of. Okay, not really, but at least you're not Wisconsin Man. What if he wants to relocate someday? Is he going to be Ohio Man in New Mexico?"

"Can't he just change his name? Be New Mexico Man or Retired Ohio Man?"

"Tons of paperwork there. They make it real painful," said Janice. "A good incentive for the hero they created to stay put if they want him to."

"Yeah, good point," said Oliver. He adjusted his arms a bit for the first time since they had gotten to cruising altitude as Janice called it. He had steadfastly refused to move them at all for a long time because it might seem a little suspicious, but now he was beginning to cramp up. He pulled himself a little farther forward too, so he could hear her more easily over the wind.

"Anyway, he was okay, just a little boring. And most particular about meeting rules." Janice gave Oliver a quick look over her shoulder as she said this and her long black hair blew across his face. It smelled amazing and Oliver had trouble getting his brain to process her statement, super enhanced clear thinking or not.

"Yeah, that was strange," Oliver managed, "but mostly annoying. I thought it would be a relaxed first meeting. Something more social for us to get to know each other but he was always talking about motions and points of order. Between him and Metal's creaking, I don't know which was worse."

"I wonder what he did before becoming a hero? Maybe that's just his personality from before and not something from the serum. At least I haven't heard of anal retentiveness being a super power before."

"At least we don't have to put up with it that often. Imagine if we were in one of those federal groups and stayed in the same headquarters," said Oliver. "But I suppose it'll be worth it if we ever need their help. The damage Metal and Buffalo can do alone will be worth it. Just look at what they did to that buffet."

"Definitely devastated that."

"Ravaged, plundered, pillaged, demolished."

"You could go on, couldn't you?"

"Afraid so, and so could they."

"Don't."

"Okay." Oliver looked over Janice's shoulder at the ground below them. It was a clear night, at least where they were currently flying, with just a sliver of moon in the sky and stars shining in abundance. Below, lights dotted the landscape, collecting in clusters here and there to show a city in the distance, as well as cars moving along stretches of dark highway. They were flying low enough that Oliver could make out mundane landmarks like parking lots or tennis courts when they flew over them. His eyes followed the dark, crooked path of a river as it cut through a city and then on out into the countryside beyond, eventually melting into blackness.

After another moment of enjoying the view, Oliver said, "You know, this flying is pretty cool."

"I've always enjoyed it. It takes a while for that part of the serum to fully kick in, usually a few extra days. You can float a bit or maybe jump off a building and glide once it starts developing, but there's nothing to compare it to when it finally matures. It's quick at that point, like turning on a switch. You can only drift or float one moment, and then, in the next, you can do it all. When it happened to me, I spent that first day flying around everywhere. What a rush," she said, shaking her head as she remembered it. Then she shrugged. "Although not quite as much of a rush as when I fry someone with a bolt of lightning or rip something apart with a mini tornado. I wonder what that says about me? Flying's very useful, though. I don't have to step on an airplane and squeeze into a seat next to someone with questionable hygiene ever again, or drive five hours to visit my parents, or worry about something being too high up on a shelf."

"Very practical."

"You should get it. Get them to spring for an add-on in the budget."

"You've seen my costume, right? I'm SuperGuy. I'm lucky they sprung for the second capital letter in my name." Janice giggled and Oliver discovered that making Janice giggle brought on even more complicated questions in relation to the clutching.

"So, what did you find in that file your secret Police Chief buddy sent you?" asked Janice after a couple minutes of silence. Oliver had told her the story of his partnership with the Chief during one of their many conversations at the conference.

"Plenty," said Oliver. "And nothing. I don't know. I'm new to all this, so I don't really know what I'm looking for. There were lots of reports and things, too many for me to read all of them yet. I got the most information from simply reading the summary the Chief included, which basically said there's bad stuff afoot, but he hasn't been able to tie it to anything or anyone yet. Possibly the mob or some crime kingpin moving into the city because he sees signs of organization behind it all. Not to mention someone tried to blow him up."

"So not terribly helpful."

"No, not yet at least."

"Well, maybe once you read through all the reports you'll see a pattern or get some ideas," said Janice.

"I hope so, but I'm not like you. I don't have a police background. I don't know if I'll recognize what it is when I see it."

"You will. That's part of the superhero makeup. You fight crime, so you're designed to recognize it now. Trust me on that. I was an okay cop before, but now I'm damn good. There's a huge difference."

"I also assumed the Police Chief and I would be buddies, fighting crime together from the start, but instead I'm stuck with this secret deal due to all the politics. I thought he'd pick up the GuyPhone or turn on the GuySignal and I'd come running, but I'm going to get phone messages and memos passed secretly through my liaison. Maybe a text if I'm lucky." Oliver shook his head slowly. "How do you get along with your Police Chief?" he asked after a moment.

"Sorry to rub your face in it, but my Chief and I get along fine. The Mayor too," said Janice. "Of course, they are men and I wear this tiny uniform, so I think that helps."

"Good point. I can't do much about that."

"Give it time. If you do your job well, they'll come around."

"That's simple enough, except if the Chief's suspicions are correct, I may be walking into a giant mess right away. If there's really something big brewing, and something or someone big behind it, well…that's just a bit more to jump into than nabbing a few regular crooks or saving kittens from trees."

"Look at it this way: If you do manage to put a stop to whatever it is, you should be in their good graces right away. There's a lot more credit in a big conspiracy than in stopping a few small crimes. But relax, it's probably not even that big of a deal. Just some small crime boss trying to increase his territory here, maybe some changes in some distribution there, enough stuff happening so it looks bigger than it is. It's not like it's going to be somebody trying to take over the world."

"Yeah. Probably not."

"Hey, could you loosen your grip a little?" asked Janice. "I don't think you're in danger of falling off."

"Oh, sorry."

16

OLIVER stood in Mrs. Lundquist's driveway watching as Janice took off and disappeared into the night, heading vaguely northwest. Most of his thoughts were about how fun it had been spending time with her at the conference and on the flight home, and he wondered if she was interested in him. There was the flirting, but Oliver wasn't certain just what that meant. He had never been good with separating the wheat from the chaff in that regard, probably because he hadn't previously inspired much flirting, so he could have been completely off. Plus there might be policies against relationships between superheroes, at least in the case of those working together officially, like in a regional superhero group. If GLAND would ruin his shot with Janice, Oliver was not as excited about being part of the club. He would have to ask Roger. He would know about any official rules like that. Speaking of his friend, Roger's car was parked by the curb and Oliver looked up to see the lights on in his apartment. It seemed Roger was visiting. Oliver also noticed the Taurus parked by the curb and wondered why it wasn't squeezed inside the garage where he had left it. That car was now his most prized possession after all. Can't just be leaving it on the street like it was an Omni or something. The Omni was also parked by the curb a little farther down. With plenty of questions for Roger, Oliver headed up the stairs to his apartment.

Stepping inside, Oliver found his home to be somewhat different than when he left. Admittedly it was a bit of a mess when he ran out on Monday morning, in a rush to make the press conference and flight out of town, but he remembered that really only being a few dirty dishes and some clothes. Now the apartment looked like a crowded warehouse, albeit a very tiny one. Cardboard boxes, packing crates, electronic equipment and miscellaneous tools sat everywhere. Styrofoam packing peanuts littered the floor. Some of the boxes and crates were stacked almost to the ceiling. Oliver's makeshift coffee table had been raised, using more of the numerous crates, to a workbench height and was covered with a variety of tools and parts. His half kitchen table was also in the midst of an identity crisis, now piled with a plethora of electronic equipment ranging from an iMac to a police scanner to several other gadgets Oliver couldn't immediately identify. A couple of thumps came from the kitchen and Roger slid out from between two stacks of boxes.

"You're back!" he said, a huge smile on his face. He rubbed his hands together in a sort of devilish way as he looked around the room happily, seeming to indicate Oliver should be feeling the same way.

"Yes, and look what you've done with the place, Honey," Oliver deadpanned. "Looks like you went with a modern warehouse style. Bold choice. Where's the forklift?"

"Oh, that would be useful," said Roger, seeming to really give it some thought, "but we could never get one in here."

"Uh, exactly what did I do to deserve this?"

"Well, essentially you left me home alone for a week with a credit card. No, don't worry," said Roger, seeing the look on Oliver's face and waving his hand to show he was kidding. "It's not that bad. It didn't cost anything. Well, just the shipping, but I had that billed to the Mayor's office. And even they can't complain too much since I saved them money. Most of the time, instead of Next Day, I settled for Two Day shipping."

"Very financially responsible of you, Roger, but exactly how did all this stuff not cost anything except shipping?" asked Oliver. He dropped his tote bag and ran a gloved finger along the top of the iMac's display on the half kitchen table. It wasn't brand new but it wasn't exactly old either, and either way it definitely wasn't cheap. He picked up an iPad sitting next to it.

"You have the Superhero Surplus Warehouse to thank for that."

"Superhero Surplus Warehouse?" repeated Oliver, setting the iPad down and turning his attention to a multifunction laser printer. It looked like it hadn't been used at all.

"Well, the DSF calls it something else, something in government speak, but the rest of us normal folk call it the Surplus Warehouse or just the Warehouse," said Roger. "It's great." His expression indicated that it was indeed great.

"So these are ours?"

"Yep."

"Okay, cool," said Oliver thoughtfully, "but how does all of this expensive equipment not cost us anything? It looks like it should cost us something. And not a small something."

"The Warehouse is the place where the equipment— all the computers, tools, vehicles, weapons, or whatever—is gathered when it's no longer needed by the hero who originally owned it, specifically so it can then be used by another hero who can't afford his own stuff. Like if they upgrade to a better car or plane, then they ship the old one to the Warehouse so someone else can use it."

Oliver gave Roger a look. "Plane? Did you get me a plane? Because I wouldn't be against that," said Oliver quickly, "not that I can fly a plane. Still be cool to sit in it."

"Well, I wasn't able to get you a *plane* exactly."

"How not exactly?"

"I actually got you two smaller flying vehicles and a little helicopter thingy. None of them really counts as a plane." Roger shrugged with disappointment at the last part. "They're all in the garage."

"Three? That's a bit more than I need, isn't it? I mean, we've established I can't fly a plane, so whether we call it a flying vehicle or a little helicopter thingy, I still can't fly one, let alone three."

"Well, flying them isn't really our most pressing issue, although they aren't as complicated as a real plane," said Roger. "Technically none of them function, which is one of the reasons why they were still at the Warehouse. Working models of any type of vehicle get snatched up pretty fast, but planes—especially planes—are gone in a split second. It's even hard to get non-working planes."

"Non-working? I thought you said they were trade-ins."

"I said they're sent to the Warehouse when their previous owners no longer need them, and if they're broken, that usually takes care of the hero needing them. Not all of the items are trade-ins because a hero has upgraded. Others are there because they've broken down or been crashed or maybe never worked right in the first place. Once in a while you can get a shot at some refurbished gear because the DSF engineers who build the new equipment also run the Warehouse, but those things go fast too. Occasionally there's even stuff from a hero who bites it, so it's kind of like an estate auction then, and in that case you can get some primo equipment. You have to be lucky to catch those things on the site while they're still available. It gets swamped as soon as the news of some hero *retiring prematurely* becomes public." Roger used his fingers to quote the two significant words in the air.

"Site?" interrupted Oliver. "You mean website?"

"Yeah, certainly. It's all online. Real time inventory. There's even an app for my iPhone. Here, I'll show you." Roger sat down in front of the computer and clicked the mouse a couple of times. Shortly a website loaded, after requesting a password from Roger, and showed various categories related to heroes and equipment. Roger clicked on links as he talked, giving Oliver a little tour of what was available. "The site is only for heroes technically, but, while you were gone, I got your hero ID number from the file so I could set up an account and start getting us some toys. Since your budget doesn't allow for us to buy any of our own, this is really the only way to get them. And there's plenty of good stuff if you just want the basics. The computer, police scanner, electron microscope, all those things were easy. Plenty of that type of stuff in the inventory. It's harder to get the really fun toys, at least ones that still work, which explains why I got three flying vehicles. Two are the same type, one was crashed and the other apparently never worked well enough to crash, and the helicopter one is just borderline useful, meaning it's pathetically slow, so you might as well walk where you're going. But it does have a nice, cushy seat."

"I'm a little afraid to ask the obvious next question," said Oliver.

"So why do we have them if they don't work?" guessed Roger, a big smile on his face. Oliver nodded, dreading the answer. "Because I think I can piece together one working flyer out of the other three."

Oliver paused for what he thought was a significant amount of time. "And you've made exactly how many flying vehicles in the past, Mr. Wright?"

"Please call me Orville, and no, I haven't made any flying machines in the past, but that won't stop me from trying."

"But it will stop me from flying them."

"What do you have to worry about? You're indestructible," said Roger, patting Oliver on the chest as he stood and stepped past him on the way to the reconfigured coffee table in the living room. "Anyway, there's a bunch of stuff in these boxes I haven't been able to get to yet, but I do have one toy you'll like which is all ready to go." He picked something up from the table and came back to Oliver. "You seem to have gotten used to wearing the mask," he said, nodding at Oliver's face, which was still covered by his mask.

Oliver reflexively touched the mask and nodded. "Yeah, you know I thought it would bug the hell out of me at first, but I had to wear it all the time at the conference and it never did. It's surprisingly comfortable."

"The mark of good styling," said Roger. "The DSF is known for making great uniforms, despite being a little hit and miss on the flying things[4]. Anyway, take that off and try this one. I modified one of your spare masks with some goggles I got from the Warehouse. It was incredibly easy. The DSF are really smart about using universal standards for connections, so interchanging parts between like components is a breeze. Makes the whole Warehouse thing much more useful. Just amazing." Roger paused at the look on Oliver's face. "Sorry, nerding out a bit there. Anyway, by pressing the button on the right side, you can cycle through the lenses. The first is just clear for normal conditions, the second is telescopic, the third is night vision, and the fourth is thermal. You simply twist the dial surrounding the button to increase and decrease the magnification. Oh, and they're UV protected and shatterproof, which is nice for the safety factor." He handed the mask to Oliver.

"What's this button on the left side for?" asked Oliver as he put on the mask.

---

[4] We admit it about the flying vehicles, they are a bit touchy. However, our success rate with uniforms is 99.95%. The costume concept and product for the hero Manscape was not very well thought out and the employee responsible has been sacked. —*The Department of Superhero Funding*

"That's for photos. Any pictures you take are automatically uploaded to the cloud and can be shared with whoever needs them. So I will have instant access to the photos here on the computer, or on my phone, wherever. Just have to type in the password for the feed. I took some practice shots. Great quality. Tons of megapixels. Makes the camera in my phone look like a Polaroid."

Oliver quickly flipped through the different modes of the mask and snapped a couple of pictures, one a macro close up of Roger's nose. "Nice," he said.

"I know," said Roger proudly. "I have another set of goggles so I'll make a backup mask as well. Plus there'll be more. As I said, I have a lot of boxes to get to yet." He waved his hand at the room.

"I guess I picked the right guy for the job," said Oliver with a smile. He looked around the small apartment crammed with boxes again. "But this isn't exactly the right superhero headquarters, that's for sure," he said, shaking his head. "Too bad we didn't get some money for that. Janice said Thunder Bay gave her an old fire station for her base and a fund for updating it. I guess I can afford to rent a larger apartment with my salary increase...but I should probably pay off my student loans first," said Oliver as an afterthought. "I guess asking the city for something is one possibility, though. Maybe we should see if they have some building they aren't using."

"Janice?"

"Huh?" said Oliver absentmindedly, still thinking about more space. "Yeah, she goes by the name Stormfront, from Thunder—"

"I know who she is," interrupted Roger, a bit of awe in his voice. "You call her Janice?"

"Yes, I met her at the conference. She found out we were from the same neighborhood, at least in hero terms, so she introduced herself after one of the first sessions I attended. She just dropped me off," said Oliver, gesturing toward the door. She flew me back from DC because I missed my flight due to—"

"Stormfront? Here?" said Roger, mimicking Oliver by pointing toward the door of the apartment.

"Well, not now. She took off."

Roger shook his head in disappointment. "Seriously dude, we have got to talk about your treatment of me. When there's someone like Stormfront around, there's got to be introductions. Got to be."

"I'm sorry, but I didn't realize you would be here."

"Well, it's not all about me. What if I turned out to be her dream guy? Then you're hurting her too. Think about her," said Roger, slightly pleading.

"Okay...yeah, I suppose that's one way to look at it," conceded Oliver. He hesitated a moment before continuing. "Would now be a bad time to ask if there are any specific rules about fraternization between superheroes?"

Roger stared at him. "Ouch. You certainly know how to hurt a guy," he said with a despondent sigh. "As far as

I know, there aren't any official rules, but I don't think serious heroes let that sort of thing get in the way of their duties. And remember for next time that introductions are still the norm whether you have a crush on the girl or not. I'd still like to meet whoever I can. And don't assume I'm not here because I'm always going to be here with all this work to do. I basically moved in during the week. In fact, I hope you don't mind because I took over your bed. I figured you wouldn't use it since you don't need to sleep anymore. Oh, and your landlady downstairs is seriously creeping me out. Always peeking out at me from behind the curtains when I walk by. Very suspicious type, she is. You think it's because I'm black? Kind of feels like profiling."

"No, that's just standard Mrs. Lundquist. If she sees as well as she hears, she probably didn't even realize you weren't me, let alone black. Although I wonder what ideas she might have in her head after seeing all these boxes and crates coming in. Couldn't have missed all of these." Oliver pulled off his new mask and gloves and flopped down on the couch. He didn't feel tired, but he felt he should feel tired, especially after the long week at the conference and the flight back home.

Roger moved a couple of small items off the other end of the couch and sat down also. "Well, with the space issues, the Mrs. Lundquist issues, not to mention that pathetic option you have for showering in the bathroom, I think getting new digs should be one of our priorities."

Oliver nodded slowly. "I'd have to say you're right."

"That and getting you some kind of flying vehicle."

"Funny, that isn't as high a priority for me," said Oliver. "But I did like flying with Janice. Despite the obvious appeal of Janice herself, it was just damn cool. Fast, easy. She recommends it."

"No doubt. It's the number one rated power among superheroes. Superhero Tech did a poll asking what power a hero would least like to lose and that was named the most. It was also the most desired power for heroes who didn't have it. It's a no-brainer. You really can't beat flying."

Oliver nodded. "I can't really think of a downside, at least to her type of flying. For your flying vehicles on the other hand, the downside would be the crashing and dying in something you MacGyvered up after reading a couple airplane magazines and Flying Machines for Idiots."

"That's not fair. I'll read at least four or five issues before I build it. Besides, we need a new place first because Mrs. Lundquist's garage isn't going to cut it as a viable workspace. Maybe that city property idea you mentioned would be the right place to start. You could have Emma check into it, maybe through the Chief. There's got to be something sitting out there unused."

"Yeah, I suppose so. Hopefully Emma will be in good spirits now that her workload is just me. As for the Chief…Well, I'm sure he'll be happy to hear I want something else." Both men sat quietly for a few moments.

KURT CLOPTON

"So what are you going to do now?" asked Roger. "It's your first night in town as the official, fully orientated superhero. Feel like you know what the hell you're doing?"

"Not a clue," said Oliver. "Didn't really think about what I was going to do when I got back. Shouldn't I just take it easy here on the couch? After all that's happened in the past week, I should be exhausted."

"But you're not," said Roger, matter of factly.

"Nope, not at all."

"Of course not. You're not wired to sit on the couch and put your feet up anymore," said Roger. "But never fear, I know what you have to do,"

Oliver looked at him expectantly. "And that is…?"

"Patrol," said Roger with a simple shrug.

"Patrol," said Oliver, mostly to himself. He nodded. "That does sound like something I would enjoy doing nowadays."

"It's what you guys do. You should take your inaugural run around the city at night and make sure everything's okay. And if it's not, you fix it."

Oliver sat there for a few seconds, thinking about it. "You know, I think you're right," he said with a nod. Standing, he pulled on his newly reconfigured mask, making sure it was perfectly straight. Then he took a second to make sure the rest of his costume was all tucked and in order. Last he tugged on his gloves, made a fist with one hand and smacked it into the palm of the other. "It's time to do the hero thing." With that he stepped to the door and walked out into the cool night.

"Go get 'em, SuperGuy," Roger called after him, caught up in the excitement. With the rush he was getting from it, Roger wondered what it felt like to be the actual hero going out to fight crime for the first time. He stood there with a smile on his face, taking in the significance of the moment, imagining this was how people must feel after getting an astronaut into orbit or landing one on the moon. It was almost breathtaking.

A couple of seconds later Oliver stepped back inside. "You got the keys for the Taurus?"

17

OLIVER was walking home. He could have run and covered the miles in just a few minutes, but he didn't feel there was a good reason to arrive any more quickly. At the moment it seemed more important for him to have some quality time during which he could reflect upon his first night on patrol in the city. It hadn't been a bad night, although there was certainly room for improvement, that mostly being in the form of still having the Taurus to drive home. Oliver had spent the better part of the night in the car, cruising slowly around the city, focused primarily on the downtown and waterfront areas with the highest crime rates. The material the Chief had provided gave him that statistical information, but also showed that while those areas were traditionally the highest in the city, there had also been a steady increase in the last six months. There were similar increases in other areas, some even out in distant suburbs, and Oliver wondered if there was a pattern he wasn't seeing. Something more than just the overall increase. Maybe he would figure out the big picture with more time, but this particular night was about routine patrolling, and the reports didn't do anything to help him there. The easy solution to that was the police radio. Oliver simply listened to the calls they were receiving and decided whether he could be of help. He could have used his communicator to listen in on the police band, but he preferred the radio in the Taurus to having all the noise right in his ear.

Unfortunately, the bulk of the calls were not exactly hero worthy, being things like routine traffic stops, public disturbances or simple complaints, so Oliver just continued to circle around, getting used to the city at night and his new job. There was one shaky moment after Oliver discovered the Taurus was equipped with lights and a siren, and he accidentally pulled over a garbage truck, but it wasn't until about four in the morning that a call went out really requiring his attention. A high speed pursuit had started on the south side of the city and was heading in Oliver's general direction, so he decided it was a good time to make his debut.

"Let's get in the game," he said to himself, whipping the car around in a quick U-turn and heading south. Listening to the ongoing commentary on the police radio, Oliver kept himself in the path of the pursuit until it was close enough that it would have to pass him on the current street. He pulled the Taurus to the right curb and got out. Tugging on his gloves to make sure they were snug, Oliver walked to the middle of the street and then slowly south in the direction of the oncoming pursuit. He heard some high noon gunfight theme music coming from somewhere, then realized he was humming it himself. The road was four lanes wide with two lanes going in each direction and the additional width of a parking lane on each side. Parking meters lined the curb next to the street, and Oliver fleetingly wondered if he should have dropped a quarter in for the Taurus but guessed he was exempt, being on official business. Or maybe he didn't have to pay after eight o'clock. He should have read the signs. Realizing he was getting sidetracked, Oliver concentrated on the scene. A delivery truck was on the left side of the street, down about fifty yards and parked so it was angled back toward the sidewalk for easy unloading. This meant it was blocking the parking lane and most of the first lane on that side of the street, but, at this time of night, there was very little traffic, except for the high speed chase in question.

Oliver heard the police sirens as soon as he stepped out of his Taurus and could now see the headlights and flashing police lights of the cars coming his way. He positioned himself just short of the delivery truck so the car had less space in which to maneuver around him, and he planted his feet, waiting. It didn't really occur to Oliver that he had never done anything like this before until the car was less than a block away. In fact, he realized he hadn't given much thought to how he was going to stop the car, although he had a sneaking suspicion the superhero part of his brain had already worked that out. Unfortunately, to what was left of the regular Oliver part of his brain, that plan looked a lot like letting the car hit him. Oliver gave a little credit to the serum at that point because at least this realization didn't seem to bother him. It was just how he did his job. This first time anyway. He reserved the right to work out new options in the future if this hurt like a bitch. A few seconds later the fugitive car was only yards away and Oliver threw up a hand to signal stop while at the same time bracing himself for the impact. The pursuing police car sirens were deafening and the lights flashed in a variety of dazzling patterns as they roared toward him. With the headlights of the fugitive car bearing down on him, Oliver closed his eyes at the last second and waited for the impact. A howling screech sounded as the car braked in that last instant and Oliver flinched in anticipation of the collision. But it didn't come. The screeching continued, followed by a repetitive metallic popping coupled with a slightly delayed tinkling after each pop, and finally one loud, thundering crash.

Oliver opened his eyes to see the pursuing police cruisers coming to a halt around him, sirens stopping and their lights reflecting off the surrounding buildings. Brand new tire marks scarred the pavement in front of him and swerved around the hero toward the curb to his right. There they straightened out and disappeared, but not before one tire had gone up on the curb and a new type of trail began, this one made up of parking meter pole stumps. There were close to six stumps along the edge of the sidewalk, a couple with the tops still attached but bent down to the pavement, while the rest of the meters and their former contents were strewn all over the general area. This mess made a rather obvious path leading to the final crash of the fugitive car, which was right into Oliver's Taurus. Police officers had approached the subject car and were pulling out the driver, who appeared to be completely unhurt and fairly oblivious to anything around him. Oliver could only stand and stare at what was left of his Taurus, its front end crumpled almost all the way back to the windshield, which itself had the pole of a parking meter sticking out of it. He wasn't an expert on automobiles, but Oliver guessed the damage was probably what insurers called totaled. Near enough, anyway. To add insult to injury, it appeared a small fire was starting underneath the two cars.

"I just got that," was the only thing Oliver had said about it at the time, but he repeated that same sentence over and over like a mantra during the walk home. One of the police officers had offered him a ride, but after watching the fire department extinguish the small blaze that had been his new car, Oliver felt like he needed some solid alone time. He knew it was just a Taurus but it was still his new job's only perk—ignoring all the super power stuff—not to mention a big step up from the Omni. How was he supposed to cruise around the city on patrol in the

Omni? So not cool. The sun was just starting to rise when Oliver finally reached Mrs. Lundquist's house and walked up the stairs to his apartment, thinking about the one useful thing he had learned from his first night on patrol. Park far away and walk to the fight. They hadn't covered that at the convention.

Inside his apartment, Oliver found a bit more activity than he expected. The smell of coffee filled the small space, along with sounds reminiscent of a bustling office. The printer was shooting out paper, some kind of movie or live feed was playing on the computer and the local news was on the television. Above it all was a grinding sound emanating ever so appropriately from a grinder being used by Roger on a piece of metal atop the makeshift coffee table/workbench. When he noticed Oliver in the doorway, Roger stopped the grinder and removed his safety glasses.

"Don't you sleep?" asked Oliver, "Or at least go home once in a while?" Shutting the door behind him, he pulled off his gloves and mask and dropped them on a convenient crate.

"Like I said before, I sort of commandeered this place, so I don't need to go home, and I slept plenty. At least as much as I could bear. It's tough to let all this new stuff sit here without opening it up and seeing what we got. It's a lot like Christmas morning really, only it's lasted a week and the presents are all the size of crates, and each one is cooler than the next. So really, a lot better than Christmas. And there's a lot of boxes yet to go." Roger gazed around the apartment, looking a bit exhausted yet very content. He was in his happy place.

"Is it me, or is this even more of a mess than it was last night?" asked Oliver.

"Same amount of mess really, just not as much is contained in boxes anymore," shrugged Roger. "I was looking for something specific and had to open a few things before I found it. Sorry about that."

"I suppose it doesn't matter, I'll probably be out saving the city most of the time anyway, right?" said Oliver, resigning himself to the current state of his apartment. He sat down on a crate. "That reminds me, after my first night on patrol and all the wisdom I've gained, I believe the job requires that we make transportation a priority. Flight would be nice, especially if it was the actual super power as opposed to a flying machine of your creation, but other non-flying vehicles would be good too. Motorcycle maybe, or an ATV. Something like that. Really anything." There was a pause. "You know, for back up...or extras...emergency reserves. For just in case," added Oliver lamely.

"I'm getting the feeling something happened to the Taurus?"

"Quite a lot, really," said Oliver. "Whole lifetime's worth of stuff in a few minutes." He noticed a slight smile on Roger's face. "But it seems you already know, don't you?"

Roger nodded. "It's already been on the news. They covered your first big arrest in the wee hours of the morning and some of the footage showed the cars burning. I thought I recognized what was left of an unmarked police car. The news didn't report it, so they must not have realized it was an official car, let alone yours. I'd say that makes your first outing as the official city hero a success as far as anyone else knows. Still tough to lose the car, though."

"I don't know, I didn't exactly have much time to bond with it. And it didn't really seem dedicated to the fight for truth and justice, seeing that it flamed right up the first chance it got. Probably a good thing it's gone since it was a fiery death trap posing as a comfortable, roomy ride with an above average sound system," said Oliver, his tone hinting at self-pity. He clapped his hands and rubbed them together. "So that brings me back to the question of transportation. Obviously I'm in need of some kind of replacement, at the very least another car, but I was hoping maybe the Warehouse where you got everything else would have something with a little more punch than the Taurus. Maybe a muscle car, or a crotch rocket. Hell, I'd settle for a hybrid. Otherwise, maybe the flying vehicles if we can get one that works, or can we find some way of getting me the ability of flight? I don't suppose they have unused add-on flight serums there, like one that arrived in the mail the day after the hero was tragically knocked out of a plane? Any ideas?"

"Well, you'd have to check with Emma about the car situation. You might be able to get a replacement through the city immediately. It should all be insured. But that's just going to be another Taurus, or something similar," said Roger, shrugging. He nodded toward the computer. "I can get on the Warehouse site and see what's available, but we'd have to be really lucky to nab something in good working order. We might be able to get some non-working or half destroyed cars, but that'll require a lot to get them going, like time and space where I can work on them—we don't have a budget for paying someone else for repairs or for building anything new. The same goes for the flyers. Really, we need more space whatever the case."

"What about sponsorships?"

"Sponsorships?"

"Yeah," said Oliver, "Like with NASCAR. We don't have the budget for buying a car, but maybe someone will pay us to use their car. An endorsement. The Coke Burger King Dodge Charger. At the post-battle news conference I'll do all the requisite name dropping. Like 'the Coke Burger King Dodge Charger ran great today and the Schwab air to air missiles were right on target.' Heck, maybe I can even get someone, like an airline, to give me the money for flying."

"Yeah, and you could wear a big Delta Airlines cape once they buy you the ability of flight," said Roger.

"Yeah!"

"No."

"No?"

"Sorry buddy," said Roger. "It's a good idea, but you can't do it. As a superhero, you just can't sell yourself. It's not legal. It could be seen as someone or some company buying influence with you, so heroes aren't allowed to do it. Although villains can. They make an absolute killing in endorsements."

"Really? That doesn't say good things about our society."

"Nope."

"Shoot. I thought I was on to something there."

"It's not that it hasn't been considered before," said Roger, "and many people think it might happen someday, especially if the economy slows and smaller cities or states start to lose their heroes because they can't fund them. Then maybe there'd be enough pressure to change the rules, but even then it's believed there will be monetary caps on the endorsements so it won't be possible for one big company to completely fund a hero. It'll look more like NASCAR as you said, patches for twenty different companies all over somebody's costume."

"That sucks. I don't want much, just a new car."

"Well, without the possibility of the Coke Burger King Dodge Charger, the first thing we need is for you to contact Emma and ask about a replacement car," said Roger. "But you should also check with her on the space issue."

"Yeah, I'll do that. She's probably not going to be happy about the car considering it was my very first patrol. That's not a good first day."

"I believe I'm legally obligated to note that the day's not over yet," said Roger.

"As far as I'm concerned it is. I'm going to call Emma and take my beating, then I'm going to sit down and read through the rest of the file the Chief gave me. If I have any luck left at all those tasks will keep me inside the apartment and out of trouble." Oliver paused a moment and sighed. Then he said, "Comm, call Emma." A second later he could hear ringing on the other end.

"Stay inside and keep out of trouble," said Roger. "Now that's what I want for the motto of my city's hero."

"Bite me," replied Oliver. He turned away from Roger when he heard Emma answer the line. "Good morning, Emma," he said as cheerfully as possible, thinking he might be able to change their whole rapport with a new start. The words that greeted him back assured him it wouldn't be happening. He had forgotten it was still very early and Emma didn't seem to be a morning person, so he decided to forget mending things for the moment and just move on to what he needed.

"So you wrecked the car," said Emma in summation after listening to Oliver's convoluted explanation of the night's events and their consequences.

"Not me personally, no, but it is wrecked. It was an innocent bystander, really. If you catch the local news you can probably see video of it burning. Quietly. In the background. Bystanding."

"Burning?" asked Emma. "So, more than just wrecked. Like totally gone?"

"Yeah, basically. I'm no mechanic, but it didn't look great before it started on fire. Sorry, I know it's early and it might take you a few minutes to get all this processed, so I'm just going to move on and you can quiz me later," said Oliver. He asked about a replacement vehicle and then gave her the mission to find them some vacant space as soon as possible.

"So after your very first day on the job the only things you need are a new car and a new building?" said Emma once Oliver had finished.

"You might try putting a slightly different spin on it when you talk to the Chief."

"I don't think the earth's rotational speed would be enough spin to make this sound good," replied Emma. "But the space issue does have merit. I just wish you wouldn't have crashed the car."

"Don't lead with that then," said Oliver, "and I have to stress once again, I didn't crash it."

"Whatever the details, I'm fairly certain the Chief will already know, being there were cops around."

"Well, just do the best you can, thanks. Comm, end call," said Oliver, cutting the line. Roger was at the computer going through the Warehouse inventory in search of anything useful, so Oliver grabbed the Chief's file from his conference tote bag and went outside onto the stairs to read. He felt a real need to make some headway on the reason he was now a superhero and putting up with all this crap.

18

GRAY Matter really enjoyed research. Simply adored it. And this was the epitome of research. Sure, on a very basic level he was just watching television, but this was some real quality television. Practically PBS or the History channel, or one of those critically acclaimed shows on HBO. So it counted as research. Not to mention this was more entertaining than watching something like pro football because there were no commercial interruptions, no time-outs, and no ungodly long halftime shows; just nonstop big hits. Gray Matter wasn't the only one enjoying the show however, since most of the city of Milwaukee had now tuned in to see their rookie superhero battling it out with some mysterious supervillain on live television. Mysterious that is, except to Gray Matter. He knew the man's identity because he had hired him to come to town in the first place. The supervillain had been tasked with putting SuperGuy through a variety of tests so Gray Matter could observe and assess his new foe. Simple, basic research. With explosions.

Sadly for most of the viewing audience, they only had the local television news coverage for watching the battle, which meant they would miss the beginning of the fight and what they did see wouldn't even be filmed very well. That wasn't really the fault of the local television stations; they usually didn't have the experience or the equipment to cover an expansive, fast-moving story. The soup and half sandwich fundraiser for the local pet shelter? They'll nail it. Picking up a small cloud formation on the Super Duper Double Doppler Plus storm radar? They'll have blanket coverage with a ticker scroll and regional map graphic showing affected counties, all of it obscuring the view on your 52" screen of your favorite show, but thank goodness you know it's raining. The haphazard local news coverage would in no way be mistaken for the product of some brilliant cinematographer who knew where the action would take place and how to set up the cameras to best take advantage of angles and backgrounds and lighting.

This had been a big problem for Gray Matter. He couldn't leave it in the hands of local television hacks. He needed to see every punch, kick, and small tactical warhead explosion perfectly framed and in high definition. It was his research project after all. He wouldn't be satisfied if CNN were doing the work. At first he had considered buying at least one local television station so he could staff it with extra cameras and operators, who he would then have conveniently in place to cover the story, but there hadn't been enough time. So instead he had decided to simply disguise several camera teams as local television crews and place them along the route where the fight would happen, in addition to remote cameras in spots where they couldn't place an actual cameraman. This allowed Gray Matter to watch the battle from beginning to end in amazing detail on the wall-mounted monitors behind his desk. Most of the monitors showed feeds from his men or the remote cameras, but three were tuned to the local television stations so he could watch their live coverage as they got on the scene. Once those stations had broken into their regularly scheduled programming, all of the monitors on the wall showed the battle from different vantage points.

And a battle it was. The Cyclone—as the supervillain was normally known, but now in a different costume so his identity would remain secret—had methodically followed each of Gray Matter's instructions, using natural or secretly placed weapons along a prearranged route through the city to test SuperGuy's abilities. Fire, water, sound, bullets, rockets, electricity—you name it, it had already been used on the hero, or soon would be. And so far SuperGuy was performing admirably, although not beyond Gray Matter's expectations since he possessed a copy of the original hero position description. But a person, even an evil genius, could never be too careful. He just wanted to make certain there were no surprises due to some late addition to the budget giving SuperGuy powers not listed in the original document. Suddenly an explosion flashed across the monitors on the wall, caught in various angles by the different cameras. Gray Matter pushed an uncooperative lock of hair off his forehead as he leaned in to see the results of the blast.

Oliver flew backward as the shockwave of the explosion slammed into him. He had seen the object thrown by the supervillain but discounted it, thinking it was only a piece of metal since the costumed man had just picked it up off the ground, but he was now carefully reexamining that conclusion as he sailed through the air. He figured he had nothing better to do with his time. Flailing his arms about didn't help; he had already tried that.

"Flying would be really useful right now," Oliver muttered to himself, knowing at least then he could recover in the air instead of having to wait for the indignity of impact. Unfortunately for him, this time the impact wasn't just a one shot deal. After slamming into what he realized was a wall as he passed through it, Oliver's momentum from the blast kept him going and he proceeded to plow through six more walls in quick succession before skidding to a stop on the thinly carpeted floor of a small apartment. Sitting on his butt, Oliver looked up to see an early twenties slacker guy on a ratty sofa holding a small container of yogurt in one hand and a spoon, one end of which was in his mouth, in the other. Dust was slowly settling on everything and something metal clattered to the floor behind Oliver. That was followed by a thud and the sound of breaking glass. The scent of petiole was strong. The slacker guy looked at Oliver for a couple of seconds, then slowly rotated his head back to the television in front of him. Then more quickly at Oliver, then right back to the television again, then to the hole in the wall and back to the television. A big smile spread across his face once he pulled the spoon out of his mouth, and Oliver steeled himself for the excitement that was a fan meeting a superhero, something he had experienced several times in his first week of work. Strangely, it didn't come. The guy stood up, dropping his spoon and yogurt on the sofa. He was practically quivering with excitement, which was typical for an excited fan, but then he ran out the hole and continued to bound through the intervening apartments until he reached the outside wall. Once there he began to jump up and down and wave his hands in the air. This wasn't typical of an excited fan. Oliver stood and dusted plaster, splinters, and—oddly enough—feathers, off his uniform. Then he noticed the television, which was showing a shaky helicopter camera shot of a big hole in the side of an apartment building that presently had a guy jumping up and down and waving from it.

"Okay, little ego check there," mumbled Oliver as he started walking back through the path of destruction he had inadvertently made. He carefully scanned the wreckage as he went but didn't notice anyone else at home in the various apartments. As he passed through one of the last walls, he grabbed a broken water pipe now spraying across the room and bent it back on itself to stop the flow. "No one will notice the pipe I fix, they'll only see the six or seven tiny holes," said Oliver.

At the outer wall he paused next to the guy waving to the cameras, and who was also now taking a cell phone video of himself waving to the cameras, and said, "You're going to spend your precious few seconds of fame just waving? At least have the presence of mind to drop your pants and moon the world." Then Oliver stepped out of the hole and dropped the six stories to the street below. He didn't really think twice about doing things like that now, which was an example of how much his perspective had changed. If someone would have told him on his first day that he would be doing such things a couple weeks into the job, Oliver probably wouldn't have believed them. There had to be some transition time, right? Start with some bike safety presentations, maybe nab a particularly devious jaywalker. Work your way up. But maybe getting blown up a couple times right off the bat accelerates things a bit. Another factor was the serum. It was made so the hero would have a natural confidence in his unnatural abilities from day one. You wanted your hero ready to go, not sitting around in a perfectly good bullet proof body trying to get up the nerve to actually step in front of a hail of bullets.

Oliver had not exactly been content to wait and see what he could do either. He had spent most of his first couple of days on the job testing his powers and their limits, along with Roger's very enthusiastic help. His powers, as he already knew, weren't mind blowing, but they were still rather cool for a guy who had been slightly below average on any type of scale you cared to use a couple of weeks before, and his limits seemed pretty, well, limitless so far. Of course, at a certain point some things began to hurt a bit, like falling more than ten stories was hard on the knees or punching more than twenty or so rocks into dust in a row was tough on the knuckles. However, the pain was fleeting and nothing Oliver couldn't handle. Higher falls would produce a bit more pain and require a little more recovery time, but it would take a fall from an airplane to really slow him down. Anything from a structure within the city was essentially nothing. Roger wondered if there might not be some way to predict the amount of pain and recovery time from a fall in a mathematical formula. Oliver decided Roger's time would be better spent finding him a way to fly so he could avoid the pain, the recovery time, and any math.

As for other experiments, Roger had enjoyed shooting Oliver when they decided to try that, but most other things were really just different ways of falling. Fall off of something (traditional falling), run as fast as you can into something (horizontal falling), or let something hit you at a high speed (lazy man's falling). Looking back now, they hadn't really attempted much more than the several varieties of falling and the bullets, although Roger used a lot of different calibers, just to be thorough, he said. This was why the present fight was proving to be so useful to Oliver. So far he'd been shot (by a surprising number of calibers), electrocuted, set on fire, shot some more, remained under water for almost ten minutes (a portion of the fight had taken place in Lake Michigan), hit with everything imaginable from bricks to better than average-sized sailboats, and finally now blown up. At this point, Oliver thought he had a really good grasp on what he could take, and it seemed to be a lot. The only thing bugging him was that he wasn't exactly dishing out much punishment in return. The villain always seemed to be a step ahead of him, grabbing the next weapon before Oliver had picked himself up off the ground from the last one. It was beginning to wear on him, not to mention being annoying.

As Oliver looked up the street to where the villain now stood, he wondered if it was his lack of superhero battle experience that explained why he was taking all the punishment. The bad guy was only about forty yards away and seemed to be biding his time, waiting for Oliver to get back in the game. The villain was dressed in a basic two-tone, mostly dark blue costume with a cape and a mask that obscured most of his face. Oliver would have said it was a pretty generic uniform if it wasn't for the fact that he had the market cornered in that regard. This guy was flashy in comparison. Oliver didn't recognize him, but he wasn't surprised since he didn't have the knowledge of superheroes and villains that Roger possessed. Oliver took his eyes off the villain for a quick second to scan the area around them. Somehow they had managed to circle back around to almost where the fight had started in the first place. Oliver even glimpsed his Omni parked about a block down on one of the side streets, which now seemed a little too close to the action. Deciding that if he was ever going to change the momentum of the fight he needed to start dealing out some damage, Oliver picked up a section of wall that had fallen to the street from the hole he had made in the apartment building. The piece wasn't very large overall but it was made up of several heavy chunks of masonry connected with rebar that could do some real damage. Oliver spun around once to gather momentum and flung the piece of wall at the villain. It looked to be right on target and was traveling at a high speed when the villain easily sidestepped the projectile and let it fly by him. Then he leaped into the air and flew off down the street, keeping one eye on the hero. Oliver however, was keeping his eyes on the section of wall he had just thrown. It certainly hadn't endangered the villain in the least, and now Oliver cringed as it plowed into the first of several parked cars on the side of the street, knocking each one into the next until they finally slid to a stop in a pile of crumpled metal and shattered glass about halfway down the block.

"Well, that's bad," said Oliver. He shook his head and turned his attention back to the villain flying away down the street. Oliver had chased him on foot earlier in the fight so he knew he couldn't catch him because the guy could fly much faster if he wanted. Still, the villain hadn't tried to get away before and it didn't seem like he was going to start now. "Why would he?" asked Oliver with a sigh. "He's not exactly in danger. Seems only hazardous to be a building or parked car at the moment."

The villain gained altitude and turned east, flying for several blocks and landing on the top floor of a partially constructed building. Standing among the steel beams, Oliver's opponent looked back across the distance and gestured for the hero to follow. Despite the distance, this was easy for Oliver to see thanks to his enhanced vision. It might have even seemed super cool if he weren't getting his butt kicked by the guy.

"Yeah, yeah, hold on," said Oliver, noticing the time on a sign for a local bank. He sprinted down a side street. A couple of seconds later he whipped around the corner in his dark blue Omni and headed east. It wasn't faster to use the Omni—Oliver could easily run the distance more quickly—but he knew his time on the parking meter was about up and he didn't want a ticket. There were a lot of cops around right now due to the fight, and he no longer had the protection of an official city vehicle. He really missed the Taurus.

Oliver's communicator beeped and a generic female voice stated 'Incoming call from Emma Simms.' Oliver automatically said, "Answer call."

"What the hell are you doing?" asked Emma.

"Um...superheroey things?"

"Oh, that's what you call it. Looks a lot like putting random holes in buildings and rearranging parked cars into piles of trash. I'm watching it on TV. So is the Mayor, who decided to call and yell at me about it."

"Well, I hope that wasn't too uncomfortable for you. Me, I just got blown up. Again. You know, explosion, flames, hotness. But enough about me, let's talk about you."

"Don't be a smart-ass."

"I'd stop but it seems to be the only thing I'm doing successfully at the moment, besides getting my ass kicked up and down our lovely city. Plenty of punishment. Mostly physical but you've added a nice emotional element to it now, so thanks for that."

"Okay, okay, I'm sorry. Look, the Mayor would just appreciate it if you would do a little less damage to your surroundings. Personally, I've never liked that area of town. In fact, if you get a chance, toss a car through that mall on 4th. A hot pretzel stand and an Orange Julius is not a food court."

"Okay, gotcha. Will try to stop breaking things. Comm, end call," said Oliver. The tone sounded to indicate the line was cut. "I wonder how I send my calls straight to voice mail on this thing?"

Parking a block short of the building for safety, Oliver jogged to the construction site and leaped over the chain link fence surrounding it. He landed on top of a bulldozer and bounded off that to a crane arm, which he ran up until he could jump across to the seventh floor of the building. He quickly leaped through holes in the floors until he reached the fourteenth. From there he took it more slowly, knowing the villain was waiting on the highest floor, which was about the sixteenth. He scaled the steel skeleton of the building over those last two floors, trying to be as quiet as possible to give himself some kind of advantage, but it did little good. As he poked his head above the sixteenth floor, the villain reached down and pulled him up by the neck of his costume and tossed him out into the open. Oliver rolled as he landed and came up on his feet, ready to deflect whatever attack followed, but none did. The villain walked over to a large object in the center of the floor and pulled a tarp off of it. Oliver expected to see some piece of well used construction equipment that was then going to be hurled at him, but instead it was a shiny metallic object. And that shiny metallic object looked a lot like a large menacing gun mounted on a stationary base.

"Uh-oh," said Oliver instinctively. He'd been shot several times so far and while being shot again didn't really worry him, he guessed by the look of the gun this was different. The villain confirmed it with the first words he had bothered to speak.

"Well, we're getting to the end of it," he said, almost sounding like Oliver's dad when they were finally about to wrap up some long, boring project around the house. The guy flipped a switch that started the gun humming ominously.

"What? Are you going to surrender?" asked Oliver.

"No, I don't think so. And don't bother trying yourself, it's not an option," replied the villain.

"Hadn't really considered it," said Oliver, taking a couple steps backward and looking around for something that might be helpful. Seeing nothing, he started to leap off to the side, hoping to get out of range of the weapon, but even before he could start his jump, the villain pulled a gun with lightening speed and blasted him with a ray of bright yellow light. Oliver stood half-crouched, ready to jump, but didn't move. Not that he didn't want to, he just suddenly couldn't. He felt as if every part of his body had instantaneously fallen asleep, complete with the prickling feeling that accompanies it. Oliver was essentially frozen in place.

"Don't get fidgety there big guy," said the villain. He waved the gun back and forth. "This is a nifty little paralyzation ray a friend gave me. Won't hold you for too long, but we only need a minute to get this done."

"Your friend's a jerk," muttered Oliver. It was a little slurred but it was all he could manage with a paralyzed tongue. The villain didn't respond, just adjusted a dial on the gun without taking his eyes off him. Oliver could feel the effects of the ray already wearing off, but it wasn't happening quickly enough. He was suddenly aware of the news helicopters hovering in the distance, catching all of this live, which was looking more and more to Oliver like the end of his very short career. It made him a little angry and he tried speaking again. It came out a bit more clearly. "You've shot me a bunch of times already and it didn't even hurt, so why bother? Come out from behind there and fight me for once."

"I'd like that, I really would, but that's not the plan. And you're right, I have shot you a lot, but I haven't shot you with this. I know you're new to the profession, so let me explain. This isn't just a normal type of weapon. This is what we call a superhero quality energy ray, meaning it's strong enough to hurt guys like us. A blast at full power will put you out of commission at the very least, if it doesn't kill you outright. But don't worry, we're not going to start that high. We want to see what you're made of." The villain smiled and pulled the trigger.

Oliver had started to say something else in hopes of delaying the seemingly inevitable, but those words quickly disintegrated into a howl of pain as a short burst of deep red light shot out of the gun and into his right thigh. It wasn't at all like being shot by a gun, which to Oliver felt like being tapped by a finger or hit by a snowball depending on the caliber. This burned as if someone were pressing a red hot ember to his skin, only it burned worse than anything he had ever felt before, and that burning didn't stop on the surface but seemed to run completely through his thigh and out the other side. Oliver staggered backward several feet from the power of the blast but he managed to stay upright despite still feeling the numbness of the paralyzation ray. An acrid smell hung in the air and Oliver leaned over as much as he could to examine the wound. No gaping hole existed in his thigh as he feared there might be, but his costume was melted away exposing his skin and the dark red burn that now marked it.

"See, I told you it hurts," said the villain, again adjusting the dial on the gun's base. "And that was just a low setting. Let's see how something a little higher appeals to you." He took aim again and squeezed off another blast. This one hit Oliver in the left shoulder and tossed him backward onto the floor like a rag doll, landing with his head just inches away from the edge. The pain was tremendous and it took all Oliver had for a couple of seconds to keep from passing out. He lay on his back sucking in air as his arms and legs shook uncontrollably. He took the shaking as a sign that he might not be paralyzed anymore, but since it was uncontrollable, it still wasn't really a positive. His communicator beeped just then and the female voice said someone was calling, but Oliver didn't catch who it was because his ears were ringing. Probably Emma again, to tell him something useful like don't get shot by the big shiny gun. Oliver obviously ignored the call, but the pain from the ray was another matter altogether. He couldn't ignore that. To the contrary, it was almost all he could think about. Almost. With great effort he pulled his still partially paralyzed body up to a more or less upright position, staggered one step forward and then three backward toward the edge. That was one more step than he had room for, so Oliver went off the side of the building and fell from view.

"Come on," said the villain, stepping out from behind the gun and walking over to the ledge. "Now how much more time is this going to take?" He still needed one more shot from the ray to complete the mission and collect his money. Gray Matter had been very specific about each test. The villain looked down to the street below, wondering how long it would take this SuperGuy to pull himself together and get back up there, if he even had the guts to come back up. But he would, it was built into the serum. A hero would always keep coming back. The villain just wondered how long it would take for this hero—who was still pretty new—to shake it off and get back up. He considered flying down and hauling the hero back up, but he couldn't see him on the ground below, so maybe he was already on his way. That was pretty impressive because the guy was definitely taking a beating. The villain turned to go back to his gun and prepare for the last shot but stopped suddenly. The hero was already back and, quite unluckily for the villain, standing behind the gun.

Oliver rolled the dial—conveniently labeled *Power Level*—to the full position and took aim at the villain's chest as the blue clad man turned around and started back toward the gun. The thought that he should give the villain a chance to surrender streaked fleetingly through Oliver's mind before he brushed it aside and pulled the trigger. The villain had a hand half-raised in defense and was starting to say something as the beam of energy caught him square in the chest and sent him flying off the building like a football kicked off a tee. Oliver, ever energy conscious, flipped the power switch off and the hum of the weapon faded. Limping out from behind the gun, he slowly made his way to the edge of the building.

"I guess that makes me 1-0," he said.

Gray Matter hit the button on his remote turning off the wall monitors and swung back around to his desk. This complicated things. He hadn't expected everything to go perfectly according to plan, it never did, but SuperGuy actually winning wasn't something he had seriously considered. At the very least, the Cyclone was to escape. Those were his explicit orders if something were to go wrong during the test. Of course, about the time the villain realized he was in trouble he was most likely unconscious the next second, which really wasn't enough time to do anything about it. He might even be dead now. Dead would be more convenient for Gray Matter, but not likely considering Cyclone's level of power. The villain was probably alive, just incapacitated for a while. Definitely more than enough time to be taken into custody. Gray Matter sat in thought, slowly drumming his fingers on his desk. Finally he looked toward the side of the room where Alex stood, and the young man came over.

"Yes sir?"

"Ask someone from legal to have representation arranged for the Cyclone. Use the firm we had handle that messy business in New York last year. They've done defense work for supervillains before."

"Won't using them be traced back to us, sir?"

Gray Matter nodded. "Yes, if someone were to look closely enough, but I think it's time to let them know who they're dealing with."

"I'll get right on it," said Alex, turning smartly and heading for the door.

Meanwhile Gray Matter spun his chair back around and flipped the wall monitors on again. The three with the local news feeds were still on but all of his operators had shut down and cleared out. One local channel showed a view of SuperGuy standing at the edge of the building looking down, his costume burnt away at the shoulder and thigh, skin seared red underneath, the effects of the battle obvious in his exhausted expression. But he was triumphant. If the man hadn't quite been a hero before, he was now. It was an impressive sight— even on local news—and made Gray Matter smile. He knew a challenge would only make him stronger, his plans more ingenious, and it seemed he might have found himself a worthy adversary.

19

OLIVER cringed. He was falling yet again. This was going to hurt. Not horribly bad.y, but he knew he was going to feel it and there wasn't anything he could do about it. This was probably the worst part of being a superhero he had discovered so far. For a superhero, a lot of things slow down. They don't literally slow down, but since superheroes can process the activity around them so quickly, it sure seems that way to them. This allows them to react to threatening situations well before any normal person would even realize there was danger. In Oliver's current predicament, he figured a normal person would have time to realize the danger, but probably not much more than enough to blurt out the obligatory 'Oh, crap,' before impact. Oliver however, being a superhero, had what seemed like tons of time during which to decide exactly when he wanted to utter his 'Oh, crap.' He opted to say it somewhat early this time (yes, this wasn't the first time), maybe so he'd be sure to get it in, or maybe because it was just as useful to do that than to bother fighting with the controls of the flying machine anymore. The one silver lining in this plummeting cloud for Oliver was the thought that at least this was the last functioning flying machine they had left, not that it was actually functioning, and he could now be done with all the crashing.

Suddenly the engine sputtered as if it were catching and Oliver had just enough time to grab the stick in hopes of pulling it out of the dive before it died again and he and the machine slammed into the ground. Ending up lying on his back, Oliver watched the dust settle around him and a small trail of black smoke begin to rise into the blue sky. Pieces of twisted metal surrounded him with a few reaching upward half-heartedly like the remains of a forest after a tornado has passed through. The quiet moment of utter devastation was broken abruptly by the white smoke hiss of a fire extinguisher as Roger came to the rescue.

"What did you do!?" yelled Roger as he sprayed the engine area of the wreck.

"Crashed. Seems pretty obvious."

"But you were fine. You were cruising."

"True, I was," said Oliver, still resting amidst the wreckage. "Sadly, the machine realized that too and decided to do something about it."

"Come on, you can't blame the machine again. It was running perfectly. We'd gotten everything fixed."

"Obviously not everything," said Oliver, getting up and knocking bits of the wreck out of his way. "Why don't you just let it burn? Put it out of its misery. Or put me out of its misery. Or is it put it out of my misery? Not really sure, but there's heaps of misery here. And smoke."

"No, we can't lose another one completely," said Roger, spraying the ruins a couple more times. He circled around the machine, examining it. "The engine is still mostly intact. I can piece something together with the frame of the first one, the wings of the second and the good engine parts of the fourth. We'll get it in the air again." He nodded at the machine with confidence.

Oliver walked over to where Roger stood looking at the engine and proceeded to chop his arm down through the center of the mass of metal. One half of the engine teetered and fell over onto the ground, leaking various fluids. Straightening up, Oliver asked, "You sure about that?"

Roger stared at the innards of his flying machine. "That's cold, man."

"I just couldn't stand to see it suffer," said Oliver, turning and walking away. Roger gave the engine one more spray and then followed as Oliver continued talking.

"I'm done with this piecemeal flying machine crap. It's more accurate to say 'crashing machine' anyway. I haven't even gotten one of these things out of the yard yet." The yard Oliver was referring to was a roughly four acre open space behind their new headquarters building where they had been test flying Roger's machines. Oliver stopped abruptly and Roger almost ran into him. "Yeah, that's it. I want the real thing. We've got to find a way to get me the flying component of the serum. All this crap would not be needed if I just got that." He started walking again.

"Well, it's not free. It's not like these machines, we'll never get it through the Warehouse," said Roger. "There's no other way except to pay for it."

"Well, then we'll have to find a way to pay for it," said Oliver, walking through the large garage door into the headquarters building. "Maybe we can take advantage of my new popularity."

"We already got this place out of that," said Roger, following Oliver inside. "I don't think they're going to give us a bunch of money too." He dropped the fire extinguisher next to the door and hit the button to close it.

"This didn't cost them anything. It wasn't being used and no one was going to buy it, not in this part of town," replied Oliver, gesturing vaguely at the building around them. He walked inside one of the old offices that had become their control room, in true superhero headquarters parlance, and flopped down on a chair. Roger did the same, but shortly got up to fiddle with some of the new computer and communications equipment he had been setting up in the room. A week had passed since Oliver's fight with the supervillain, now known to be Cyclone in disguise, and a lot had changed. Foremost was Oliver's status in Milwaukee, which was directly related to the fight, but second was the new headquarters. They probably would have gotten the building anyway since the city owned it but no longer used it, nor had any plans to, but SuperGuy's sudden immense popularity helped speed things along.

There had been plenty of support from the devotees of superheroes before the fight, but they were only a small segment of the population. Oliver's epic battle across the city in front of all those viewers had earned him the respect of an overwhelming majority of Milwaukee inhabitants. There were huge headlines and some glowing editorials in the Milwaukee Times Herald News Observer, not to mention a record number of positive reader comments on their website, as well as on the city government's official website. Several local television interviews, public appearances, and speaking engagements followed on the heels of the fight, although technically one of the speaking engagements, the address to the Milwaukee Flower and Garden Society, had been arranged beforehand. The interviews and speaking engagements were things Oliver didn't think he would have ever done before becoming a hero, let alone actually enjoy, but now the charisma and confidence that was hot-wired into his brain thanks to the serum allowed him to do it without a second thought. He didn't even use notes, preferring to just wing it most of the time. It didn't stop at the local notoriety either. Stormfront had given him a congratulatory phone call because the battle had received national, and in her case pseudo-international, coverage. She even mentioned that Metal and Buffalo were using the publicity of the battle to announce the formation of GLAND since SuperGuy was one of the founding members.

The new headquarters was probably the most tangible reward of Oliver's popularity though, and so far the most useful. It was an old city maintenance building, mostly used for road repair and snow removal vehicles in its prime, so it had a large amount of indoor parking space as well as some office space. On the downside, it was located in one of the most run down and worst crime areas in the city, but that was also a good reason for it to be chosen. Plop a hero right down in the middle of the mess and you get things done much more quickly. That and nobody else in their right mind wanted the place. The bulk of the building was simply garage. It was a huge, open expanse of ancient cement floor with decades of stains and marks and a high, almost three-story ceiling with metal rafters and large, dingy yellow skylights. Off to one side was a vehicle maintenance area with two bays equipped with lifts able to accommodate large vehicles and a bunch of miscellaneous abandoned equipment. On the side opposite the maintenance area were two floors of storage rooms and offices, some of which had barely been looked in by the new occupants and still contained tons of junk from whoever had inhabited the building in the previous decades.

The huge garage door they had entered led out to the large, fenced yard they now used for testing, and was mirrored by another huge garage door on the front of the building leading out to the street. Both of these garage doors were large enough to accommodate the oversized vehicles that had originally been stored in the building, but there was a second, standard-sized garage door next to the front one, which made it much less overkill to use when they drove their personal cars inside. Four cars were presently parked on the far side of the floor just off to the side of that smaller garage door. One was Oliver's new city government Ford Taurus, the replacement for his previously totaled one, which had miraculously appeared at his apartment the day after his victory over Cyclone. It had the additional perk of being dark blue. The second car was the crumpled hunk of metal that had been Oliver's first Taurus. Someone somewhere had a sense of humor and it had been waiting in the garage when they showed up to check out their new headquarters. The third was Roger's new silver Honda Civic Hybrid he had bought immediately after receiving the first check reflecting his raise. The fourth vehicle was Emma's older Jeep Cherokee. It wasn't new like the others, but she had no need for a new car, being happy enough with the location of her new office.

Emma had seen the advantages of a new headquarters beyond just what Oliver and Roger were looking for when they requested it. Once she had procured the new site, she had happily moved out of her tiny cubicle in the city government office building and into the 'Garage' as they had come to call it. For her, the move had a few bonuses, one of which was the larger, private office, despite how much cleaning she had to do to make it inhabitable. An office opening onto a garage for a few decades wasn't the best option for cleanliness, but it was better than her old cubicle. That tiny rectangle may have been cleaner but it was still in the city office. Despite Emma's new official position, it didn't keep people from dumping work on her. Everyone knew she was only supposed to be handling Oliver, but since she knew how to do everything else, like travel, equipment requests and purchase orders, they kept asking her to help them out. Basically her job had not really changed at all, it had just gotten busier. Knowing it wouldn't end until she was out of sight, Emma jumped ship as soon as she secured the Garage from the city. It also had the additional bonus of being a shorter commute from her apartment. If she could just get the smell of tires and gas out of the room, it would be perfect.

The office area was made up of five rooms on the lower level and four on the second level. The entire structure of rooms sat in the back right half of the main garage space, opposite the vehicle maintenance area and seemed as if they had been stuck in there as an afterthought, like somebody had decided to build this two story structure in the back corner after they figured out they could use things like an office and bathroom in there. Stairs on the end led up to the landing on the second level. The control room, as they had come to call it, was the first one on the left on the lower level, tucked in the corner against the back wall. Emma's office was the next one over, and the third was filled with all the junk they had emptied out of the first two. The next room was a kitchen/break room, and the last room on the lower level next to the stairs was a bathroom with a shower. They had cleaned these last two rooms right away. So far all of the second floor rooms were unused, but Oliver and Roger already had plans for a major renovation that would give them each living quarters since neither wanted to bother with commuting to where they would undoubtedly be spending all of their time anyway. Plus there was no rent, which they both thought was a good thing.

Roger had spent the first couple of days in the Garage setting up all the various equipment he had procured from the Superhero Surplus Warehouse, as well as installing and networking a state of the art security system for the building. He hadn't been overly excited about the questionable neighborhood when he first heard about it even though he'd be working with a superhero, but when he realized he could get a ton of amazing security toys through the Warehouse and make the building more secure than any place in the city, he was happy. In the control room was a bank of video monitors on one of the walls showing various security camera views, in addition to computer monitors displaying the status of other security features like motion detectors, sound detectors, and alarms on every window, door and skylight. All of these fed into the main computer network so anyone knowing the right passwords could monitor security from any computer in the building, or from other locations, like another office or from home. Roger also put an app on everyone's phones and iPads so they could monitor from those as well. Oliver didn't know why Roger needed to be that thorough but figured it was mostly just because he could.

Roger had burrowed under one of the tables in the computer room and appeared to be wrestling with a mess of cables behind another new, obscenely large flat screen monitor, which Oliver had only noticed now.

"Is this a new toy?" asked Oliver, leaning forward to examine the monitor. "I thought you were done with all this stuff."

"This is the video communication system for GLAND," came Roger's slightly muffled voice from underneath the table. He wiggled his way out and took a seat back in his chair. "I had the monitor sitting around extra, but the rest came in this morning. See the camera there?" he said, pointing to a small device mounted on the top of the monitor. "Smile pretty for that. Anyway, I think it's all ready. We could run a test, call someone up if you want. Anyone in the group will do, though some will look better in HD than others."

Oliver pulled off his gloves and set them on the table. "Call someone up? Somehow I'm guessing it's not Creeper you have in mind?"

"I could go all coy on you here," said Roger with a shrug, "but who are we kidding? Stormfront, of course."

"Honesty, huh? I like that you're giving it a try. Okay, then. Let's call her up."

"Excellent," said Roger with a smile. He leaned forward, turned the monitor on and pointed to a keyboard sitting on the table. "This keyboard is the shortcut to everything. Each member of the team is assigned one of the function keys—I wrote their names above the key—and you just need to hit the key to start," Roger pressed the key labeled Stormfront and text appeared on the monitor asking him to verify the command to call Stormfront, "and when you get that you just hit Return." Roger pressed Return and two windows appeared on the monitor, a larger centered one and a smaller one above it to the left. The smaller one showed the view from their camera on top of the monitor, which at the moment was displaying an extreme close up of Oliver's nose and upper lip, while the larger window had the words 'Calling, waiting for answer' written across it. Roger looked up from the keyboard and noticed the close up view of their camera. "Oh, let me fix that," he said and proceeded to tap more keys and click on various things with the mouse arrow.

"Might be a good idea," said Oliver, just as the larger window switched to a picture showing Stormfront, who was sitting down in front of her camera.

She gave an odd look to the screen and hesitantly asked, "Oliver?"

"How'd you guess?" replied Oliver as he sneaked a peek at the smaller window on his monitor that still showed his nose, just even closer now. "As you can see, we are still doing a little troubleshooting."

"It's not bad for your first try. You should have seen what The Creeper's camera showed the first time he called me. And the second. I sensed a pattern so now I take his calls on audio only." As she said this, the camera view of her started to change, zooming in slightly.

"Oh, I didn't know you could do that," said Roger, still working away at the keyboard. Then the picture of Stormfront zoomed in more to just encircle her face. "Whoops, it's a bit touchy."

"I'll have to keep that in mind if he calls me," said Oliver, still talking to Stormfront. "Maybe we'll just set that up in the preferences before I even have to deal with it. At least my imagination has me thinking I don't want to wait to make that decision."

"I wouldn't wait," replied Stormfront, "I'm still nursing some mental scars. You might as well save yourself from those." Suddenly the picture of her zoomed in a little more, then zoomed back out again to just her face.

Oliver took his eyes off the screen and reached over and slapped at Roger's hands. "Would you quit screwing around, Rog, and fix my camera. Hers is fine." Then Oliver returned to the conversation with Stormfront, but she was no longer there. Actually she was, but not her face. Now the camera showed mostly her hair and what Oliver thought might be part of her ear. "What'd you do?" Oliver asked Roger.

"What?" said Roger, who then noticed her picture. "Crap, I didn't do it. You hit my hand."

"Well, just fix it."

Roger tapped several keys and clicked the mouse furiously for a couple of seconds. "I lost it. I don't have control anymore. What did you hit?" he asked, staring at the keys.

"I don't know, I hit your hands. What did you hit?"

"If I knew, I'd fix it, SuperDork."

"Is there an owner's manual?"

"I don't know."

"Guys?" said Stormfront. "Can I interrupt for a second?"

"Oh, uh, yeah," stammered Oliver.

"You know I can see the video too, right?"

"Uh, yeah, I'm sorry about that. We were trying to fix my video and...failed somewhat."

"Who's we?"

"Oh, that's Roger, my tech support guy. He really wants to meet you sometime. He's a big fan," said Oliver. Roger took time out from pecking keys to hit Oliver in the shoulder, which he regretted immediately as he yelped slightly in pain.

"That's nice," said Stormfront. "Here, I'll do it." With that, the camera view zoomed back out to where it was originally.

"Great," said Oliver. "Thanks."

"Hey, how'd she do that?" asked Roger.

Oliver ignored him and continued, "I'm sorry about that. Look, why don't we let you go and we'll get this thing fixed. At least we know it works, besides the human error issues."

"Sure, no problem. Thanks for the call. It was good seeing you again," said Stormfront.

"Yeah, good seeing you too," said Oliver. Then he whispered to Roger, "Okay, hang up or whatever it is you do." Roger just cringed at him and shrugged, mouthing, 'I don't know.'

After a few more seconds of grumbling back and forth, Stormfront interrupted them again. "Don't worry guys, I'll do it. Just FYI, Command plus D will switch the camera back to the default view in the active window, hit the tab key to cycle through different windows, and Command plus W closes the communication. Like this." With that, Stormfront's hands went to her keyboard and the screen went blank.

Oliver sighed and rubbed his forehead. "Well, I'd count that as a success. At least up to the standard to which we've become accustomed."

"True, I didn't have to break out the fire extinguisher," replied Roger.

"So, any other new things on the agenda?"

Roger held up a finger. "Now that you mention it, I have two new things for you. Well, one of them isn't new at all, but it's new to you," he said, stepping over to a shelf and grabbing something. He returned and set a Snickers down on the table in front of Oliver. "Found that inside the old candy machine in the break room. It has to be at least twenty years old. Dare ya."

"Okay," shrugged Oliver, picking up the candy bar and unwrapping it. "So this is one of the things, what's the other?" He started eating the Snickers. It was about the tenth old thing they'd found in the place that Oliver had eaten. The first time he had done it to gross out Roger, but it had come back to haunt him with Roger daring him to eat anything he found that could even slightly be construed as food. The point was since Oliver wasn't susceptible to food poisoning, it was funny to see the looks on other people's faces when he ate something utterly grotesque. It was a lot of fun around Emma.

"Oh, the other thing is the really cool one," said Roger. He pulled a sheet of paper off the printer and handed it to Oliver. "Probably more cool now that we're out of the flying machine business."

Oliver looked at the paper. "What is that? A missile?"

"No, it's a small submarine. A mini-sub. In complete working order—that means I don't have to fix it up at all," said Roger. He looked adoringly down at the picture over Oliver's shoulder, almost as if he were showing a photo of his newborn child.

"A mini-sub?"

"Yes, it's perfect. I don't know why I didn't think of it before, but moving here to the new headquarters only blocks away from the lake was a kick in the pants. I was looking at all those boats on the water as I was driving here and thought we should have something as well. There's undoubtedly going to be some point at which you'll need to do something on the lake, so I checked out the Warehouse to see what there was. I was looking for a speedboat at first, but when I saw this baby, I jumped at it. I couldn't believe we could get one, but I suppose they aren't in as much demand as other vehicles since not everybody's on water. Plus it's cool. A mini-sub. Don't you love it?"

"Sure, it's great. I just don't know how much I'll use it."

"Who knows, if not for fighting crime, at least we can cruise around in it. Maybe water ski. It's more than fast enough, being a superhero quality type of mini-sub. Oh, and until we find some way to get you flying, it's easily the fastest way to Thunder Bay, if you were ever wanting to go up that way."

Oliver gave a little nod. "That is a bonus. Is it here yet?"

"Will be tomorrow. I arranged for it to be tied up down at the Police dock. They'll look after it and everything. They weren't too excited to have another thing to take care of but when they found out what it was, they didn't mind. Everyone likes a new toy, especially a mini-sub."

"Does it shoot stuff or anything?"

"Oh yeah, it's a Bond car for water, baby."

"Nice. Now we're talking," said Oliver, with a nod and a smile. There was a light knock on the door and Emma entered.

"Sorry to interrupt, but the Police Chief called and wants to meet with you. He said he has new information."

"Will this be a super secret meeting?" asked Oliver, amusing himself. "Perhaps on the top of a skyscraper in the middle of the night or under a pier down at the docks? Or at least the parking garage again."

"But only in the middle of the night," added Roger. Oliver nodded in agreement.

"Actually he said to come by his house after six. He should be home by then. Not exactly middle of the night, but it might be getting close to twilight by then if that helps," said Emma. "He did say to make sure you came to the back door, though, so no one sees you visiting. I doubt that has as much to do with your super secret thing as it does with property values or his reputation in the neighborhood. You know, not consorting with young men dressed in questionably tight clothing and all that. He also said, and I quote, 'My wife will probably insist you stay for dinner, so be ready for that, and by ready I mean with an excuse. You're not staying.' End quote. Cute, isn't he?"

"Ever so much," said Oliver.

20

SERGEANT Przybylinski liked a good glass of whiskey, but since he was a tad on the frugal side, he often settled for a good enough glass of whiskey. He had discovered a quiet little pub not far from work and more or less on the way home that kept a decent Scottish blended whiskey behind the bar at an acceptable price, and he had started a tradition of checking their stock at least a few times a week. He nursed only one glass per night, not wanting to seem like a drunk, and he knew that with retirement he would have to be even more careful not to let all the free time end up as more drinking time. Or not. It really depended on if there was anything decent on television. Of course that style of retirement wasn't looking as probable as it once was now that his mother had begun to have serious health issues. He thought the world of her. She was probably the only person on earth he could never be mean to, but helping her with her medical bills was really beginning to hurt the sergeant financially. If it kept on like this for much longer, his retirement was going to be much less than he imagined, if he was going to be able to retire at all anytime soon. Money. Unfortunately it was the topic that most often occupied his thoughts during these quiet whiskey breaks.

The sergeant was about halfway through his glass when another patron sat down beside him at the bar. This slightly annoyed the sergeant since he liked this establishment because it was quiet and never busy, like now, so there were plenty of other stools open at the bar and no need for someone to be sitting right beside him. He was debating between scaring off the intruder or just finishing his drink and leaving since he only had a few more sips. Not surprisingly, being scary was winning the internal debate, but before he could begin to terrorize anyone, the other man spoke.

"Sergeant Przybylinski?"

The sergeant turned his head slowly toward the speaker, who was a younger man with well-groomed short hair, dressed in a nice suit and tie. Sergeant Przybylinski was immediately reminded of a stockbroker or investment banker, something slick like that, although his mother would have called the man 'clean'. However, the sergeant could see the dirt beneath the surface of guys like this. Came from being a cop for so many years.

Sergeant Przybylinski chose not to reply, figuring this kept him well within scary territory.

"Sergeant, I'm sorry to bother you, but I was hoping we could have a short talk," said the young man with a pleasant smile. He seemed very non-threatening. "Perhaps I could buy you another drink while you listen to my proposal," the young man said. He motioned to the bartender. "Maybe something from a higher shelf." Sergeant Przybylinski's eyes widened ever so slightly as he watched the bartender reaching for a bottle somewhere in the range of great to greatest whiskey. The man continued, "My employer is interested in having a very simple business relationship with you. Just a friendly association, built on the exchange of information...and money. Very lucrative for both parties. You would provide us with a little bit of information, and we would make sure that your future is very secure, no matter what expenses might arise." He paused and gave the sergeant another smile. "Oh, I'm sorry, I haven't introduced myself. My name is Alex."

Oliver knocked on the Police Chief's back door at precisely 6:12 and, as he waited, glanced around to make sure no one had observed his arrival. Wearing sweat pants and a sweatshirt over his uniform and keeping his gloves and mask tucked in his waistband, Oliver had left his car at a park two blocks away. He then pretended to be like any other runner as he ran through the park and along the street until he neared the Chief's house, at which point he had darted up the driveway and jumped over the fence into the backyard. This last bit had been done at full superhero speed, so he was gone in the blink of an eye, and he doubted anyone would have noticed unless they were specifically watching him. Even then they probably would have done some soul searching about what medications, prescribed or otherwise, they were mixing nowadays. Oliver turned back as the door opened.

"Hello Chief," said Oliver. "Just past six at the back door as requested."

"Mr. Olson," said the Chief, pushing the screen door open. "Come in." The Chief was still wearing his uniform but he had taken off the jacket and loosened his tie. He showed Oliver through the kitchen and down the hall to his study. The study was exactly what Oliver would have imagined from the big, old two-story house, a lot of dark wood with built-in bookcases, a fireplace, and one large dark wood desk. What Oliver didn't expect was to find other people there. The Mayor was standing over by one of the bookcases, either closely examining the titles or posing for a portrait, it was hard to know for sure, and Emma was sitting on a sofa next to another woman Oliver didn't recognize. She had short brown hair and glasses and sat with what seemed a laughably large briefcase on her lap.

"I'm sure you remember the Mayor," said the Chief as they entered the study. The Mayor smiled but didn't move from his spot on the other side of the room. He believed it was a good power position and didn't want to lose it just to shake hands. The Chief continued. "This is Lily, the Mayor's personal assistant." He gestured toward the young woman who smiled shyly and shifted the big briefcase a bit. "And you know Emma, of course. Here, have a seat." He pointed Oliver to one of the two leather chairs facing the sofa. A very tasteful dark wood coffee table occupied the space between.

"Why didn't you say you were going to be here?" Oliver asked Emma as he sat down. The Chief sat down in the other chair as the Mayor took up another power position by leaning on the desk.

Emma shrugged. "I don't know. Why, did you want to carpool?"

"So I guess this is the first official meeting of the secret superhero committee," said the Mayor. He smiled. "I'm just joking. I'm not sure why the Chief insists on this much secrecy, but when he told me earlier today you two were meeting, I wanted to be a part of it. I even offered to do it at the mansion, but our Chief likes his mystery." There was just the slightest tinge of bitterness in this last comment as the Mayor thought about the publicity lost by not having his prize superhero over for dinner at the mayoral mansion, but he resolved to do just that this weekend. Black tie, city celebrities and his superhero. He could see the cameras flashing like crazy now. Maybe Oliver could bring a date too, like that Canadian super hottie he'd been linked to in the media. "I want to start out by saying that you've been doing a great job so far, Oliver. Just great." It was true. The Mayor's numbers had jumped right along with Oliver's after his battle with Cyclone. At this point, re-election seemed a given, but the larger the margin of victory the better for the Mayor. "If there is anything I can do to help, please let me know. In addition, Lily here has a list of public events and appearances we would like you to attend in the next couple of weeks. I also have a thought about a little dinner on Saturday night, so keep that open." Lily went about digging into her briefcase and handed Oliver a couple sheets of paper listing events. She handed a copy to Emma.

The Chief waited politely through the Mayor's opening comments, still cursing himself for even mentioning this meeting. He had merely been trying to keep the Mayor apprised of their progress against what he considered a major crime problem, but the Mayor only saw the publicity side of it. He waved off the copy of events Lily tried to hand him. Instead, he grabbed a folder off the coffee table. "This is what we've compiled on Cyclone. His history, his record, that sort of thing. Lots of stuff there, but nothing I noticed offhand that would explain his attacking you or any connection to Milwaukee before now. That alone makes me believe he's got some connection to our mystery crime problem. He's got a high-classed legal team from New York defending him and they've already thrown up a billion roadblocks to the charges, not to mention getting to trial. I doubt we're going to get anything useful out of him."

"Maybe I could talk to him directly," said Oliver, taking the folder and flipping through it.

"Not a chance his lawyers would let that happen, even if he were agreeable," replied the Chief. "Maybe Emma could do some more digging into it for you. This file is just the routine stuff from the criminal database. I don't want anyone at the office to see we're interested in this guy beyond what we would normally do in this situation, but I have a feeling this is a good opportunity for us to find something useful."

"Okay," said Oliver. He finished flipping through the last few pages of the file, and while it would seem to anyone else he had merely been skimming the pages while listening to the Chief, he had actually managed to read and analyze the material and agreed with the Chief's assessment. He handed it to Emma. "I guess that means you can make use of some of that shiny new equipment we have, as long as Roger has it all set up. See what you can find out about his legal team, there seems something odd about that part of it."

Emma put the file in her lap. "You know I've never done anything like this, right? I didn't get a serum to make me a criminologist or a hero's research assistant or whatever."

"Just ask Roger, he probably knows some shortcuts or places to look," said Oliver with a shrug.

"Or just Google it," said Lily. "You'd be amazed at what's out there. Thousands of hits for SuperGuy already."

The Chief shook his head. "A major crime syndicate against us and Google. They don't stand a chance."

"Oh, that reminds me," said the Mayor. "We probably need to get something about SuperGuy on our official city website."

"Already done," replied Lily. "It was added as soon as he became official and we even have video clips from the Cyclone fight right on our homepage. Lots of hits. Almost overloaded the server shortly after the fight. IT guys have it under control now."

"And what about all those cool social app thingies? With pictures and the comments?" asked the Mayor.

"IT guys have it all set up," said Lily. "Accounts up and running on all social apps. Sending out pictures, videos, alerts for appearances, everything."

"Excellent," said the Mayor, practically beaming. He didn't usually poll well with the cyber geeks, so maybe this would help. "That's why I love you, Lily: You're always a step ahead of me." He rubbed his hands together with delight, not noticing as Lily blushed and fiddled with her briefcase. "I suppose that pretty much wraps up our meeting then? I want to talk to Oliver about Saturday night."

"Actually there is one other thing, Mr. Mayor," said Emma. She looked at Oliver and mimicked flying with two hands out in front of her and some slight sound effects.

"Oh, right. Flying," said Oliver, turning to the Mayor. "I've done enough already to see that I need the ability to fly. I was wondering if there was money in the budget to get me the add-on flying serum."

"Oh, the budget, yeah. Hmm," mumbled the Mayor. "Well, it's late in the year and there's not much of anything left. That might be kind of hard right now." Lily had been reaching into her briefcase for the latest budget numbers but stopped when she saw the Mayor's hesitancy. She knew there was money in certain places, but the Mayor might have plans for it. The Mayor mumbled negatively a little more before finally asking, "How much does something like that cost?"

"I have it right here," said Emma, who pulled a sheet of paper out of her own sensibly sized briefcase and handing it to the Mayor. He looked at it and groaned slightly, then handed it to Lily. She saw that while it wasn't cheap, there was plenty left in the budget to get it done. It was just if the Mayor wanted it done.

Oliver watched all this and decided how best to proceed. "Actually Mayor, you might find that it will pay for itself in a very short time. Consider the amount of damage caused during the fight with Cyclone that could have been prevented had I been able to fly. When I got tossed around all I could do was wait to crash to a stop. Helpless. But with flying I can stop myself in mid air, without the assistance of large structures." The Mayor looked at Lily, who nodded slightly at the point. Oliver went on. "It will also make me much more visible. Right now I'm driving around in an unmarked police car. I don't think people are all that impressed waiting for the hero to arrive on the scene and parallel park. Flying is much more visible, much more impressive. Basically just an airborne advertisement of your tough anti-crime policy. Thousands will see me flying over the city every day."

The Mayor thought about it, and the more he thought about it, the more he liked it. It was basically a big campaign advertisement that wouldn't cost him anything out of his campaign fund. He smiled and nodded to himself, and then he looked at Lily. "Do we have enough in the budget to do this?" he asked. Lily nodded. The Mayor looked at Oliver. "Well then, SuperGuy, I believe we'll be getting you off the ground."

21

Being a superhero isn't for the faint of heart, or for the person who prefers to ease into things. It may only be your first week on the payroll, but this is a job that requires you be ready to stand toe to toe with a supervillain from the word go, and in the case of our hometown hero, SuperGuy, he showed he had the goods. Less than two months into the job and only five weeks past his already legendary battle with Cyclone, SuperGuy sat down with our own Milwaukee Times Herald News Observer Entertainment Editor, Les Williams.

LW: SuperGuy, what's it like to be SuperGuy?

SG: A little strange. Lots of surprises, lots of getting blown up so far. And falling. An unreasonable amount of falling.

LW: What causes all this falling?

SG: Well, gravity obviously. It's a bit relentless. And gullibility. Well, it's not gullibility really, I just need to stop trying to fly in things that are supposedly made to fly but don't actually fly. Rather big flaw. And when you're dealing with that, gravity is not your friend. Especially if you're a flightless superhero. I'd wear a parachute if DSF uniform regulations didn't prohibit it[5].

LW: What motivates you?

SG: Inspirational posters. Especially ones with kittens or puppies, or three-legged puppies. Those are killer. Or anything with a 'seize the day' motif. Really all the usual stuff. No, I'm kidding. I don't really need specific motivation, it was in the serum. So I guess you could say it was the drug. Drugs motivate me. Well, that doesn't sound good. But it's essentially hardwired into me now. At least that's what they tell me. But I do like puppies.

---

[5] Except for Basejumper. She wears multiple parachutes of various sizes as part of her wingsuit, many of which are weaponized (albeit slow and occasionally inaccurate due to windy conditions). —*The Department of Superhero Funding*

LW: Let's talk about being hardwired. Are you sometimes resentful of not having a choice?

SG: No, I don't mind. At this point I think I would make this my choice, if I had one. Sometimes we don't realize all the possibilities out there. We may believe there's only path one or path two to choose from, but then by some strange twist of fate something new opens up to you…well, it's kind of an easy choice. You don't even consider those other paths anymore because the new one is obviously the best. Besides, I've already got the funny uniform, what else am I going to do?

LW: Speaking of that uniform, how do you feel about it? I mean, that creates as much talk as your crime-fighting exploits.

SG: Well, it's taken some getting used to. Not the costume so much, it's really very comfortable, very well made, and as I've learned it's also very easy to clean. It's really the staring and general lack of eye contact that's a little much. And it's inspired some rather explicit emails being sent to us. That's a little creepy. But for the most part I'm thinking about it less and less every day.

LW: What can you say about Stormfront?

SG: She hasn't sent any emails that I know of.

LW: I mean, there have been rumors to the effect that you and she are an item. Is that true?

SG: I don't know. I've really only talked to her via video since we met at the orientation. That doesn't really constitute a relationship, at least for those of us who get out of the house. She's nice, though.

LW: Is it true she's attending the Mayor's Gala with you?

SG: Yes, that's true. I don't think the Mayor would let me come if she wasn't.

LW: That sounds a bit like a date.

SG: Eerily close to a work function really. But I hear the food's great and the band is excellent. Never been to the Mayor's place.

LW: You'll love it. Great garden. Good place for an evening stroll. Quite romantic.

SG: I'll keep that in mind.

LW: You threw out the first pitch at the last Brewer's game. What was that like?

SG: Great. I threw a change-up just off the outside corner, a little low, which was good since it was a little harder than I thought it would be.

LW: The catcher didn't make the play, did he?

SG: No, never even saw it.

LW: They ever find the ball?

SG: Yes, they were able to dig it up about fifteen feet back.

LW: What's the best thing about SuperGuy?

SG: Probably eating anything I want, or not eating anything I want. Either way. That's kind of nice.

LW: What's the worst thing?

SG: The gaudy uniform.

LW: Are there any rules or philosophies you live by as SuperGuy?

SG: Some. I'm still pretty new at it so it's sort of a work in progress. So, like always assume whatever it is, it's going to blow up. That's right up there at the top. Or try not to fall more than twelve stories. Not good on the joints and I tend to start making holes at that height. Don't fly anything Roger builds. The first rule pretty much applies to that too. And don't piss off Emma.

LW: I don't know if I'm surprising you with this, but it was just announced a short time ago that your mother has signed a book deal.

SG: Really? No, I hadn't heard. Can't see how that's going to be bad.

22

"YOU know, it's no trouble for me to fly all the way to the front door," said Janice, with a smile. Oliver couldn't see the smile since he was behind her, but he knew it was there.

"You really think you're cute, don't you?" he replied.

"Not child actor cute, but superhero cute."

"Nope, we covered this. Land short and we'll walk in. I've got a tiny bit of dignity left. Soon enough I'll be able to fly and it won't even be an issue," said Oliver. "And quit giving me trouble or I won't ask you to any more big parties, no matter how much the Mayor begs. Heck, I would've had you land in his backyard if it wasn't so important for him that we be noticed arriving in the first place."

"I understand. My mayor's the same way. They love their publicity." Janice swooped down and landed lightly in the street about a block away from where the lights illuminated the front gates of the Mayor's mansion. Paparazzi and fans surrounded the entrance and a string of limousines crawled along the street as they waited their turn to let out their guests. Oliver didn't want any of the paparazzi getting a photo of him being towed in for the party. It was a little embarrassing, and he was so close to getting his own flying serum.

Oliver let go of Janice and straightened his mask even though it didn't need it. He slapped his gloved hands together and said, "Shall we go to the ball?"

"Certainly," said Janice as they started walking toward the front gates and all the attention. It was a gorgeous night. A full moon floated high in the sky, and occasionally a stray cloud would drift across it for effect. It would have been an even more stunning visual if not for the huge spotlights outside the front gates of the mansion which were lighting up the night like a Hollywood premiere, not to mention the incessant camera flashes. The sounds of crickets and other night noises could be easily imagined, but they were being drowned out by the noise of the party Oliver and Janice were quickly approaching, and the smell of a late summer night in Wisconsin would have been wonderful except for all the limousine exhaust.

Once they got close enough to the gates to be noticed, Oliver and Janice were surrounded by paparazzi and fans. Camera flashes blinded them while they were simultaneously assailed by a cacophony of yelled questions and sporadic mindless screaming (only some of it coming from Oliver). The latter was mostly from the fans, although some of the reporters couldn't be ruled out. It's a thin line. There probably weren't that many paparazzi, this was just Milwaukee after all, but it seemed a few photographers and reporters had made the trip down from Thunder Bay. There was even one reporter and camera crew from a nationally syndicated entertainment show, and the heroes stopped to give them a short interview. Oliver gladly let Janice handle most of the questions since she was more experienced at this sort of thing, only occasionally throwing in a word here and there when the reporter seemed to require it. After that they negotiated the rest of the path to the front door, stopping a few times for pictures with fans along the way. It was all very surreal to Oliver. A couple months ago he might have been watching this on television while sitting on his crappy sofa eating soggy corn flakes. He thought fleetingly about whether that reality might prove to be the better option in the long run, not knowing how this whole hero thing was going to turn out. He could be burnt to a crisp by some fire powered supervillain next week. Then Oliver looked at Janice arm in arm with a fan taking a selfie, and it was obvious that walking into the party with the hot girl was way better no matter how much a guy liked his corn flakes or how soon he was burnt to a crisp.

Inside, Oliver got his first opportunity to see the big house did indeed live up to his personal definition of a mansion. With all the attention and the crowds and the flashbulbs and the canopies outside, he hadn't really noticed much about the exterior of the building itself, but inside things were elegant, upscale and quite shiny. And quiet. Much more quiet. Apparently rich folks in tuxes and party dresses didn't make it a habit to scream questions at people about their dates. In fact, a lot of them seemed not to notice Oliver and Janice at all, which was a bit of a relief to Oliver as he took a moment to look around the mansion. They had passed through an entryway larger than Oliver's apartment and much better furnished before entering a large ballroom that was the hub of the gathering. Near the front of the ballroom, hallways led off in either direction to what Oliver was certain would be wings of the mansion, while the back wall of the room was mostly windows with numerous doors leading out to the gardens. The mansion had originally been built in 1887 by—no surprise here—a rich guy. Someone who had moved up from Chicago after making buckets of money in the mercantile exchange. The ceiling was ridiculously high and gorgeously decorated with leaves and cherubs and other things Oliver couldn't really identify but were probably important parts of the motif. Several chandeliers were spaced throughout the giant room, bathing everything in a bright golden glow. Oliver was still staring upward when Janice grabbed his hand and pulled him farther into the party. He hadn't noticed, being all caught up in the ceiling, but the Mayor's assistant, Lily, had approached and was leading them to her boss.

"I assume the man with the big smile and the waving arms is your host?" said Janice as they weaved through the crowd toward the Mayor, who was indeed waving his arms in order to get their attention even though Lily was leading them right to him. The Mayor was standing amidst a group of people, one of whom was the Deputy Mayor with his standard sour-looking expression, and some other well dressed and well fed members of the city's upper crust. Oliver steeled himself for what he figured was the start of a long night of meeting people who may or may not care if he existed, but he did notice a couple of Brewer players, one Buck and even a legendary former Packer quarterback in the room, so maybe he'd at least get to meet them.

"Here we go," said Janice, who seemed to know what he was thinking.

"SuperGuy and Stormfront," said the Mayor as they got to him. He shook their hands as if they were his biggest contributors. "I am so honored to have you here," the Mayor continued. "And I'm especially thankful you could take the time to come down from Thunder Bay, Stormfront."

"My pleasure," said Janice.

"Here, let me introduce you to a few people," said the Mayor, mostly to Janice. Oliver got the feeling he was just along for the ride at this point, but he didn't let it bother him. He wondered if it would be cool for him to sneak off and check out the buffet. He didn't need to eat, but he figured if there was ever going to be a time to simply enjoy food for the sake of food, this might be the buffet. The Mayor introduced them to the Deputy Mayor, a couple of Miller bigwigs and the manager of the Brewers. Oliver wanted to talk to the Brewer's manager about why they couldn't find anyone worth a damn to bat leadoff, but the Mayor didn't dawdle, keeping the group moving along and introducing new people. After several more introductions the Mayor finished with a short man in a tuxedo and gray pinstriped vest with matching bow tie. He had a full head of slicked back white hair set off by dark, intense eyes that stopped just short of beady. He smiled happily as the Mayor and heroes approached.

"SuperGuy and Stormfront, I want to introduce Raymond Joyce of Joyce Industries," said the Mayor. "A very good friend and supporter."

"And an even better contributor," said Joyce, chuckling.

"Well, let's just say you're damn good in all of those roles," laughed the Mayor. "Mr. Joyce owns a number of companies in the city and employs a good number of our city's men and women."

"And you're the new defender of those citizens," said Joyce, reaching out to shake SuperGuy's hand. "A real pleasure to meet you."

"Nice to meet you, Mr. Joyce," said Oliver. "This is Stormfront." Mr. Joyce shook hands with Janice as the

Mayor excused himself to speak with another nearby group.

Mr. Joyce turned his attention back to Oliver. "So how are you coping with your new position? Up to speed and everything?" he asked.

"Ah, well, getting there. Learning as I go, to say the least," said Oliver, smiling at Janice. She had received more than her share of calls for advice in these first several weeks.

"Really?" said Joyce. "Not as simple as throwing on the suit and running around?"

Janice laughed. "Not as simple as that. But Oliver's picking it up quite quickly."

"If by picking it up, you mean getting knocked all over downtown by the occasional supervillain, then sure, I'm a natural," said Oliver.

"From what I've been told, you acquitted yourself quite admirably in that fight. Even coming out the victor, despite the odds," said Joyce.

"Yeah, I wonder what those were? I would've liked to have put some money on it," said Oliver.

"About 83,406 to 1," said Joyce, "but that's just a rough guess."

"Really? That's rough?" said Oliver. Joyce just smiled and shrugged.

"I wouldn't have thought the odds were that good," said Janice.

"I would be offended at that if I didn't completely agree," said Oliver. "Hopefully next time I can get the odds a little more close to even."

"A little more time and experience and I'm sure you will," said Joyce. "But of course, if they were in your favor, then it wouldn't have been quite as heroic either. Well, it was a pleasure meeting you, Stormfront, and you, SuperGuy. I will not monopolize your time, as I'm sure the Mayor will want you back soon enough." Joyce shook Janice's hand and turned back to Oliver to shake his. "I do look forward to having you in our city, especially once you've reached your full potential, as it were." With that the diminutive man turned and disappeared into the crowd.

"Neat little guy," said Janice.

"Yeah," agreed Oliver, nodding his head slowly. "If by neat you mean a little off."

"Sure, but how many of these people haven't seemed a little off? I don't think their interpersonal skills are the best when dealing with us common folk. It can be difficult to have a conversation with someone who doesn't sleep on a pile of money when they go home."

"I suppose that's true. It's gotta be hard," said Oliver, looking around the room. He spotted Roger and Emma over by one of the garden doors. He grabbed Janice's hand and guided her that way. "What are you two doing here?" he asked, once they reached them.

"Emma got us invites," said Roger, sipping a drink as his eyes scanned the room. An impressive feat for him considering Janice was right there.

"Sure, I got us invitations after you pestered me about them nonstop from the moment you heard about the party," replied Emma.

"Why not?" said Roger. "This kind of thing is a perk of the job."

Emma nodded begrudgingly. "Well, it's not bad. But I can't afford this dress and it's going to cost me a favor with Lily. Not to mention she didn't even give us invitations with a plus one. Just us only. I had to walk in with him," she finished, gesturing at Roger.

"Hey, easy there. I'm not that bad. This tux is a pretty good quality rental. I won't even hold you to leaving with me if you find something better. At least I won't pass up the opportunity."

"Classy," said Oliver.

"Hey, before I forget," said Emma, smacking Oliver on the shoulder, "I got a new land line put in for a phone in your room at the Garage and gave the number to your mother. She keeps calling and I'm tired of taking messages. Not your secretary, remember. I hooked up an answering machine, so now she's all yours."

"Great," said Oliver. "At least I was smart enough not to give her the number for the communicator."

"Just make sure you call her or answer the phone once in a while, or I'm betting she'll be back to calling me. Then I might just give her the communicator number," threatened Emma.

"Be a good superhero, Oliver," said Janice, "Call your mother."

"I will, I will. I've just been a little busy and most of her calls are about her book now. She keeps asking about things I don't remember. I don't think she remembers. Gotta be tough to write an autobiography if you don't remember anything. I'm beginning to think she was doing a little drinking back when I was growing up."

"Can't blame her," said Roger, still scanning the crowd with his coolest cool guy smile.

"There's more," said Emma. "A call from someone named Kate?" She took a drink of champagne, trying to hide a slight smile.

"Really?" said Roger, turning back to their conversation. "That's interesting."

"Who's Kate?" asked Janice, picking up on Roger's sudden interest.

"Nobody," said Oliver, a little too quickly.

"She's not nobody," said Roger. "She's Oliver's ex. Dumped him right before he won the lottery here. I bet she's kicking herself for that."

"Doesn't matter now, does it?" said Oliver.

"Well, she just said she wanted to talk," said Emma. "She said you two were...close."

"Close," said Janice. "That's sweet."

"Okay, okay, enough already. We weren't that close. She dumped me via voice mail, if you must know. I'm sure if we were more serious she would've gone to the trouble of a text with emojis." Oliver grabbed a glass of champagne off a tray a waiter was offering. He drained it and looked at the empty glass. "I sure wish this had an effect. It might make you guys bearable. And you," he said, looking at Janice, "you don't need to be helping them. You should know better. Isn't there a superhero code or something?"

"Yes, but I believe there's an ex-girlfriend clause," she replied with a smile.

"Relax, SuperGuy," said Roger. "Just tugging on your cape."

"One last thing," said Emma. "How do you feel about doing a reality show?" Oliver just looked at her without answering, not sure if she was serious.

"No way!" Roger looked back and forth between Emma and Oliver. "Really?"

"Apparently," continued Emma. "I got a call from a cable network about it today, and then someone called from the Superhero Union. Seems like they're kind of behind it, think it will be good publicity. The network wants to begin filming right away, get in with a brand new hero. See what it's like for someone just starting out."

"Great, so every single time I get blown up it will be on camera, not just every other time," said Oliver.

"You are a natural at getting blown up," said Roger. "Come on, you've got to do it. It'll be great."

"Great for you. You'll get on television and won't get blown up."

"That depends. I'd consider getting blown up too if the money was right," said Roger.

"You've got to do it, Oliver," said Janice.

He looked at her. "You think it's a good idea?" he asked, surprised.

"Oh, no. Definitely not," she replied. "But you heard Emma, the Union supports it. And that means they want you to do it. Which means you have to do it." Janice shrugged at him sympathetically.

"Have to?"

"Yes, unless you want whatever cooperation or equipment you get from them now to suddenly become much harder to get," she said. "They can be real jerks sometimes."

"Hey, wait, the Warehouse?" said Roger, fear clear on his face. "They'd take away the Warehouse?"

Janice looked at him. "Yes, definitely. You won't be able to get anything if they aren't happy with you. Equipment, intelligence, enhancements..." She let that last word linger there.

"Flying?" said Oliver. "They'd take the flying away?"

"I've heard worse," said Janice.

"But we've already ordered it."

"But we don't have it yet," said Roger.

Oliver thought for a minute and then sighed. "Well, I guess I'm doing a reality show now. From superhero to reality show star. It's hard to believe I have become a loser quite so quickly."

"Come on, it'll be fun," said Roger, clearly happy with the decision. "Besides, you've always been a loser. Dressing up in spandex didn't change that."

"Thanks, Buddy," said Oliver. "Look, I'm going to run to the little superhero's room. I'll be back in a minute." Oliver started off through the crowd, wondering how different it would be with cameras following him all the way to the bathroom too. He found the men's room and stepped up to a urinal, thinking it was a little strange to have a bathroom with urinals in your house, but there must be exceptions if your house was a mansion. He also appreciated the fact that the costume makers at the Department of Superhero Funding were good enough to give him a fly to use in situations like this. Of course, it was designed so well he didn't even realize there was a fly to use for the first three weeks, but now things were much easier. Number two wasn't so simple. Oliver's thoughts were interrupted by another party attendee stepping up to the urinal beside him.

"We meet again so soon, SuperGuy," said the white-haired Raymond Joyce. "Small world."

"Mr. Joyce," said Oliver with a nod, mostly directed at the wall in front of him since eye contact at a urinal was a difficult proposition. An awkward silence followed.

"How do you handle the relationship?" asked the billionaire CEO. "If you don't mind me asking."

"The what?"

"The relationship. With the woman you're here with," said Joyce. "The tall one."

"Oh, Janice. Stormfront. I don't know if you could call it a rela—"

"I don't mind telling you I have a little difficulty talking to women." Joyce shook his head as he stared at the wall. "We're both in the same sort of positions, really. Powerful men, a bit of fame. It's hard to have a normal relationship with someone. Hard to even know how to approach a woman."

"Sure..." said Oliver. "Well, I don't know that—"

"How did you go about asking your young lady out?"

"I suppose I just asked her," said Oliver. "But this is a special function and the Mayor wanted her to attend as well. I guess that made it easier. I kind of had an excuse." He walked over to the sink to wash his hands.

"Right," said Joyce, nodding. "Excellent idea. Of course she's a superhero so it makes sense. I doubt the Mayor would care either way if a waitress came."

"A waitress?"

Joyce shook his head. "Doesn't matter," he said, zipping up and heading to the sink also. "I guess I missed my chance. This might have been a pretty impressive first date."

"Maybe, I don't know," said Oliver, trying to follow the man's train of thought. "Um...I guess it's a bit over the top, really. Maybe she, the waitress, would have appreciated something a little lower key. I know I'm not used to this kind of thing."

"Good point," said Joyce. "Still, it was an opportunity. I hate to miss opportunities. You never know how many you'll get." Joyce dried his hands on a paper towel and dropped it in the trash can. "I look forward to seeing you again, SuperGuy. Thanks for the advice."

"You're welcome," replied Oliver, not really sure he had given much in the way of advice. He watched the short man leave, dropped his own paper towel in the trash and went out the door. Weaving his way back through the crowd, Oliver spotted Janice near where he had left her, but Roger and Emma were gone. "Where'd the kids go?" he asked as he walked up.

"I think the pull of the buffet became too much for Roger to resist, and Emma went along for logistical support. I think he needed her to carry an extra plate or two," answered Janice. She looked around the room for a second and then nodded at the door leading out to the gardens. "Hey, you want to take a walk? I'm a little tired of being..."

"Leered at?" finished Oliver.

"Yeah, pretty much."

"Well, let's go."

The two superheroes stepped through the nearest door onto the biggest patio Oliver had ever seen in his life. He would have thought it a terrible waste to cover so much grass with stone, but then he saw the size of the garden beyond and figured the green space was holding its own. There were other people talking in small groups here and there, and a few people, mostly couples, were strolling through the garden. It was still warm and a slight breeze rustled the leaves of the nearby trees.

"If I were a gentleman I would offer you my coat, or at least my cape, but I've got nothing," said Oliver. "I realize we don't feel the temperature, but I would still seem like a smooth operator."

"Were you a smooth operator before you became a superhero?" asked Janice as they walked down steps into the garden. They passed a couple walking hand in hand and so totally absorbed in their conversation with each other they didn't notice the two superheroes. The muted conversations and footsteps of other people walking among the meticulously manicured hedges and trees seemed to float by from all directions. Janice turned down a secluded and empty path.

"Oh, god no. Not a smooth anything," said Oliver. "Definitely not. But I think once in a while if the planets were aligned just so, I could pull off a decent line or two. Maybe seem like an okay enough guy. I got dates."

"And one of those dates was this Kate?"

"Yeah."

"But you weren't terribly close?"

"Even less than I thought."

"That's too bad," said Janice, brushing her hand against some leaves on one of the hedge walls as they walked along.

"Actually, I don't think so," replied Oliver. "Not much at all. I'll just write it off as experience. I'm not smooth but I'm hoping to bumble my way towards a little closeness again someday."

"Not smooth, huh?" said Janice, stopping and stepping in close to Oliver. Their bodies touched just barely. "I don't think you give yourself enough credit."

"Well, I'll work on my self confidence," said Oliver, and he leaned in to kiss her. Just as his lips touched hers, there was a blinding flash. Oliver's first thought was this was one of those kisses that came with fireworks, but he and Janice broke apart amidst a few more flashes, which he now recognized as cameras. Two of them, operated by paparazzi who now pushed farther out of the bushes in which they had been hiding. Oliver was just beginning to think about how he should handle this when Janice grabbed him and flew up into the night sky, quickly leaving the cameras, garden, and mansion far below. And Oliver had to admit, kissing while floating high above the night-shrouded earth was pretty cool.

23

"HOW come it's taking you so long to put that together?" asked Roger. They were in Roger's room on the upper level of the garage, and Oliver was attempting to assemble a microwave cart while Roger finished up the connections on his flat panel television. It wasn't as simple as a television of course, it was also patched into the whole garage headquarters system so Roger could monitor everything from his room whether that was checking the security cameras or using the communications system, among many others. Lots of things had changed in the office area of the Garage in the past week. Since the building itself hadn't cost them anything, the new occupants were given a decent budget for renovations and, with a slow economy, there was no shortage of people ready to do the work. Oliver, Roger and Emma had done some quick planning and got crews in immediately to begin the renovations.

The first project was somewhat simple, which was to knock down the wall between the control room and the second office, to make a much larger and more useful space. It hadn't taken long for that first office to become packed with equipment, and they wanted to add a conference table for meetings. Emma had moved from the second office to the third to make way for the expansion. The next projects were Oliver and Roger's living quarters on the upper floor. Since the offices weren't terribly large, they had decided to simply knock out the walls between the first and second offices and the third and forth, creating two bigger rooms. Then the crews added bathrooms and kitchenettes in the middle, building out from the adjoining wall. The rooms weren't super spacious but they made decent efficiency apartments which were more than enough to satisfy Roger and Oliver.

"So, how long is it going to take you?" asked Roger again.

"I have no idea," replied Oliver, a bit of defeat in his voice. "The directions are in English, but apparently I'm not as fluent in that language as I thought I was."

"Ah, another shortcoming of the serum. Nothing in it to cover assembling products made in China with directions written by someone whose first and possibly even second language isn't English and probably wasn't allowed to see the product they were writing the directions for," said Roger. He finished connecting a last cable and pushed the flat panel television back against the wall.

"Think there's a serum booster that would cover it[6]?" asked Oliver. He stared at the directions for another moment and then tossed them aside. Grabbing a drill and a very long wood screw, he proceeded to drive the screw through the side of the cabinet and into a couple of other boards that hadn't been cooperating. "There, that should do it," he said, setting the drill aside and moving the cart into place next to the kitchen counter. He grabbed the microwave with one hand and plopped it on top like it was a made of cardboard. "Perfect," he said. "I just wouldn't recommend rolling it around much. Or using the drawer. Not that you could get it open now."

"Great," said Roger. "Would have been cheaper to stack up a couple of small crates, not to mention just as useful."

"But I would have been robbed of a great sense of accomplishment," said Oliver.

There was a knock at the door, which was standing open, and Emma walked in without waiting for an invitation. She looked around at the small apartment and nodded. "This isn't too bad, Roger. Nicer than my apartment, except for the garage smell."

---

[6] An IKEA Furniture Assembly Booster (IFAB) has been an ongoing research project for years. So far it has proved unsuccessful. We're only human. —*The Department of Superhero Funding*

"Thanks, I'm liking it."

Emma dropped a stack of papers on the coffee table and sat down on the couch opposite the wall with the flat panel television. There was another small chair stuffed into the space with the couch, but little other room. A divider stood right behind the chair, separating the living room area from Roger's bed.

"I've been researching Cyclone and his big time New York lawyers for connections to Milwaukee, and I think I've found something," said Emma once she was comfortable. "Of course I'm saying that as a person with absolutely no experience in doing this sort of thing, so I could be completely wrong. But I don't think I am. I got some confirmation from the Superhero Union's research department. It was a low priority request since we're small time and it wasn't an emergency, but they helped run down a couple of things. Regardless, I'm pretty proud of myself and my amateur detective work," she said with a satisfied smile.

"Joyce Industries?" asked Oliver, walking over and sitting down in the small chair.

Emma's smile disappeared instantly. "How did you...?"

Oliver answered somewhat distractedly. "I had a pretty good guess from all the other material from the Chief. I narrowed it down to two or three possibilities, but I was betting on Joyce. Especially after meeting him at the Mayor's Gala. There was just something about him."

"Wait," said Roger, his attention being pulled away from the television he had tuned to a baseball game. "What did I miss? We found the bad guy? And how'd we do it so fast?"

"*We* didn't do anything," said Emma. "And I apparently didn't do anything. Just wasted a ton of time researching law firms and companies and shell companies and the shells of shell companies. Why didn't you tell me you already knew?" she asked Oliver.

"Because I didn't know for sure," said Oliver. "I only had a guess but you confirmed it. You did good research. I know it would be faster if we had some kind of crime stopping supercomputer to sift through all the facts for us and spit out an answer instead of my guesses and your research, but we don't. Or do we? I'm getting ahead of myself. Roger, did you get us a crime stopping supercomputer?" Oliver looked at Roger for an answer but he wasn't listening.

Roger picked up some of Emma's printouts. "Joyce Industries? The bad guy is a corporation?" he asked, somewhat crestfallen. "No supervillain, just a boardroom of guys in suits? Crap, I hate it when these criminal conspiracies turn out to be corporations or oil companies or politicians. That's so boring."

"It's not a whole boardroom," said Oliver. "Aren't you listening? Just one guy named Raymond Joyce. You know, the weird short guy with the slick white hair I told you about at the Gala. He's the guy behind it all. And he could be a supervillain. We don't know for sure yet."

Roger paged through a few more of the documents. "Joyce Industries is huge. That guy must be loaded. Why would he bother with masterminding a crime syndicate in Milwaukee?" asked Roger. "It's not like it's New York or L.A. Doesn't seem like it's worth the trouble."

"It's not really a crime syndicate in Milwaukee," answered Oliver. "That's just a cover. An overall increase in crime to cover for a few specific ones so those won't get noticed and be connected to each other."

"What specific crimes?" asked Emma.

"A kidnapping, an arson and a stolen chemical formula to name the big three, besides other minor ones. There were also some financial deals that, while legal, would have helped show a pattern if things weren't such a mess due to the crime increase."

"Now wait a second. A minute ago you said you had a good guess it was Joyce Industries and you needed my information to confirm it, yet you seem to know the whole plan. Exactly how good of a guess did you have?" asked Emma.

"96.9 percent probability," answered Oliver.

"And we need a crime fighting supercomputer," said Emma. "Right. Sounds like you just spit out the answer."

"Okay, I'm sorry. I didn't mean to make you feel bad, it's just that the information I read needed to…I don't know, sort of cook for a while before I knew what was going on."

"So not so much like a supercomputer as a crock pot?" said Roger.

"And a generic crock pot at that," said Oliver. "Anyway, after letting all the information simmer for a while, to keep with the cooking metaphor, things just kind of fell into place. But I still needed your confirmation, Emma."

"Okay," said Emma, with a nod and slight smile.

"So, are you going to call the Chief and go arrest this guy?" asked Roger.

"Nothing to arrest him for," replied Oliver. "We can't really connect him personally to any of the crimes, being the…uh…good at crime guy that he is. We just need to stop him." A baseball manager on television was throwing and kicking his hat. It looked nice in high definition. You don't often see foolishness look so crisp.

"Stop him from doing what exactly?" asked Emma. When Oliver didn't answer, she prompted, "Oliver?"

"Oh, he's developed a chemical to enslave the entire world population," said Oliver absentmindedly.

"Enslavement and world domination?" said Roger. "Wait, was this whole conspiracy crime syndicate thing really complicated?"

"I'd say so," said Emma. "The amount of paperwork I sifted through finding the connection from Cyclone's lawyers back to Joyce Industries was staggering."

"I mean needlessly complicated?" asked Roger.

"Isn't that all law-related stuff?" said Emma. "But yes, the Union research person I spoke to did mention there were several more layers than one usually sees in these situations."

Roger turned to Oliver. "And the details of the crimes the Chief gave you, you said there were many done just to cover up a few, right?" Oliver nodded. "Almost like it was more trouble than it was worth?"

Oliver nodded again. "Yeah, it kind of made the odd ones stand out more when you really looked at it. Lot of extra work put in there."

"Yes!" said Roger, raising his hands in the air. "Yes, yes, yes. World domination and overly complicated plans? This Joyce guy is definitely a supervillain. Corporations just want the cash. They don't do enslavement. Well, except tobacco companies. Sweet!"

"Isn't it wrong to be that excited when you find out someone's trying to enslave you?" asked Emma.

"And the whole rest of the world," said Roger, still obviously thrilled. "It may be wrong, but I think in this case it's appropriate. Our first time out and it's for all the marbles? It could have just been some guy trying to corner the market on light beer, but we got somebody trying to take over the world. That's the holy grail of evil plans. That's pretty cool."

"Pretty cool?" Emma shook her head. "You are really messed up. Okay, well, what do we do now?"

Oliver scratched his ear as he thought. "That's the thing, I'm not exactly sure what to do next," he said.

"That's easy," said Roger. "I'm surprised it isn't hard-wired into that superhero brain of yours. You've got to do the face-to-face."

"The what?"

"The face-to-face. You gotta go meet the man. Well, I know you already met the man, but you didn't know it was the man, so it doesn't count. Now you've got to confront him. You know he's the bad guy with the evil plan, he undoubtedly knows you're the good guy because of the funny suit, so you have to call him out. Maybe he'll make a mistake because of the pressure, giving something away, or maybe you'll pick up on a clue there, or maybe the two of you will just have a pleasant talk and decide to make a regular thing of it. Sunday afternoon tea. I'm not really sure. It's just the way it's done."

"That sounds kind of dangerous," said Emma.

"Oh, it's not at all," replied Roger. "There's sort of an unofficial cease fire to these things."

"*Unofficial*," repeated Emma, the doubt clear in her voice.

"Okay. I guess I could just go to his office. That's easy enough," said Oliver. "Do you think I need to make an appointment?"

"Oh, no. He'll see us without one," said Roger.

"Us?"

"Oh, yeah, I'm going with you. This is your first face-to-face. I wouldn't miss it for anything."

24

"**BARCODE** Boy," said Roger.

"Excuse me?" said Oliver, without looking at his friend beside him.

"Barcode Boy," repeated Roger. They were standing in an elevator staring at the digital display above the doors. The red numbers were rising steadily as they ascended to the top floor. "I imagine that's what they would call your sidekick. SuperGuy and Barcode Boy. Oh, wait. That's not going to fly with a black guy. Your sidekick could only be some small white guy with a name like that. Just one more way to keep the black man down. I'll have to come up with something better. I was just thinking about what my sidekick name would be since I'm on this mission with you."

"Mission? It's more like a meet and greet the way you described it," said Oliver. He was a little put out that he was having to use the elevator to get to this meeting instead of flying up and landing on the roof or balcony or something cool. The elevator was definitely not cool. Not superhero at all. Oliver took his eyes off the numbers and looked around the interior of the elevator. It would have been obvious his brow was furrowed in thought had he not been wearing a mask. "Do you find it disturbing there's no elevator music? I would have expected elevator music. It's a nice elevator. Pretty fancy. Would have thought there'd be music. And not thin sounding or tinny, a really solid system. Full sound with good bass."

Roger shrugged. "Didn't really notice there wasn't. Probably best. You don't want a Barry Manilow song playing in your head during the face-to-face. Might throw you off your game."

"I have game?"

"I'm making assumptions. You know, serum and all."

"Sure, but do I even need game for a meet and greet?"

"Well, I shouldn't really say it's that simple," said Roger. "The face-to-face meeting is a little more than a tea party. There is the potential for violence."

"I thought you said there was an unofficial cease fire in these first meetings, which is why you were coming along, and why I'm letting you."

"That's true. I guess it's more the potential for potential violence. Sort of a very subtle, yet menacing thing. Does that make sense?"

"You need to ask?"

"Of course, there is also the chance the guy's a real nutter. Then I suppose the unofficial rules of the game don't really apply and I could be screwed," said Roger, looking somewhat concerned. "I didn't think about that."

"Well, if things do get ugly, do your best not to get killed. I would feel bad."

"Don't. I deserve it for coming along when I should know better."

"Fair enough." The elevator came to a halt and the doors opened with a ding. Oliver walked out. "Come on then, Barcode Man...or Person or Guy, whatever you want to be called."

"Those all suck," said Roger. "Leave the sidekick names to me."

"This from the guy who came up with the racially insensitive 'Barcode Boy'."

Having had their arrival announced when checking in at the main reception desk in the lobby, Oliver and Roger were met by a young man in a dark suit who introduced himself as Alex, Mr. Joyce's personal assistant. He led them through a set of double doors that were flanked on either side by desks. Both were currently empty but messy enough to look regularly used. It was almost six o'clock so Oliver guessed their owners might be gone for the day, which was a better thought than they had been sent home so there would be no witnesses to Oliver and Roger's disappearance. Beyond the double doors was a spacious office with a large desk on one side and a sofa and chairs on the other. All of the furnishings were extremely nice, and even Oliver, whose knowledge of furniture began and ended at cardboard boxes covered with a mostly clean sheet, could tell they were also extremely expensive.

"Nice office Mr. Joyce has here," said Oliver as he took it in. There was no Mr. Joyce to be seen.

"Oh, this is not his office," said Alex, "this is mine."

"Really?" said Oliver. "I thought that was you out there." Oliver pointed toward the desks they had passed as they came in.

"No, those are my assistants," replied Alex.

"Cool, assistants to the assistant. Nice," said Roger.

"So where is Mr. Joyce?" asked Oliver.

"Right through here," said Alex, waving a hand at the far wall and walking toward it.

Oliver hadn't noticed anything more than a wall when he first looked around the room but now he could see the oversized double doors set into the wall in such a way they were not easily seen. Not purposely hidden, just made to blend into the wall. Alex knocked and then opened the doors without waiting for a response. He stepped to one side and held out an arm as invitation for Oliver and Roger to enter. Inside was a vast room which made Alex's office look like a closet. It wasn't the regular one-story-sized height you would assume an office building to have. Instead, the ceiling on the low side was at least two stories tall and sloped upward to about three stories in height where it met the opposite wall. That opposite wall was all windows showing an amazing view of downtown Milwaukee with the lake in the background. All that brightness was balanced on the other side of the room by a wall of black marble. Against that black marble sat one gray couch with a couple matching chairs opposite it, all of them situated around a small coffee table. The couch might have been large, but against that wall it seemed tiny. Directly across from the double doors was the only other furniture in the room, a massive, dark gray desk. It had to be big if it could still be considered large in the cavernous room. Part of the wall behind the desk was covered with nine flat panel monitors, all of which were currently on but had the sound muted, each one showing something different. The local television channels were all displayed as well as CNN and a few other major news and financial channels.

Behind the desk was a large gray leather chair and in that chair sat the small man with bright white hair Oliver had met and spoken with at the Mayor's gala. Mr. Joyce wore a gray pinstriped suit with a gray tie, shirt and vest. He wasn't entirely easy to notice in the immense room dominated by the desk, high ceilings and the walls of video screens, black marble and windows. Oliver and Roger had slowed after entering as they took in the size of the room and its contents, but now Oliver focused on Joyce and walked across the floor to the desk, followed slightly more slowly by Roger. Mr. Joyce got up from his chair and came around the desk to greet them.

"SuperGuy," he said, offering his hand and shaking Oliver's vigorously. "It is a great pleasure to see you again. And this is Mr. Allen, I presume? I'm Raymond Joyce," he said to Roger, while shaking Roger's hand. "I'm honored to have both of you here."

"It's good to see you again," said Oliver, a bit hesitantly. Immediately after saying it he realized it probably wasn't the best way to greet the person you just recently discovered could be your arch nemesis, but he was a little taken aback at how genuinely friendly and enthusiastic Joyce was. It's hard to be a jerk in the face of that. Maybe it was the serum helping him to be cool in the situation, but Oliver had never been a very confrontational person. Now he was slightly confused as this face-to-face thing wasn't starting out quite like he thought it would. The feel was all wrong. He had been imagining various scenarios ever since they decided to make the visit. Most of them took place in poorly lit, back-room offices filled with cigar smoke and bad guy muscle surrounding a mobster-looking boss who spoke ironic pleasantries through clenched teeth. Here there was no smoke, no muscle, no irony and the lighting was gorgeous. So much natural light from those huge windows.

"Here, please sit down," said Mr. Joyce, pointing to a couple of chairs Alex had just brought over to the desk. Joyce walked back around to his own chair to sit while

Oliver and Roger settled into theirs. "Can I get you anything to drink? Oh, or maybe something to snack on?" He checked his watch. "It's actually pretty close to dinner. I could have my chef fix something."

"Um, well…" said Oliver, not really sure what the snacking etiquette was in the whole face-to-face confrontation thing.

"I'm feeling a bit hungry," said Roger.

"You are?" asked Oliver, looking over at Roger. He held up a hand to Mr. Joyce. "I'm sorry, could I have a word with Roger?" Mr. Joyce just nodded and smiled pleasantly. Oliver stepped over to Roger and pulled him out of his chair, leading him several feet away. He spoke quietly. "We can eat?"

"Why not?" said Roger.

"I don't know. I don't know the rules."

"There really aren't any, like I said. Sure, there's the cease fire, but past that I don't know. You chat for five minutes or five hours if you want. Eventually there'll be some threats, possibly veiled, possibly obvious, which will confirm he's the bad guy with an evil plan and you're the good guy who's going to stop him. You can find you hate him because he's truly evil or maybe you end up feeling sorry for him because he's really just misguided due to some childhood trauma, but beyond that, I think it's just filler. I don't see a problem with a little snack, or maybe something more substantial. Apps at least, or maybe a couple of dinner courses. You heard him, he's got his own chef. That screams good eating. Oh, and cocktails. I bet he's got nothing but top shelf booze."

Oliver thought about it for a few seconds. "What about poison?"

"Poison?"

"Yes, what if he decided to poison us?"

"Okay, that's a bit paranoid. I thought the serum would have taken care of the irrational part of your brain already, but I suppose it's a big job. Look, poison wouldn't affect you anyway. Bit of a downer for me, but if the food's good…I mean, private chef, man. I'd take the chance," said Roger with a shrug.

"Okay," said Oliver. "So we eat?"

"And drink," said Roger. "Hell, yes."

They came back over to the desk and sat down in their chairs again. Mr. Joyce looked at them expectantly. "So, any decisions?" he prompted.

"Dinner would be good," said Roger before Oliver could speak. "And maybe drinks, if you're open to that."

"Great," said Mr. Joyce. "Alex, please have Tony fix enough for two more and have a table brought in. And bring a wine list for Mr. Allen." Oliver did not need to look at Roger to know how big his smile was at that moment.

"Right away," said Alex, turning and leaving by the double doors.

They sat there staring at each other for a moment before someone spoke. Oliver was a little surprised it was him, but he felt he needed to say something before it got too uncomfortable. He wanted it to seem as if this were all just everyday stuff for him so he asked the first thing that popped into his head. "So, Mr. Joyce, how are things with your friend? The waitress, wasn't it?"

Joyce looked justifiably surprised by the question and thought about it for a few seconds. "Oh...well...I'm not...Have either of you dated a waitress before?" he asked. Oliver and Roger exchanged looks and managed to mumble negatives. "Really? No? Seems like there are so many waitresses yet no one I ask has ever dated one. At least not recently, or an actual waitress. A server at the Ponderosa buffet doesn't count, does it?Tell me, do you think it's appropriate to ask one out on a date while they are working? Or should you wait until they are off...although it might seem a little untoward to approach them away from work..." Mr. Joyce trailed off as he stared out the window.

Oliver was about to attempt some kind of advice when he noticed breaking news coverage on one of the local television channels behind Mr. Joyce's head. They were showing live helicopter footage of a major fire in a building just a few blocks away. As he watched, each of the other local stations broke into their programming and began showing coverage of the fire. Oliver glanced over at Roger to see he had noticed it too. Mr. Joyce was completely unaware and continued to talk about waitresses. Oliver stood up and interrupted him.

"I'm sorry Mr. Joyce, but it seems I may have an emergency," said Oliver, gesturing at the screens behind the white-haired man. His communicator beeped and an automated emergency message began playing in his ear telling him about the situation and the location. Oliver stepped over to the windows to see if he could see the fire from there. It was just out of sight, hidden by other buildings, but he could see a lot of smoke. He looked back at the televisions and out the window once more. Roger came over for a look out the window as well.

Oliver turned back to Mr. Joyce. "Look, I know we're supposed to have a nice little give and take here, at least that's what I'm told being new to all this, but it appears I've got to run. I suppose we could re-schedule but I doubt delays really help me while they're probably very helpful to you, so I guess I just need to know whether or not you intend to continue on your present course with all the various crimes. You know, the thefts, kidnapping, arson and the whole world enslavement thing," said Oliver. "Really set on it?"

"Oh." Mr. Joyce seemed somewhat startled by the question, and took a few seconds to think it over. "Yes, I think so. I see no reason not to. If anything, you make it sound even more enticing a venture than I had considered it before."

"Oh. Well, I wasn't really going for that, but great. Um, nice meeting you. Sorry to miss the food." Oliver took a few steps back, got a running start and jumped through one of the large windows. Both Roger and Mr. Joyce stared at the gaping hole through which Oliver had disappeared. Bits of glass dropped and shattered on the floor. Roger took a couple steps forward and leaned out, trying to see where Oliver landed. He couldn't, but he did see an outcropping one story below had kept any glass from falling all the way to the street. He stepped back.

"He didn't really have to go out that way, did he?" asked Mr. Joyce.

Roger glanced at him, then back at the window. "No, probably not. But he can be a little passive aggressive. I think I'll just take the elevator when I go," he said, pointing vaguely toward the door. He patted his pants pocket for his keys. "I'm glad I drove. Sorry about the mess, Mr. Joyce."

Mr. Joyce just smiled. "Oh, don't worry, Mr. Allen. And please, now that we have had our official introductions," he said with a little bow, "you can call me Gray Matter." Roger nodded, realizing with a name like that, they were definitely dealing with an actual supervillain. The double doors opened and several men carried in a dinner table and chairs, which were quickly arranged and set with dishes and glasses under the direction of Alex. Another group followed closely behind, a couple of men sweeping up the broken glass on the floor while others sealed the window with clear plastic sheeting. Those men disappeared out the doors as a waiter brought a wine list to Roger.

"Thank you," said Roger, taking the list with a little uncertainty.

"You will still stay for dinner, won't you, Mr. Allen," asked Mr. Joyce. "I know Mr. Olson had to leave, but there's no reason for more food to go to waste."

Roger looked from Joyce to the wine list. He didn't know anything about wines but the names sure seemed expensive. And the dates. Most of them were older than he was. But without Oliver here... "You won't poison me, will you?" he finally asked.

"Poison? Oh, most definitely not," said Mr. Joyce. "You have my word. Much too early in the game for that sort of thing, don't you think? Eventually there might be a good reason to kidnap you for leverage against Mr. Olson, but not yet. Besides, I'd like to pick your brain a bit about this whole dating conundrum. You seem like the kind of man who might have some insight. And look, our food is already here." Joyce gestured toward the table which was now fully decked out with a gray table cloth, ornately decorated plates and salad bowls, and very shiny silverware. The waiters were finishing setting out the food, of which there was a lot and it all looked beyond good. Not to mention the smells drifting over were amazing. Roger looked back at the supervillain in front of him. A man he now knew was undoubtedly an evil genius with a presumably nefarious plan to enslave the world and destroy anyone who got in his way, including Roger himself.

"I could eat," said Roger.

"Is that her?" asked Roger.

"Yes," answered Mr. Joyce. He said it with a combination of longing and fear that was almost palpable. A soft rain fell steadily on the two men as they stood outside the diner in the increasingly darkening evening. At Mr. Joyce's insistence, they were pretending to have a casual conversation while looking for the waitress, Alice, who was at work during the dinner rush. Joyce had added a long gray raincoat to his ensemble and held a surprisingly black umbrella. Roger held a matching umbrella given to him by one of Mr. Joyce's assistants.

"So, are you ready to do this?"

"Are you sure this is a good idea? I feel like we're rushing it. I don't want to rush it."

"Would you stop it with the rushing talk? From what I can tell, you are in no danger of rushing anything."

"But if we are, then bad things could happen. First impressions are everything. It could all be lost in a second. I say one wrong thing and that's it, it's all over."

"Seriously, it's not that big of a deal. You need to relax," said Roger. "Breathe. Remember what we talked about. You're not making the plunge now, you're not asking her out, you're just going to make some non-threatening small talk. Not even a lot. Don't talk her ear off, just stick to the two or three sentences we planned. See how she responds and proceed accordingly. Right now you simply want to get your foot in the door, get noticed, maybe make her smile. We're not trying to change her world in one passing conversation, just have a simple, pleasant exchange. Concentrate on that."

Joyce made a sound like a groan, but with extra dread.

"Look, you can do this," said Roger. "You're the CEO of a huge corporation and a supervillain. You're in charge of thousands of people and you run every kind of legitimate and not so legitimate business there is. You juggle trying to kill off superheroes with taking over companies and swindling retirees out of their savings. You can handle a couple of idle comments to the waitress taking your order. Now get in there and order some pie," finished Roger with a flourish. Joyce nodded and, with a not terribly convincing look of determination on his face, pushed the door of the diner open and went inside.

Roger stood in the rain for a second longer, before turning and heading for his car. "How can this guy possibly be a threat to enslave the world?" he said. He figured he could keep the umbrella.

25

"Do I get a cape?" asked Oliver.

"You really want one?" asked Emma. She was sitting at the conference table in the expanded control room watching Roger and Oliver open the box from the DSF containing the flying serum. It was like watching two boys on Christmas morning, only those kids wouldn't be as excited as these two grown men were. Granted, this probably was the best present ever.

"Capes are cool," said Roger while trying to tear the package open. "God, they use really good tape."

"It's not so much for the coolness, or the flying, it's so I can cover myself when needed," said Oliver. He pantomimed covering himself with a cape as he did it. When he saw how Emma was looking at him he complained, "Did I tell you about the ladies from the Flower and Garden Society?"

"Yes, we've heard," sighed Emma. "No podium, just the lone microphone stand and strong lighting. And they were creepy. Let it go."

"No, that's just it. There was a podium when I first arrived. They dragged it off to the side and left me with just a microphone. You should have seen it. Three old ladies dragging this big wooden podium. I asked if I could help but they just giggled and averted their eyes. Creepy. Old ladies shouldn't be creepy. Weird or crabby, sometimes wise, but not creepy."

"I said, let it go," repeated Emma, exasperated. "You won't have to give them another speech, although they have already contacted me about having you back. Too bad for them you're more in demand now."

"Fame will set you free," said Roger, "Or at least keep the creepy old ladies at bay." He tugged at a flap on the box some more, then handed it to Oliver as he got up. "Man, this is really good tape. I gotta get a knife."

"Oh, and you can't have a cape. At least not yet," said Emma.

"Why not?" asked Oliver, holding the box as Roger rummaged through a nearby desk.

"Surprisingly enough, getting you a serum booster to fly was much easier than all the paperwork it will take to alter your uniform," replied Emma.

"Oh, that's true," said Roger as he returned with a box cutter. "The DSF doesn't like changing uniforms.

They've got a bit of an ego about their creations. They don't want folks making changes just because they dislike their gloves or something."

"Look, just get the paperwork started to get me a cape. At least try. Maybe it'll take months, but it'll be worth it for me."

"Damn it!" said Roger. "Broke the blade. This is really good tape. I wonder if it's hero quality?" Roger got up to find a replacement blade.

"Forget it Roger," said Oliver, taking the box and popping it open as easily as a pop top on a can of soda. "Nope, not exactly hero quality.

"Careful, don't break anything," warned Roger. He cringed as Oliver stuck his hand in the box.

"Yes, that's paid for," added Emma. "No returns."

"Okay, Rog, you get it out," said Oliver, removing his hand and giving the box to Roger.

Roger took the box and set it on a table. He pulled out a large piece of molded packing material, setting it aside as carefully as a surgeon might a harvested organ, then reached in and pulled out a silver metallic cylinder. Very similar in shape and design to the original serum container, it had an opening on one end with the words *Insert Finger Here* etched in the surface and on the side there was a glowing green display that read *Full*. Oliver grabbled the cylinder from Roger, who was doing this all a little too reverently, and stuck it on his finger. He felt nothing but watched as the display changed from the green *Full* to a red *Empty*.

"Well, that was simple enough," said Oliver. "When can I start flying?"

"You have absolutely no sense of occasion," said Roger. Oliver shrugged. "Well, you won't be flying tomorrow. It works basically like the original serum in that you'll see some slow change over the first several days, like you might be able to float slightly or jump a little farther, but it will take at least a week or ten days before you're really flying. So don't go testing it by jumping off a building in the next five minutes. Not that it would matter much for you. Just might upset the folks you land on."

"Speaking of upsetting," said Emma, "I thought you might want to know there are about three unauthorized biographies in the pipeline for you. Pretty much a race to see who can get one out first."

Oliver shook his head in surprise. "What's there to write about? I didn't do anything before SuperGuy, and I've barely done anything since. Are they going to get my report cards and interview my third grade teacher? Hey wait, my mom isn't writing one of them, is she?"

"No, I don't think so," said Emma.

"She's probably too busy writing her book on how to raise a superhero child," said Roger.

"Yeah, Chapter One: Make sure they survive until they're eighteen and can move out. Chapter Two: Superhero Serum," said Oliver. "I think that would pretty much cover it."

"But you fill it out with little anecdotes about toileting accidents and catching you with adult magazines under your mattress," said Emma.

"Adult magazines?" said Roger. "You're giving him too much credit. He squirreled away an underwear catalog at best."

"You bet," said Oliver. "JC Penney all the way. Those Younkers girls were just trashy."

"So true," said Roger. He added a dreamy, "Ah, Younkers girls..."

"Another thing," said Emma. "You've got several websites devoted to you now with plenty of pictures, some of them not so innocent. Most of the more revealing ones are obviously Photoshopped, but I do have to say your senior photo from high school is pretty special. The combination of the pose, the sweater, and the hair is almost mind-blowing. I would say the hairstyle was a mullet if I didn't think mullets had died out at least fifteen years before the photo was taken. Either way, a really classic look." Emma held up a printout of the picture. Roger started laughing.

"Oh, that sweater. I loved that sweater," said Oliver. "Well, you two laugh all you want. You better just hope there aren't any bad pictures of you out there, because you know they will add support people to the sites eventually." Oliver smiled. "Actually, if this reality show thing goes through, you guys will be stars too. That means dedicated websites, creepy fans and doctored photos for all." Both Emma and Roger stopped laughing.

"Oh, crap," said Emma.

"Ditto," said Roger. "I better go visit my mom and destroy all the old pictures I can find. She'll be holding them in front of the first camera that comes to her door. She doesn't know any better."

"Oh, crap," repeated Emma.

Oliver nodded and smiled. "Well, there you go. Now you sound like a girl who's got something to hide. I like it. You can feel my pain."

Roger's phone beeped and he checked it. "It's Joyce," he said. "A text." He read it and then sat in thought.

"Wait, did I miss something?" asked Oliver.

"You usually do," said Emma.

"A text from Joyce?" said Oliver. "What's up with that? You're pals with the supervillain who has the plot for taking over the world? Why doesn't that seem right?"

Roger shook his head at Oliver. "It's nothing sinister," he said. "I'm just helping him with the waitress. A little coaching."

"The waitress? The girl he wants to ask out?"

"Yes," said Emma, not waiting for Roger to answer. She got up from her seat and moved around to look over Roger's shoulder at his phone. "Did he ask her?"

"No," said Roger. "He says, 'Tried. Got nervous. Ordered pie again. Don't like pie.' God, he's hopeless." Roger shook his head sadly.

"Poor guy," said Emma, the sympathy plain on her face.

"Poor guy?" said Oliver. "Poor guy? Bad guy, remember? Evil supervillain? If that's not redundant. I think maybe you two could use a little reminder that he's the evil, evil bad guy. Bad. And evil."

"Oh, just give him a break," said Emma. "Not everyone's serum makes them an instant stud muffin, irresistible to the ladies."

"Give him a break? What is wrong here?" said Oliver.

"Just relax," said Roger. "I thought maybe it was an opportunity to mess the guy's world up a little. Maybe he can't efficiently put his plan into action if he's distracted by this. Or, if I want to be idiotically optimistic, maybe I help hook him up, he gets all happy and decides not to enslave the world." Roger shrugged. "Harmless."

Oliver thought about it for a second. "And—I just want you to consider another possibility here—what if he doesn't get hooked up and it all goes really, really badly?"

It was Roger's turn to think. "Oh. It goes really south and he ends up both evil and bitter? Could be a problem. Good point."

"That's what I'm saying. Thank you."

"We just can't let that happen," said Emma. "We've got to get them together, Roger."

"Yeah, forget all the fancy gadgets and flying machines," said Oliver sarcastically, "just get the bad guy a date. Don't think about the innocent woman you're trying to match up with the guy with the twisted brain either. What does she matter?" He paused for a minute.

"Well, you keep up with the supervillain dating game. In the meantime, I guess I'll do a little work. Emma, you have that list of Joyce Industries holdings in the area?"

Emma broke away from Roger and his phone and walked over to her files on the other side of the conference table. She searched for a minute and then pulled out a stapled set of papers. "Here it is. All the buildings and businesses in the area owned by Joyce Industries or any of its subsidiaries." She slid it across the table to Oliver.

"Wow. That's a lot," said Oliver as he quickly flipped through it. "I didn't think there'd be so many."

"Whatcha gonna do?" shrugged Emma as she inched back around the table to Roger, who was texting again.

"So...I guess I'll be going at this the old fashioned way. Investigating. Not that it's old fashioned to me because I've never investigated anything before, but now I'm supposed to be good at it. You guys could probably help if you want, maybe take a few places and drive by, see if anything looks promising..."

"No, no," said Emma, talking to Roger. "Don't say that. He can't tell you're being a smart-ass in a text. He doesn't know you."

"Oh, yeah. That could be bad," said Roger. "How about this?"

"Okay, I'll just start going through the list and checking these places out," said Oliver, inching slowly toward the door. "See if I can find anything suspicious, any kind of base of operations for this evil scheme of his."

"No, not quite," said Emma. "Here, gimme." Roger handed her the phone and she started typing. He leaned over to read it.

"Wait, girls like that?" asked Roger.

"Sure, some love it."

"Right. Good to know," said Roger with a nod. "You sure he can handle that? He could just end up with a lot more pie."

"Okay, then," said Oliver, in that uninspired way one does when they know the conversation's over for them. "I'll go investigate. You two play love connection." Oliver got only vague grunts of response from his two friends, so he shrugged, pulled on his mask and headed for the door. "I'll just spend all night driving around looking at various buildings for signs of evil, world-enslaving schemes. Stupid evil schemes. Wish I could fly already."

26

"**ABOUT** time you guys got here," said Emma as Roger and Oliver walked up to her outside of a meeting room. They were back in their old stomping grounds at the city government office building, specifically on Oliver's floor. A piece of paper with the words 'Video Training Room' was taped to the closed door. Emma gave a little nod toward the sign and said, "Not that it would have mattered much since they're running late. I don't know how long it will be before they're done."

"Well, I'm getting used to being late when I'm with the hero here," said Roger. "There's always something holding him up. Autographs, rescues, not at all subtle and rather annoying flirting."

"You could have gone on. You didn't have to wait," said Oliver. He said it quietly and without much enthusiasm, feeling he should defend himself but knowing it was just going to cause more problems.

"Oh, I had to wait," replied Roger, smiling at Emma.

"So, by the way you described the options, I'm going to guess it wasn't an autograph or a rescue," said Emma.

"It wasn't anything," said Oliver simply. Then he tried to change the subject. "How long do we have to wait?"

"It was Joan," said Roger, ignoring Oliver and answering Emma's question. "She ambushed Oliver outside her office and had him rearranging furniture before I even knew what was happening."

"It wasn't like that. She just had me move her desk a little."

"She had you move almost everything in there and most of the stuff is built in," said Roger. He leaned toward Emma conspiratorially. "She even had him up on a ladder putting things on top of her filing cabinets."

"I have to assume she held the ladder," said Emma.

"Oh, yeah," laughed Roger. "You've got to be safe. Can't have a superhero falling off the second rung of a step ladder."

"She's just lucky your flight hasn't kicked in yet or you wouldn't have needed the ladder, or her holding it," said Emma. "Must have been quite a show for her."

"I should have worn my coat," said Oliver, his face showing his embarrassment. "Definitely next time I'm in this office."

Between little bouts of laughter, Roger managed, "And she kept handing things up to him to put on top of the cabinet...not for storage, just anything...off her desk...her stapler and her...lamp. Oh god, I couldn't believe it. Her whole desk is up on top of those filing cabinets now." Roger leaned his back against the wall and slowly slid down, giggling all the way. Soon he was sitting, curled up in a ball with tears in his eyes. "The phone...ahh, I can't stand it...she gave him the phone...off her desk...ohh, god..."

"Okay, can we let it go now?" pleaded Oliver. Roger just continued to giggle with the occasional snort.

"Okay, big guy, we'll give you a break," said Emma after she stopped laughing herself, but it took awhile. "There is something else I needed to tell you. I forgot about it back when all this started but I got a reminder today."

Oliver looked thankful at the change in topic. "What's that?"

"Surprisingly enough, a physical."

"Physical?"

"Yep, there's a mandatory physical for the superhero position," said Emma. "I set up an appointment with a doctor, here's the time and place. You just need to have him sign this form." She handed Oliver a card with the details and a form.

"A physical," said Oliver. "For a superhero?"

"I don't think they thought this one through," said Roger, who had finally stopped giggling enough to stand up.

"They probably meant for it to be completed before you took the job," said Emma, "but in the rush to get the position filled, it got missed. But it's a requirement for the position, so it's got to be done. Have to put a check mark in the little box."

"Despite the obvious illogical nature of it all..." said Oliver.

"Yep, despite it all."

"Just don't screw up and fail the physical. That would be hard to explain," said Roger.

"Okay, let's settle down here," came a familiar voice. "There are people trying to work and a training going on."

They all turned their heads toward the voice, but Oliver already knew who it was. "Sergeant Przybylinski. You haven't retired yet?" he said.

"Can't afford it," came the man's quick reply. "Nobody made me a superhero and gave me a raise. I still work for a living."

Oliver was tempted to comment on the sergeant's work habits because of all the torture he had endured in the past but decided it wasn't worth it. "You work?" Whoops, it was worth it. "Well, I'd love to stand around and chat about all the good old times, but we have a training session that's about to start."

"Oh, I know. I'm coordinating the trainings today, so we're going to get to spend a little time together," said the sergeant with a smile.

"Little being the key word there," replied Oliver. "Our session is only supposed to last…" He looked to Emma.

"Twenty-five minutes," she said.

"Oh, sure, that's right," said Sergeant Przybylinski, "but that's just your group session. You, being the actual superhero, have your own individual training session to do."

"I don't recall being told about that," said Emma.

"Oh," said Sergeant Przybylinski. "That might be my mistake. I don't coordinate the training sessions very often, so I probably missed something. Anyway, Mr. Olson's here now so he might as well just do it after your group session." He smiled innocently at Oliver.

Oliver stared at the sergeant for a moment before replying. "Sure, no problem. Like you say, I'm already here."

"Great, I'll have it ready," said Sergeant Przybylinski. He started to walk away but turned back. "Oh, it is a bit long, by the way."

"I'm sure it is," said Oliver. The sergeant smiled again and walked over to the meeting door to consult a clipboard.

"He hasn't changed," said Roger. "Still a lovely human being."

"Is that what he is?" asked Emma innocently.

"You traded him for the likes of Gray Matter. Not to mention all the average bad guys on the streets or any other supervillains that happen to come along," said Roger to Oliver. "All in all, I'm thinking you came out on top."

"I'd have to agree," said Emma. "Gray Matter seems like a delightful man in comparison."

"Well, speaking of our delightful evil genius supervillain, we're kind of stuck. I spent half of yesterday and all last night working my way through that list of Joyce Industries holdings. I checked close to forty different locations and they were all clean as far as I could tell, not that I know exactly what I'm looking for."

"I think you'll know it when you see it," said Roger. "That super detecting part of your brain will recognize it."

"I hope so, and soon too. I'm not even a fourth of the way through the list yet. With junk like this training and oh, surprise physicals to waste time, it's going to take days to get through the rest of the locations. I'm afraid we don't have that kind of time. We've got to find the place where he's getting this drug ready to disperse, however he's going to do that, and shut it down," said Oliver.

"Well, it's got to be on the list, some part of Joyce Industries," said Roger. "Hopefully it's not hidden better than that or we'll never find his secret warehouse or factory of evil, or whatever it should be called."

"Factory of Evil. I like that. I mean I like the name, not factories of evil in general," said Oliver. "I've just been thinking of it as his distribution center, but I guess that should at least be a *secret* distribution center."

"Factory of Evil is much catchier," said Emma. "That's what I'd go with."

"That makes it unanimous," said Roger. "Factory of Evil it is. Glad we got that taken care of. Now we just have to find it."

"I think we can assume it's not small. It's not in somebody's basement or a one bedroom apartment above the corner shop; it'll be a much larger operation than that. It just seems like Joyce owns a billion warehouses and factories around the city. We have to find a way to narrow the search or we'll never stop him," said Oliver.

"He does own half the city. That's a lot of possibilities," said Emma. "And it's assuming we found all Joyce's properties and didn't miss some shell company buried under three others. It might not even be on the list."

"And that's only if it's in town. He could be doing it somewhere else entirely," added Roger.

"Possibly," said Oliver, "but I think it's here somewhere. I just have a feeling. I think he'd want something this important to be close by."

"Okay, Olson, you and your pals can go in now," said Sergeant Przybylinski from next to the door as the last person from the previous group filed out. Each one of the departing employees looked as if some part of their soul had been slowly stripped away, drown in the fetid pool of a plugged office drinking fountain, stomped on by an otherworldly evil half elephant-half filing cabinet beast, and burned in a small fire of training handouts. Oliver knew that look; he used to be that look. But despite the grueling trial, they had completed their training session and learned something new and valuable. Maybe one of them. Probably not. It was all common sense stuff anyway. As Oliver and the others walked in, the sergeant picked up two DVDs from the cart just inside the door of the meeting room. "Have a seat anywhere, plenty of room. Here's the first video for all of you," he said, putting a disk into the machine at the front of the room. "This second one is just for the hero." He held it up to show Oliver and then set it on top of the television.

"Emma, will you give me a ride back to the Garage so I don't have to wait for the loser?" asked Roger.

"Absolutely," answered Emma as the music started playing with the opening credits of the first video.

Sergeant Przybylinski hit a switch on the wall to dim most of the lights. "Make sure you sign the form before you take off or you won't get credit for the training," he said with a smile and shut the door.

Oliver was still thinking about Gray Matter's secret factory of evil as he opened the door to the parking garage and walked toward his car. Truth was he was thinking some about the secret factory of evil and some about Joan. To her credit, she wasn't easy to shake and a couple hours of boring hero training video didn't exactly occupy the mind. He was also thinking about Janice, and feeling guilty. He hadn't done anything wrong, apart from putting a number of items on top of a filing cabinet that shouldn't be there and probably pissing off the feng shui gods, but he still felt a little guilty. Oliver was reaching for the handle of his car when someone called his name.

"Olson."

Oliver turned to find Sergeant Przybylinski strolling toward him from where he had been waiting between some nearby police vans. "Sergeant Przybylinski. Another training video you forgot? I know I signed the form. Or maybe you didn't get enough time to reminisce inside? Want to go for a drink and catch up?"

"No thanks. I've got a girlfriend."

"Good for you. When will she be paroled?"

"Look, I'm not here for the clever banter," said the sergeant, coming to a stop and shoving his hands in his pockets. "I think I have some information that might be useful to you."

Oliver leaned back against his car. "How so?"

"I overheard some of your conversation earlier about that guy, Joyce," said the sergeant. He took one of his hands out of his pocket and rubbed his bulbous red nose as he glanced around the parking garage, making sure they were alone.

"Yes?" prompted Oliver, taking a quick scan of the garage himself now.

"So he's some kind of bad guy? An actual supervillain?" asked the sergeant.

"Yes, the real thing," said Oliver.

"It sounded like you were looking for a place of his, something big and special for some reason."

"True."

"Well, I have sort of a...relationship with Joyce, or at least one of his guys."

"That doesn't sound good."

"It's not quite what you think, or what they think for that matter. They think they have me as a mole in the department."

"Actually, that was pretty much what I was thinking," said Oliver.

"Well, that's not it. Listen. They've been paying me for information about ongoing investigations. Most obviously any that start to focus on Joyce Industries or anything they are involved with. I've been giving them meaningless crap for a while and they keep paying me. I was just playing them, no way I'm going to give them real information. I thought they would have learned by now. Anyway, at one of my last meetings with this guy I'm dealing with, Alex, he got a phone call I mostly overheard. They were talking about a place which needed to be carefully guarded, a cereal factory in Glendale. Sounded funny they needed to guard a cereal factory at all, so it stuck in my head. I figured it was because of corporate espionage and some secret cereal formula or something. When I heard what you said earlier about looking for a place this guy Joyce has, I decided it might be something you needed to know about. These guys may think they bought me, but they never did."

"So you decided to be a good guy?"

"I may be an ass, but I'm still a cop."

Oliver nodded. "Yes, you are."

"Good luck," said Sergeant Przybylinski, extending his hand.

Oliver took it and shook. "Thanks." Sergeant Przybylinski turned and walked away. Oliver watched him go and then opened the door to his car. He had the next step in his investigation.

27

ALEX entered the diner and looked around, finally spotting Mr. Joyce in a back corner booth. Alice was there taking his order. Alex watched as Joyce said something and smiled in a hopeful way. Not being able to see Alice's expression from his angle, Alex had no idea if she was smiling too, but she nodded and walked off toward the kitchen. Joyce proceeded to take out his phone and begin texting furiously.

"Undoubtedly to his new top advisor," said Alex under his breath as he made his way back to the booth. He sat down across from Mr. Joyce.

"Ah, Alex."

"Mr. Joyce." It was always Mr. Joyce in public, although he had taken to wanting to be called Gray Matter in the office.

"Glad you could join me. Would you like something to eat?"

"Sure, sir. I am feeling a bit hungry. I could use a menu, though." Alex had been forced to eat in the diner enough to know all the choices on the menu, but it gave Mr. Joyce an excuse to call Alice over again, which he did after a couple more quick texts. He apologized to her for being a bother and made a self-deprecating remark that almost passed as charming. Alex had to admit that whoever Mr. Joyce's mystery love advisor was, they were making progress. Both apologizing, albeit for nothing, and being self-deprecating in the same moment? Alex had never seen either behavior before on their own, let alone in consecutive sentences. And it seemed as if Alice was indeed a little charmed herself. What were the odds? After Alice had gone to put in Alex's order, Mr. Joyce got down to business—after a couple more texts.

"So, did you find out if our mole has double-crossed us?" asked Mr. Joyce.

"Yes, he did. Our surveillance caught him giving the information to SuperGuy in a parking garage a short time ago."

"Excellent."

"When do you believe he will come?"

"Oh, tonight, certainly," said Mr. Joyce. "I doubt as a rookie superhero he has much patience and we didn't leave him a lot of time in which to act, so he has little choice." Mr. Joyce looked longingly at Alice as she refilled a man's coffee cup at the counter. If she smiled too much, that poor customer would have a very bad night once he left. "This means we need to get ready for guests at the factory. After dinner, of course." There was a beep from Joyce's phone and he picked it up. Another text. "It's from Rog." He read for a second, then looked up at Alex. "You won't mind eating at another table, this is important."

"Of course not, sir," said Alex. He stood and walked over to a stool at the counter as Joyce went back to texting.

*   *   *

When Oliver arrived back at the Garage, he found Roger and Emma in the control room, each parked in front of a monitor.

"Guess what? I know where the factory of evil is," he said as he stepped into the room and dropped his gloves and mask onto the chair beside the door. Both Emma and Roger turned away from their computer screens.

"Really? Was this another one of your 'I knew it but the dough was still rising' osmosis things, because you weren't very confident earlier," said Emma.

"Yeah, that act is going to get old after awhile," asked Roger. "You pretend not to know something, get us all worried like there's no way to solve the puzzle, then you walk into the room and boom, answer. Might get annoying."

"No, not osmosis or an act," said Oliver. "Kind of old school detective work. After putting in all those hours and doing the hard-nosed investigating, I put two and two together and got a tip. Turns out it's a cereal factory over in Glendale, just north of the interstate. It was on the list, just hadn't gotten to it yet. Still have to check it out to know for certain too. Emma, can pull up the information on it?"

"Sure," nodded Emma, turning back to her computer.

"Where'd this tip come from?" asked Roger.

"Sergeant Przybylinski of all people. Seems the sergeant has been earning some extra income via Joyce Industries. Claims he's given them nothing real, just been leading them on for the fun of it, and the cash, but he overheard this bit of information." Oliver sat down at the communications station and hit the F key on the keyboard that initiated a call to Stormfront. The monitor displayed the text *Calling*.

"I can't say I'm surprised the sergeant was selling info," said Emma without turning from her screen. "Of course I'm even less surprised he was screwing them over for the money." She tapped a couple more keys. "Here it is. A cereal factory owned by a company which is owned by a another company which is owned by Joyce Industries. In Glendale as you said."

"Going for a surprise inspection?" asked Roger.

"Yes and no," replied Oliver. Roger was about to ask for clarification when the communications monitor beeped and displayed a picture of Stormfront, who was just sitting down in front of the camera.

"Hi, Oliver," she said. "Sorry I was slow answering, I had to check who it was. The Creeper keeps calling about any little thing he can think of so I've been 'out of the office' a lot lately." She made little air quotes as she said it.

"Ah, well, even though you are mostly happy to see me just for who I'm not, I'll be content with that," said Oliver. "Listen, we've had a couple interesting developments here recently and I thought I might run them by you." Oliver recounted what all they had learned about Gray Matter and most recently the cereal factory.

"And you say this cop hasn't been giving them any information?" she asked after Oliver had finished his summation.

"According to him, he's given them nothing."

"And he overheard this about the factory?"

"Yep."

"So it's a trap?" asked Janice.

"Almost certainly," answered Oliver. He ignored the looks he was getting from Emma and Roger. "I thought you might like to buzz down and check the place out with me. It being a trap and all."

"You do know how to touch a superhero girl's heart, don't you? Unfortunately, I've got a big event here tonight. Charity thing for the mayor and all the pretty people but it's not all partying. There's a gang with delusions of grandeur that's going to rob it. I'm going to foil it and all that. It could take all night. Can I get a rain check?"

"Sure, absolutely."

"Hey, how's the flying coming?"

"It's not yet. Can't even float," answered Oliver. "I might get a little drift in a fall off a tall building, but that could just be wishful thinking."

"Well, it'll come. We'll have to plan a nice evening flight over the lakes once it's ready," said Janice. "And be careful tonight. Remember, it's a trap."

"I know, I'll be careful. You do the same."

"I don't have to. It's my trap," said Janice, reaching for her keyboard. The screen went black.

"What's this about a trap?" asked Roger as soon as the communication was over.

"Just exactly that," answered Oliver.

"When did you find that out?" asked Emma.

"Popped into my head during my conversation with Sergeant Przybylinski. Just a little too convenient to be fed the secret location by the guy they're paying, especially if he's double crossing them with something he's overheard. Life just isn't that easy. So, have you guys found anything in the way of background?"

"I haven't found anything more than that Joyce owns a lot of stuff," said Emma. "A *lot* of stuff. Including a certain cereal factory now." She handed Oliver a printed page about the factory. It was little more than they already knew, just a basic history, the shell ownership information, and the size of the building.

"I was able to scrape together some stuff on the hero boards, but it's mostly rumors," said Roger.

"Hero boards?"

"Yeah, a private discussion board on the internet. Kind of like the Superhero Surplus Warehouse, but for information. Mostly heroes and law enforcement people posting, but also some special assistants like me. The Department of Superhero Funding hosts it. Not many people had heard of Gray Matter but one of the DSF moderators knew of a spoiled brain buster serum going for a very high price a couple years back on the black market."

"I thought you said that wasn't unusual," said Oliver.

"Yes, but it was in this case. It was a very high price and the serum was very big on the brain end of things," replied Roger.

"Very big?" said Emma. "What exactly does that mean?"

"Well, you know how these serums all give the basic powers to heroes? Like the minimum strength and speed, plus the cosmetic stuff?" asked Roger. The other two nodded. "Well, they do make a few of these special brain ones that don't bother wasting space on the body stuff, they just pile it all into the brain. That being said, he'll still have the invulnerability, they all do, but he won't look it. Won't have the speed or the strength or anything like that. Probably can't take even close to as much punishment as a regular hero before he's incapacitated, but he'll still survive. I don't exactly understand how it works, it's a lot of chemistry, but it does explain why Joyce is five foot nothing and a hundred thirty pounds."

"And no matter what he's hyper-smart," said Oliver.

"And hyper-evil, most likely," said Roger.

"Not a good combination," said Emma, "unless you're a supervillain."

"I'm kinda feeling bad about helping set him up with the waitress now," said Roger. "Just seems kind of mean."

"You never know, maybe she's an evil waitress and it's a perfect match," said Emma.

"Well, let's hope," said Oliver with extra fake enthusiasm and crossing his fingers. Then they all sat there quietly for a moment until Oliver suddenly stood up and grabbed his gloves and mask off the chair by the door. "I guess I better get going. This trap won't get sprung on its own."

"If you know it's a trap, why not call the Chief and go in with the cops?" asked Emma.

"He can't do that," said Roger with a scoff. "It's an honor thing. It's like the face-to-face meeting; it's just the way it's done. If the bad guy lays a trap for you, you've got to go in. It's what a hero does."

"But that's silly. It's a *trap*," said Emma, emphasizing the last word as if the two guys weren't quite hearing it.

"I have to go in alone *because* it's a trap," replied Oliver, pulling on his gloves. "I can take a beating, but

I'm not going to call in some cops who might get killed. It's kinda my job. And I'm told it's good work if you can get it." He slipped on his mask. "Don't wait up. I might be late," he said and walked out the door.

28

OLIVER dove behind a metal support just as a small missile fired by one of his mechanical foes streaked past. The missile exploded on a wall behind him, showering the area with debris and pelting him with shrapnel. Smoke drifted toward the ceiling and the air was filled with a burning scent, yet Oliver could see no flames. Obviously these heavily armed machines were there to exterminate folks like him, probably specifically him since they seemed like overkill for normal cereal factory security, but do it in a way that wouldn't cause too much indiscriminate damage or burn the factory to the ground. Certainly a sensible policy if you wanted to stay in business but an awfully difficult task if you were going to arm your killing machines with missiles. While they were very accurate, they also tended to explode, which can cause a bit of a mess, and if the target in question is not easy to hit, then the damage begins to add up. Still, Oliver was getting a little tired of all the running and jumping and diving. Not to mention the shrapnel. It doesn't even break the skin, but the constant stinging is annoying.

"Why not arm them with stun guns? Or paralyzing rays?" Oliver yelled toward the factory ceiling. He didn't know for certain anyone was watching but assumed there were security cameras. "Or paralyzation rays? Is it paralyzation? Paralyzing? Paralysis?" Oliver ducked instinctively as another missile exploded nearby. More stinging. "Probably not vital we work that out now." Without knowing exactly what the machines were, Oliver had taken to calling them Killbots in his head, and occasionally out loud with a naughty word or two attached when he felt really strongly about it. That was usually right after he failed to dodge a missile or machine gun burst. The Killbots were basically very fast miniature tanks that fired missiles, machine gun rounds and smaller hero quality lasers. And while those lasers were small, they still hurt; Oliver had been pegged by them several times already. Putting it out of his mind, Oliver dove across the aisle and rolled into better cover behind some heavy looking metal cylinders. He had been doing the very same thing, among other evasive and attacking maneuvers, continuously for about forty-five minutes, starting almost immediately after he entered the cereal factory by a rear door. It was almost as if they knew he was coming, which was the case, but it didn't stop Oliver from bitching about it to himself as he dodged missiles and lasers.

Oliver had no real idea where he was inside the huge building or where he was trying to get to, but that wasn't an issue at the moment since he was being given no time to do anything but keep evading attacks. He had dispatched seven Killbots since the start of the fight but more kept showing up. Right now there were at least two in front of him and three or four coming up behind, so he couldn't stay stationary for much longer. Risking a peek, Oliver stuck his head out from behind cover and scanned the area in front of him. Another Killbot had joined the two in front and they all fired on his location just as he pulled back to safety. A missile exploded against one of the metal cylinders, rocking it back and forth and causing it to start making some rather scary rumbling sounds from within. Oliver stepped back as he listened to it.

"That doesn't sound good," he said, eyeing the cylinder as a laser flashed by and numerous bullets ricocheted around him. The large container continued to rumble internally and steam began leaking out from underneath it. "Probably time to move on," said Oliver. He remembered seeing a side passage off the main aisle about ten meters down on the left. That wasn't far but it also happened to be only a short distance before the intersection where the three Killbots were currently sitting. Oliver knew he might get peppered a little making a run for it, but he had to get moving, especially since he could hear the trailing Killbots closing in on his position. Ripping the rumbling metal cylinder off the ground, Oliver swung around as he stepped out into the main aisle and tossed the huge object at the feet of the closest Killbots behind him. They now showed themselves to be more nimble than Oliver had thought as the first two easily rolled to the side, out of the cylinder's path as it tumbled past. The next two weren't so lucky. They also tried to maneuver out of the way but whatever was rumbling inside the cylinder finally won the battle and it exploded, propelling the two Killbots backward out of sight.

Oliver didn't see anything after that because he turned and sprinted forward as the three Killbots in front and the two left behind began to fire. He could feel bullets bouncing off him like raindrops and the unmistakable searing heat as a laser hit his right calf. He dodged left to avoid a missile from the front and realized his luck as he also happened to dodge one from behind at the very same instant. His eyes followed that one as it continued forward and exploded against the lower part of one of the lead Killbots, kicking its lower half out from under it and dropping the metal hulk to the ground. Successive explosions to his right kept Oliver moving along the left side of the aisle, which was perfect since that's where he wanted to go. He dove into the safety of the smaller side aisle just as more missiles exploded in front of him and machine gun bullets ripped their way along the floor of the main aisle. Rolling to his feet, Oliver didn't hesitate, having learned early on in the fight that the Killbots didn't seem to have a slow gear. There were still two in front and two behind, and they were undoubtedly closing in quickly. Besides, Oliver was really tired of getting shot, so he sprinted forward to put some distance between himself and his pursuers while seeking some kind of cover from which he could maybe put up a fight. Barring a good option for that, he simply had to keep moving. A doorway at the end of the aisle showed the only possibility of escape at the moment, and Oliver scurried for it as bullets began whistling after him, tearing into the equipment and shelving lining both sides of the aisle.

Oliver tumbled through the doorway, angling to the left to be out of the line of fire and giving him precious time to determine his next move. That move was probably finding the next means of escape. That was the plan anyway. Sometimes however, plans don't go the way you'd like. Other times, plans just suck. As Oliver climbed to his feet, he discovered the room was a dead end, with only the one door through which he had entered. Oliver was debating whether it would be better to try breaking through one of the walls, or if he should use the doorway as a bottleneck for fighting the Killbots, when a shiny metal door dropped down to seal off the entry. Looking around, Oliver saw the same shiny metal made up the walls of the room too, and he had enough experience now to know it was probably hero quality metal. For the moment, he was trapped.

"Well, I guess I knew getting trapped was a possible outcome when walking into a trap," said Oliver. "Shouldn't really be too surprised." Oliver thought for a few seconds. "Comm, Call Emma," he said, but the channel opened to nothing but heavy static. He had tried the communicator earlier in the battle but got the same result, showing Gray Matter had been thorough enough to block it. With that in mind, Oliver didn't imagine the supervillain would have done a shoddy job of building this little room either, but he started forward to inspect for any possible weak spots in the walls or around the door just to be sure. Before he could take two steps, there was a whirring sound as panels in all four walls slid down to reveal rather large, shiny guns. Oliver thought they looked a lot like the hero quality laser Cyclone had used on him.

"Not fair!" he yelled, and then they opened fire.

✳　✳　✳

Oliver finally shook off the memories of how he had gotten to this point. Maybe there was something special in the super serum allowing heroes to zip through flashbacks in these circumstances, but it just didn't seem like the best use of time for the hero at the moment. Especially when that time was rapidly diminishing due to the laser cutting through the chains suspending him above the vat of hero quality acid and rotten super serums. Oliver tried his communicator again but got the same result as before, nothing but static. Looking up to check on the progress of the laser, Oliver saw it had cut through one of the chains already and was halfway through the second. Not long and it would be slicing its way through the third and final one. It seemed to be a very efficient hero quality laser. Oliver didn't really appreciate that efficiency. Once its work was done, he would be falling into a vat that at best would spoil his day and at worst would make that day the bright spot of the rest of his existence because on that day at least he didn't spend the entire twenty-four hours as a hideous monster. Hideous monster being a really optimistic assumption of course.

Oliver shook off the feeling of impending doom and began reassessing his situation yet again, searching for some small chance of escape. The broken part of the first chain hung down loosely from where it connected to the manacles on his wrists, ending just above his head with part of the last link, the one sliced in half, still hanging on. Oliver shook his hands on the off chance the chains weren't as secure or hero quality or even chain-like as they looked, but they were and he was rewarded with the broken link coming loose and smacking him on his cheek on its way down into the vat. Although his strength was still sapped from being knocked out by the multiple hero quality lasers, Oliver was already feeling slightly better than when he first regained consciousness. Of course, 'slightly better' just meant he could wiggle a little more vigorously. The current situation called for a bit more than wiggling, no matter how vigorously done. Oliver also calculated that his current recovery rate would not be fast enough to allow him the strength required to flip himself to the safety of the rafters above before the laser finished cutting through the chains. That calculation didn't keep him from giving vigorous wiggling a couple more tries anyway, but he only managed to get himself swinging and twisting a bit wildly again. As Oliver gave up and let the swinging slow down, he began to wonder if this might be his last few moments as a superhero. Of all the things he had given thought to once he realized the whole hero thing was really happening, actually dying due to the job hadn't been one of them. It was kind of a bummer.

Looking despondently down at the vat below, Oliver said, "I wonder what the record is for shortest tenure as a superhero?" He continued to swing slowly, wallowing a bit in self pity. "And mine could end in a cereal factory. Not very heroic. Even if it is a Cereal Factory of Evil."

*　　*　　*

Gray Matter was still a bit pissed. It should have been a more majestic occasion. There should have been more gravity to it all. He had tried, right? He'd played his part, trapped the hero, been there for the give-and-take at the end. There definitely should have been better banter. To say it lacked the requisite wittiness that banter should have was an understatement. He didn't even get to explain his awe-inspiring plan of world domination. It was really mind-blowing in some aspects. Subtle here, audacious there. Really quite the magnificently evil scheme. But now it just remained a tale untold, like some dusty manuscript shut away in a drawer instead of a spectacular blueprint laid out to astonish the hero. Yes, it should have been so much more. SuperGuy should have realized that too despite his predicament, or really, because of it. In a situation such as that, there is a weight to the proceedings. Two legendarily powerful figures facing off in their final confrontation, death on the line, the fate of the world in their hands. Yet SuperGuy didn't get it. It just wasn't right and really bothered Gray Matter. He stomped his way through another door held open by Alex and abruptly came to a stop. Alex stumbled into him and apologized profusely knowing the mood his boss was in, but Gray Matter didn't seem to notice. He just stood there in the middle of the walkway and stared at the floor in thought.

"He doesn't know any better. He's too green," stated Gray Matter quietly after a moment.

"Excuse me, sir?" asked Alex, leaning in more closely to hear.

"He's too green," repeated Gray Matter, more loudly this time. "It's my fault. I'm moving way too fast. He doesn't understand the occasion because he barely understands what it means to be a hero, let alone one in a climatic battle against an evil arch enemy with the fate of the world in the balance." Gray Matter paced in a small circle. "He barely even knows me as a supervillain, let alone a nemesis with whom he shares a long history. Of course he doesn't get it."

"Well, he doesn't have much time to get it now," said Alex. His boss didn't say anything for a moment, apparently lost in thought again. "Maybe his replacement will be more aware of his role," added Alex, trying to find a positive way to spin things.

"His replacement…" mused Gray Matter. "His replacement might be better, if they choose to fill the position at all. The Mayor has this election won now, so he may wish to save the money for other things. I will either have no foe at all to inspire me, or a new one who is even that much farther behind by the time they arrive on the scene." Gray Matter shook his head slowly back and forth as he stared at a spot on the floor. "That simply will not do."

"Sir?" asked Alex, sensing a decision had been made but at a loss for what it was.

"Let him go."

"What?"

Gray Matter shook himself out of thought and turned back to his assistant. "Let him go," he repeated, and seeing he was not being understood, continued, "I cannot afford to have my arch enemy eliminated so quickly. Who will motivate me to more and more ingenious plots? Who will push me to come up with the ultimate plan of world domination if he dies tonight? Obviously someday he will die, that's a given, but it should be when it means something, not while he's still practically a trainee.

Besides, he's already won this battle. Even if he dies, his handlers undoubtedly know where he was going, and the police will soon follow and discover our plan. That part is now a foregone conclusion. However, he can escape, as will we, and the war will continue. In essence, our legendary future may be saved." Gray Matter smiled as he walked to Alex and put an arm around his shoulder. "Alex, you need to go back and turn off the laser."

"Turn it off?"

"Yes, there's still time. Turn it off and eventually he'll regain enough strength to escape, but it will take a while. More than enough time for us to still get away safely. So hurry up and get it done. I will wait for you in the car."

"Yes, sir," said Alex with a nod. He turned and began to jog back toward where they had left SuperGuy in peril.

Oliver was twisting slowly in a semi-circle, staring down at the boiling vat of liquid, when he heard the metal door open. Gray Matter's assistant, somewhat out of breath, stepped through the doorway and looked first at Oliver and then at the laser on the platform. The man started walking toward the laser and Oliver wondered why. Something was wrong and, as the man got closer to the laser, Oliver feared he wasn't even going to get the few moments he thought he had left. Perhaps the police were already here because Roger and Emma had notified the Chief just to be on the safe side (which Oliver had been wishing for a while now), or maybe Janice had foiled her plot early and flown down to surprise him. Whatever the case, it meant Gray Matter had given the order to drop him into the vat ahead of schedule. Oliver was out of time.

Gray Matter's assistant reached the laser, stepping up on the small stool to access the controls just when the second chain gave way. Oliver heard the metallic pop as the link broke in half, one part springing away and landing in the vat below while the other half remained connected to the loose end, which fell down against Oliver's arms. When it hit his arms, the broken link came loose and fell past Oliver's head. Everything was slowing down for Oliver now. He could see the assistant reaching for the controls in the background as he tracked the descent of the broken chain link in front of his face. He pushed his chest out slightly, bouncing the link off it and out farther away from his body. Then he pulled his legs up to pop the link off his left knee and up into the air. As the heavy piece of hero quality metal spun in front of him and began to drop again, Oliver swung his legs back, waited for the precise second, and whipped them forward to kick the piece of metal at his target.

Alex never saw the heavy link coming, being focused on his task of shutting down the laser. His hand was poised above the power switch when his world flashed brightly and he lost consciousness. The blow from the chain link spun him around and he fell backward over the laser controls and railing, landing on a section of large exhaust pipe that entered the wall just below. The pipe was at an angle that started the unconscious man rolling forward until it bent away to the floor, which left him falling again. Unfortunately for Alex, that extra distance out into the factory floor put him above the vat and he plunged into it with a heavy splash.

"Oh, that can't be good," said Oliver, staring down at the ripples in the vat below him. "Not good at all." Oliver's attention was pulled away from the unfortunate fate of the assistant when he realized the sound of the laser had increased. Looking up, he could see the laser's beam was thicker and slicing through the third chain much more quickly than it had the previous two. The assistant must have managed to at least increase the power before Oliver took him out.

"Okay, I no longer feel sorry for him," Oliver mumbled as he shook his hands futilely, hoping his strength might have returned more quickly than he estimated. It hadn't, and he stopped when he realized it might just break the chain faster. That effort left him swinging slightly back and forth, which in turn made him think that if he could get his body swinging as much as possible and if the last chain broke at precisely the right second, it just might toss him close enough to the side of the vat for him to catch the edge and save himself. The odds were probably not on his side, but Oliver began to pump his legs as hard as he could. He had managed to swing back and forth several times before the laser finally cut through the last chain, and while he wasn't going as fast as he wanted by then, he was lucky enough to be almost at the far end of a swing when the last link broke. Oliver's momentum tossed him slightly outward as he began to drop, and his last big leg kick caused a complication as it sent him flipping over so he was falling headfirst. To make things worse, his back was to the side of the vat so he couldn't easily grab the edge even if he was close enough. Looking down as he fell, Oliver could tell he wasn't going to reach the side. About three feet away from the edge he estimated. A lousy three feet. He had been suspended pretty high above the vat so he had a little time to really think about those three feet and how badly he wanted to reach the side of the vat. That's when he felt the drift. Slightly at first, tugging him toward the side, but then a sudden little burst tossing him as if he'd been shoved by some unseen force. Almost like an engine that catches for a second and propels you forward but then stalls. Oliver got two quick bursts out of his flying engine and he craned his neck to see how close he was going to get to the side. While the bursts had helped get him closer, he was still going to come up just short of the side, most likely bouncing off the inside of the vat and into the acid below. However, just as his back collided with the side, Oliver bent his knees back and hooked them over the top edge of the vat, holding on and suspending himself just inches above the liquid.

"Stuck the landing," said Oliver.

29

GRAY Matter was sitting in the back of his limousine when the door opened. "It's about time, Alex," he said as he poured himself a second glass of wine. Supervillainy was such thirsty work. "Were you successful?"

"I'm guessing not," answered Oliver, settling into the seat opposite the white haired villain.

Gray Matter looked up in surprise but quickly composed himself. "On the contrary, he does seem to have been successful," he said with a smile that seemed genuine enough to Oliver.

"Okay...I doubt that's true, since I'm here—and alive."

"Well..." said Gray Matter as he tapped a finger against his glass in thought. "Yes, I suppose you are right, at least to a degree. If he had been successful, you wouldn't be free yet, although you would be alive, and he should have had time to get here first. I must assume you managed to escape without him needing to turn off the laser. I appear to have underestimated you. That's good."

"Turn off?"

"Yes," said Gray Matter, taking a sip of wine. "You could say I had a change of heart. I decided our relationship was only just beginning. We have so much untapped potential, it would have been a shame to terminate it so soon."

"Oh," said Oliver, thinking back to the vat. He supposed he might have made the wrong assumption about what Gray Matter's assistant was going to do with the laser. "So he was turning the laser off?"

"Yes, that's what I said."

"Oooh." Oliver drew out the word as he thought about it.

Gray Matter leaned forward to look out his window. "So where is Alex?" he asked. "You didn't have to subdue him, did you? He's really pretty harmless."

"Um...I'm afraid he might not be coming," stammered Oliver. "He sort of fell."

"Oh," said Gray Matter. "Well, he's young and in good shape. I'm sure he'll be fine."

"Well..."

"What?"

"The vat. He fell in the vat."

"Oh boy," said Gray Matter. "That's unfortunate."

"Maybe he'll be okay," said Oliver. "Like you said, he's young and in good shape."

Gray Matter scoffed. "Oh that won't matter, not with what's in that vat." He shook his head as he thought about it. "Really bad timing though," the villain continued. "It's his birthday tomorrow. We're having a big surprise party for him. Or were, I guess. It would have been bad enough with just a fall maybe, or if you had roughed him up. Not good for pictures at least, but after the vat…I don't think we'd want pictures at all." Oliver opened his mouth but nothing came out. The silence dragged on a bit before Gray Matter went on, "Not to mention he was supposed to be in a wedding this weekend. Best man too. It's a good friend of his from college, found his soulmate I'm told. That's Saturday and then on Sunday his goddaughter is being baptized. His sister's kid. She's adorable. He always has new pictures on his phone. Loves to show them. Probably no phone anymore." A short pause. "So, actually it was a really big weekend for him."

"Uh…" stammered Oliver. He only saw the image of Alex dropping into the vat in his head.

"HA!" yelled Gray Matter. "Just kidding! I really had you there. You should have seen your face." The villain giggled while trying not to spill his wine. "Oh, you superheroes are just too good sometimes."

"So…there's no niece?"

"Hell, I don't know. Don't care," said Gray Matter. "I don't even know when his birthday is, don't know if he has a sister. Doubt he's got friends from college. He's kind of jerk from what I hear."

"Okay," said Oliver. "I guess that's better…"

"Well, forget that," said Gray Matter. "We have more important matters to deal with. Like us."

"There's an 'us'?"

"Absolutely." The villain smiled. "And the endgame. The question of what happens now."

Oliver just sat there. Still a bit thrown by the whole Alex thing, he hadn't given the slightest thought to what was next.

Gray Matter continued, "You're probably wondering if there's going to be a big fight between us. A showdown. A little mano-a-mano thing. You and me, one on one. Or maybe you're wondering if I have a secret escape plan to whisk me away and out of your clutches at the last second." Oliver could only just sit there and nod slightly. "Well, the answer's no to both. I really didn't expect to still be dealing with you at this point so I have no contingency plan. I guess letting you go was probably a misstep on my part. A last second change like that can really mess things up. But still, all-in-all, it's a pleasant surprise, I tell you. I was really a bit depressed with the way things had gone earlier. Not at all the weighty importance I wanted our showdown to have. This is so much better."

"Okay," was all Oliver could manage.

"So, should I just have my driver take us to police headquarters?" asked Gray Matter. Oliver opened his mouth, but then only nodded slightly. The villain pressed a button and spoke into an intercom. "Alan, could you please take us to police headquarters. Also, phone my attorneys and have them meet us there." He took his finger off the button and smiled at Oliver as the car started moving. "Oh, where are my manners? Things can get sloppy amidst all the fun. Wine?" asked Gray Matter, gesturing toward the bottle.

"No, thanks," said Oliver. After a moment, as Gray Matter had gone to looking out the window at the scenery while sipping his wine, Oliver asked, "So this is it? You'll have to excuse me, but I'm a little new. Do we always share a limo to jail at the end?"

"Oh, it happens more than you'd think," answered Gray Matter with a chuckle. "Besides, it's all lawyers from here on out anyway. No more fun for us and the whole thing drags on forever. You know lawyers and the justice system. I'll most likely get off on some technicality or they won't even be able to charge me with anything definite because the plot is just too huge and complicated for them to get their minds around. I'll end up having to pay some fine for tax evasion or something and that will be it."

"Well that's not comforting," said Oliver.

Gray Matter shrugged. "That's our legal system. Maybe I'll write a book too. With all the publicity, I'll make a killing."

Oliver sat there for a couple minutes thinking about vats of boiling acid and the legal system. "You know, I think I will have that glass of wine," he said.

*   *   *

Oliver and Roger were out on the floor of the Garage as Oliver experimented with just how much his flight ability had kicked in. He wasn't actually flying yet, but it wouldn't be long. So far they had discovered he could now float a few feet above the ground, jump twice as far as he used to, and drift enough on a fall that he no longer thudded straight into the ground but could angle himself enough to tumble and roll to a messy stop most of the time. That part wasn't particularly useful as it tended to be more destructive. Emma had rolled her chair out of her office and sat with a laptop while reading official emails aloud to them from various people if she deemed it worthwhile. Many of them were congratulatory on his victory over Gray Matter, although the success was being somewhat devalued by the fact the villain was already out on bail and his public relations people were doing some incredible spin. Thankfully, Oliver wasn't being targeted by them but Gray Matter was being turned into a misunderstood genius whose intent was to vaccinate all mankind from the common cold. Or the flu. Or minor skin irritations. It wasn't quite clear, but it was very compelling stuff, and it was working. 38% of area residents were saying they believed Gray Matter wasn't a supervillain, 42% weren't sure any crime had been committed at all, and 29% were less itchy.

All of the flight tests and conversation in the garage were also being recorded by the cameras and crew of the reality show that had started taping the previous day. The producers were a bit pissed about missing out on the big cereal factory showdown but were happy they were getting a hero just learning to fly. There were three or four cameras going at all times, along with several stationary ones and a feed coming directly from Oliver's mask.

"Try for the third rafter from the far wall," said Roger, pointing to the target. "That would be the record for a standing long jump."

"You got it," said Oliver, stepping behind a line Roger had made on the floor in chalk. "Of course, at this pace, all I have to do is wait an hour and I can break it again."

"Yes, but waiting is boring, and me telling you to jump for this or fall from that is far more fun," said Roger.

"Hey, what about this?" asked Emma, reading from her laptop. "Looks like a little fallout from your fun with Gray Matter. The cereal factory manager is all pissed about the damage from the fight. Lots of minor damage due to missile explosions and lasers—you'll have to explain to me how anything from an explosion is minor—not to mention major destruction due to the vat. The vat wasn't there for cereal purposes of course, but it looks like it did burst and everything around it on the main factory floor was melted or damaged by the acid inside. Apparently there was also a very distinct trail of destruction all the way across the floor leading to a very large hole ripped through one of the outer walls. Did you do that?"

"No, I left through a door," said Oliver. He and Roger looked at each other.

"The guy you dropped in the vat?" asked Roger.

"Hey, he fell," said Oliver.

"Because you hit him in the head with a piece of metal," said Roger sarcastically.

"I thought he was trying to kill me," said Oliver defensively. Then he smiled in a half-heartedly optimistic way. "But he can't be in too bad of shape since he walked out, right?"

"Walked out a wall," said Roger, "Emphasis on the *wall.*"

"And there's the part about the trail of destruction," added Emma. "The guy didn't just head down an aisle, he made his own path and his own door. *That* doesn't sound good."

"Okay, okay. You're right," Oliver admitted, shaking his head in frustration. "So what are the odds 'Vat Guy' is going to come back to bite me in the ass?"

"You mean the chances you just created another bad guy for you to fight? High, given the whole superhero and supervillain karma thing," said Roger. "But on the bright side, it keeps you working, so just call it job security." Roger smiled and looked at Emma. "But forget 'Vat Guy.' Let's talk about the important thing here. What kind of cereal did they make there? I hope it's not one of my favorites if it's going to screw up the whole supply."

"How about that?" said Oliver. "My first really big victory over a supervillain and the biggest repercussion, besides 'Vat Guy,' could be a temporary disruption in the supply of your favorite cereal. I saved you, and the rest of the world, from being enslaved by an evil baddie, but who's counting? It's the cereal that really matters."

"You're a public servant," said Roger. "You answer to the little guy."

"If it's only cereal you have to worry about, Oliver, that's probably something to be thankful for," said Emma, going back to the emails.

"Probably," agreed Roger. "Maybe you'll get a break from the big threats and we can have some normal hero life around here. Get some experience with regular crime. No supervillains, no world conquering conspiracies, no super groups. Just let you settle into the mundane everyday business of being a superhero, knocking some small time criminal heads."

"Actually, I don't think that's going to happen," said Emma, looking up from the computer again.

"Why's that?" asked Oliver, sizing up his target rafter on the other side of the Garage.

"They want to give you a sidekick."

ABOUT THE AUTHOR

Kurt Clopton works full time as a professional Olde Tyme photo model, specializing in wide brim hats and saloon backgrounds. He spends most of his spare time perfecting his mediocrity at tennis and guitar, and the rest of it watching instructional YouTube videos on how to fix whatever he has most recently broken. He lives in Wisconsin with his secret second family when he is not on the road "traveling for work."

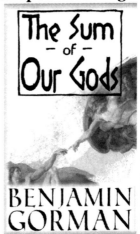

CPSIA information can be obtained
at www.ICGtesting.com
Printed in the USA
LVOW07s1829030417
529391LV00019B/182/P